THE
Kappa *Child*

Praise for Hiromi Goto's *Chorus of Mushrooms*

"Hiromi Goto expertly layers the experiences of a Japanese immigrant woman, her emotionally estranged daughter and her beloved granddaughter into a complex fabric and compelling story." –*Ottawa Citizen*

"Such a love for words is evident in *Chorus of Mushrooms*, which contains passages of breathtaking beauty."
–*Globe and Mail*

"Hiromi Goto, a Japanese–Canadian writer, has written a masterpiece of our times. . . . The readability of the text is attributable to the author's craftmanship, and one feels like reading it over and over again."
–*The Herald* (Harare, Zimbabwe)

"Not only is Goto's language precise and evocative, she has crafted a complex and poetic text that weaves realities and mysteries into a subtle pattern."
–*Edmonton Journal*

THE Kappa *Child*

Hiromi Goto

Red Deer Press

Published in Canada by Red Deer Press
195 Allstate Parkway, Markham, ON L3R 4T8
Published in the United States by Red Deer Press
311 Washington Street, Brighton, Massachusetts 02135
www.reddeerpress.com

Credits
Edited for the Press by Aritha van Herk
Cover design by Duncan Campbell
Text design by Dennis Johnson
Cover photo courtesy of Pierre Arsenault/Masterfile

Acknowledgments
Red Deer Press acknowledges with thanks the Canada Council
for the Arts, and the Ontario Arts Council for their support of our
publishing program. We acknowledge the financial support of the
Government of Canada through the Canada Book Fund (CBF)
for our publishing activities.

ISBN 978-1-55005-230-5

For my sisters, with love.

Kappa wa honto ni iruno kana? Wakaranai ne . . .
    —Naoe Kiyokawa, February 13, 1996, 3:55 P.M.

I AM A COLLECTOR of abandoned shopping carts.

Skyscrapers made of mirrors glare brilliant orange, a trick of blindness, and I creep to a stop at every intersection. I can only intuit the change in traffic lights. Thankfully, the city center lies still. The solitude bleeds into my body and instead of feeling lonely, a bubble of singleton glee swells inside my chest. My shopping carts cling, clang, clatter inside my van and the music of metal on metal is an urban orchestral production. I raise my right hand high to conduct a pothole crescendo.

This weekend is a long one, and the business shuffle turned into a mass exodus for the markets. Instead of bidding for pipes, steel cables, real estate, and crude oil, human suits are clamoring in long lineups for carcasses of meat, fowl, and the limbs of large mammals.

An angry blast of a car horn. I stop conducting my symphony to check the side mirror. A brown minivan tailgates my rusty bumper. The van veers left and burns past, a woman in a flowered hat who rolls down her window to shake a white-gloved fist. I raise my eyebrows in alarm. The weather's still cold, after all.

"How dare you finger us! May Jesus forgive your heathen soul!" Her voice is thin, barely audible through my closed window. She must be screaming for me to hear her.

My hand clamps my mouth and I laugh, turtle shoulders shaking with mirth. The flower-hat woman wants to throw something at me, but all she has is her gloved fist.

The minivan roars ahead and cuts me off. I slam on the brakes to avoid rear-ending it and a worn bungee cord snaps, my shopping carts break free. Disengaging, they smack into the back of the cab seats, ricochet the other way, burst through the rear doors to spill out onto the pavement.

"Holy shit!" I gasp, shoulder-check for accidents to ripple behind me.

The silver carts bounce, clang, tumble great acrobatics. Sparks fly and I pray. Pray there are no pedestrians.

"Holy shit!"

I careen to the curb and slam to a stop.

Thank god for Christian holidays. The streets are empty and the crosswalks lifeless. My shopping carts are strewn for three blocks. Some of the wheels broken off, I wonder if I'll have to pay for them. I slump in my seat. Helplessly, start laughing again.

Reach for the CB. "Breaker one-nine."

"Breaker one-nine, copy! Report your status, soldier."

I roll my eyes. "Gary, I'm going to be late." My boss will never fire me because he loves playing CB too much.

"What is your condition?" Gary barks.

"I have incoming wounded. I repeat. I have incoming wounded."

Gary hisses dismay. "Pull back. Return to base. We don't have airlift capability."

"I'm not finished my route," I moan. I have a work ethic, like anybody else.

"Head back, soldier. We'll call it a day." A static pause. "Happy holidays."

I'd rather go on collecting the lost carts than make the pilgrimage home. How many people are writhing through similar contortions? I don't know why I bother, but not knowing doesn't stop me. Doesn't stop my sisters from going home either. Do migrating whales ask themselves why they bother? Of course their reasons aren't the same as mine, but what's to say my biology doesn't have a navigational force over my life? My stomach gurgles oceanic and I clamp my arm over my starving middle. I might as well stock up on more Japanese cucumbers at Bernie's market while I'm downtown. But work first.

I hop out of my van to collect my maimed and scattered carts. The bright orange glow from glass buildings is a myth. The wind bites cold into exposed skin and my teeth clatter.

"Who knows?!" I shout at the empty streets. "Maybe the visit won't be so bad!" For the first time in my adult life, I'm taking someone home with me.

THE CREST OF NIGHT SPLINTERS, the moment between darkness and light breaks so suddenly that my heart fists, small and painful. I wasn't expecting the sun so soon. I wasn't expecting the end of night. I wasn't expecting anything at all, but that didn't stop me from getting pregnant. People always inquire if you're expecting *after* the fact. If anyone asks, I'll say I wasn't expecting a single thing, but pregnancy is a foregone conclusion now.

The frozen ground thunks with my plodding steps. Snow hillocks of crusted ice that won't melt until high August. I swing back my foot to kick a mound, but no, don't bother. It's not so much I want to keep all of my unsightly toenails, but I can't stand pain. And sigh sigh sigh. There are no love stories waiting for me and I'm not up to invention. Too bad, barbed wire's always easier to crawl through when there's someone else to make the space wider with a helpful hand and foot.

I leave pieces of my terrycloth housecoat on a stretch of tangled fence but what I don't realize at the time is that I leave a huge trail of dispirit which meanders everywhere I walk. When the farmer tries to plant some winter wheat in the fall, nothing will grow in the crisscrossing paths, and paranormal investigators will bring extra money into the sagging economy.

Don't get me wrong. I've come to love the prairies, but the frozen beige season that's neither winter nor spring is hardly the best time to be pregnant. And an "abnormal" pregnancy to boot! Over six months and no outward sign, no one asking if I'm in the family way with that tone of universal admiration. Pregnant in a way no one will even notice.

I've no one to blame but myself. Of course I'm not *all* to blame. Of course I *dallied,* so to speak, but not for love and not for keeps and certainly not to bring another child into this horrid life on earth. I'm not a neurotic, antisocial pessimist who thinks that all humans should stop bearing offspring because we have no redeeming qualities. That we're a blight upon our planet. But there you go. People will always believe what you deny. Why waste my breath arguing? No skin off my pregnant belly.

I should have foreseen that unusual acts are followed by unusual consequences. What else could I expect to happen, naked, on an airstrip during the last totally visible lunar eclipse of the twentieth century?

BUT I PRECEDE MYSELF. Before the fetus, there is an egg.

TWO OF MY THREE SISTERS are still sleeping, and so are my parents. I can't imagine waking any one of them for a family jaunt. We're not the sort of people that walk together, at dawn or otherwise, exclaiming at nature and the shades of lavender-pink on the horizon. The only reason I am up is heart-squeezing indigestion. None of us, me included, are morning people. My youngest sister is, though, and she's awake. Busy riding circles around the farmhouse on her new bicycle. A flashlight strapped to her temple. She's trying to balance a jar of peanut butter on top of her head while she bumps around Okasan's wishful-thinking lawn. As my sister bounces over frozen gopher holes, the beam of light swings jerkily from the grass to the walls of the house to the expansive sky. The thought occurs to me that something weighted more evenly than the butterknife-scooped contents of a jar might be easier to balance, but then I think, why is she trying to balance *anything* at all?

I don't claim to be the only sane person in an insane family. I'm not saying that I'm the only sane person in an insane world.

My Okasan suggests that I should complain a little less. That we ought to be grateful that our family came to Canada. We should see what life is like in Japan before we complain about things here. If we still lived in Nihon, Okasan murmurs, I would be happily married with two kids and my two younger sisters wouldn't even be conceived, let alone born, Japan such a crowded and expensive country. As if this should make me feel better! I stroke the unpregnant curve of my belly in a pregnant woman type of way.

A child isn't born bitter. I point no fingers as to who tainted the clean, pure pool of my childhood. Let's just say that when I realized that I didn't want to grow up, the damage was already done. Knowing that being grown up was no swell place to be means that you are grown up enough to notice. And you can't go back from there. You have to forge another route, draw your own map.

I roof a ridge over my eyes with my mittened hand, peer into the sun. Green circles lift from the solar disk and float above my head. Arms spread wide in a Jesus posture of simultaneous trust and supplication, I tip slow-motion backwards. No! Snow's not soft! But I'm halfway fallen and can't stop, crunch into the ice behind me. Ouch. Angels are out of the question. I feel like I have broken into a sheet of dull glass, but the pain is tolerable after the ice melts. The unexpected one kicks peeved feet against my kidney. Sorry already! I didn't mean to disturb you. I dig into my house-coat pocket and grab the slender, green fruit of a Japanese cucumber. What a beauty! Half the size of the grotesquely enlarged English variety, and a lovely curve in the tail. Shaped like an uppercase J. The bumpy skin tickles through the wool of my mittens and the green is bamboo-fresh. Bite off the bitter stem part and spit it toward my feet. Crunch. Chew. Wedge. Ahhh. The unexpected one is consoled.

The sun is winter-dim, the sky too pale to be called light blue. Crying is an option but one I don't make much use of. I don't think of myself as a complainer. Maybe bitterly realistic and sarcastic to boot, but it's hard to be otherwise. Especially if you're an ugly, pregnant Asian born into a family not of your choosing. The odd thing about your looks is that you never see your own face. Funny how that works. How your reflection isn't really who you are, just an image of your real self contained in glass. You go your whole life without seeing yourself as you really are. All you know is how you are treated. Just as well, I suppose. All surface and no depths make for a poor swimming pool, my Okasan says.

My teeth clatter. I've heard that once you get past the cold, hypothermia is a pleasant way to die, but if you can't get past the cold, there's no point in trying. Not that I would ever consider suicide. I can make a tragedy out of my personal life without having to die.

When I stand, the wind freezes the wet back side of my clothes into grating stiffness. My lack of foresight never ceases to amaze me. I try walking fast enough to stay warm, but when I start warming up, the frozen parts of my housecoat melt. Not much of a choice between frozen and wet. As I finally crawl through the last fence, the sun is past its apex and backing down again. And no later than 11:00 A.M.

Mice has left her bike and an empty peanut butter jar lying on the grass. Can't see the flashlight though. At least she has sense enough to take it indoors and avoid drawing attention from Dad. I sigh. This is Mice's fourth bicycle and still counting, each bike cheaper, by half, than its predecessor. She has had two stolen and lost the other and not a hope in hell of the latest seeing a longer life in her hands than three months. Well, none of my business. But I push her bike to the side of the house, the windless side. Hopefully, Dad is nursing his leg and hasn't gone out to check the fields.

I don't know why he checks the spread every day. Especially in the winter. The fields aren't going anywhere. Well, I guess they are. They lift and blow blow away to be dust elsewhere. Wishing the soil would stay doesn't help one bit and if I were Dad, I wouldn't want to watch my life scatter like that.

Mice is probably inside, sleeping off her early exercise or a peanut butter tummy-ache. She probably got fed up with the knife-slathered contents of the jar. Hard to balance, she must have kept on dipping into the jar to level the paste, dip and stick, smack, cluck cluck of tongue on palate, a sludge of peanut guts adhering to the dome of her mouth. She probably licked and smacked all of the peanut glue into her Micely stomach and now Okasan's looking for the ancient enema. Nope, Dad's still inside, his golf cart parked with a couple of garbage bags as a cover. Rocks on top to keep them from being plucked by the wind. Orange Cat sits beside one of the tires. Sniffs a paw, then lick, lick. He slides into an arch, extending toes and toenails, knowing he has an audience. The rocks are too heavy to knock off for a satisfying piss on the seat so the cat sniffs once, lifts his tail, and sprays each tire. I halfheartedly toss a pebble in his direction but he only flicks one paw before mincing across the gravel drive and into the fallow field.

Our mother's name for the cats is a running joke in the family. If you don't speak Japanese, it doesn't matter, but if you do, you'd be better off calling all the cats "Redundant."

Okasan gave us all Japanese names too, but folks couldn't remember for nothing, as the saying goes. Hard to know what was worse. Having names no one could say or being called names not our own. What's in a name? some people say. A great deal, was my conclusion. So when it was apparent no one could utter us intelligibly, I made up new names, based on the animal of our birth year. Names that would disguise and protect us. I was particularly stumped, though, by next younger sister who was born in the Year of the Boar. Who wants to be called any form of a wild pig? A bore?

"We call them inoshishi," Okasan offered.

We all started laughing, my sisters and I, because "Shi, shiii" was what our mother said to help us pee.

"I suppose we could just say, 'Shi,'" I mused, "but it might get confusing."

"Why?" my beautiful older sister demanded. "Why would it get confusing? I think *Shi* sounds pretty and feminine."

"Exactly," I sighed impatiently. "We would be saying *Shi,* but everyone would be hearing *she.* Like, if we said, 'Shi went to summer camp,' people would say, 'Who went to summer camp?' and we'd say, 'Shi did!' and they'd say, 'Who?! Who?! What's her goddamn name!'"

"Oh, I get it!" My oldest sister laughed and laughed until we stared pointedly, then she quit.

"Goddamn yuwanaino," Okasan scolded gently.

"No," I muttered. "She can't be Shi . . ." I stared at my next younger sister's face. Her perpetually frowning brow. The left eye that floated slightly upward.

"You," I blessed the top of her head, "shall so be named Pig Girl!"

Her eyebrows creased into one bushy line.

"PG for short," I amended.

PG gave a quick jerk of her chin.

"You," I turned to my youngest sister. She stared so intently I had to look away. "You will be known as Mice."

Mice hooted softly in approval.

"Make one for me! Something really nice," my oldest sister pleaded, and I rolled my small eyes inside the pumpkin expanse of my head.

"Stop doing that," my beautiful sister whined. "You're scaring me."

"Scary things aren't scary if you're not scared of them," PG chanted.

I rolled my eyes even more, but stopped when my temples started aching.

"What's mine? What's mine? Pick one for meeeee."

I held out my hand, palm forward, to silence my oldest sister, and she stuffed the slender heel of her hand into her kissy mouth. Fairly panting with anticipation. It was hard for me to believe that she was a year older. Hard for me to believe we were related.

"I anoint thee, from henceforth to be called Slither!"

"Yay! Banzai!" PG cheered and wordless Mice clapped her hands, a sharp staccato. Slither pressed her tapered fingers over her tiny ears.

"Oh no!" she shook. "No, that's just awful! It's so gross! Can't it be something nicer? Please?"

"Sorry," I shrugged, my turtle shoulders heaving, "the Name Master has spoken." I thumped downstairs. Slither trailed after me, ahhhh pleading, but I ignored her and shut myself in the downstairs bathroom. I locked the door with the small hook that dropped into the tiny loop. Even Slither could have pushed the door in if she wanted to, but the sound of the cheap metal hook slipping into place shut out my sister more than if I had hung up a sign. I heard her mincing back up the stairs.

And shortly after the day I renamed us, Dad made a big announcement.

We were moving again. Away from the coast. To the Great Prairies.

And there is an egg.

The way is darkmurky and the tunnel wetly warm. I linger briefly in the waving cilia passage, easy as a speck of sand among undulating ribbons of seaweed. Lovely and rich. How wondrous, being an egg. I am surrounded by six thousand of my egg sisters. Laughing softly, their presence a comforting murmur of water. And how I feel! The perpetual sense of potential, vibrant and miraculous. How can the infinitely possible be compared to terminal growth? Degeneration? How can an egg live in an environment that is not bathed in rich moisture? The intimacy of blood. I didn't ask to become a fetus. It's a bad sign, don't you think. How we develop, not by growing, but by splitting.

I'M COLD BUT IT'S HARD TO GO INSIDE. The new, dark pink curtains Okasan put up for Easter make the window eyes glow with an unholy light. I guess she's never seen them lit up from the outside. Creak up the three old, wooden steps to the small patch of porch. Made by Dad for Okasan's anniversary present. My hands curl to fists in my pockets and the distance from there to the latch on the porch door seems impossible. Why do I to these dinners?

"Are you coming inside?" Mice at the mesh door. She isn't sleeping after all, must have been there the whole time, watching me for who knows how long. Jesus! She gives me the willies, as they say around these parts.

"Of course!" I bluster. Take my hands out of my pockets and slap at my soppy housecoat. I look up to smile, but I just can't.

Mice stares at me, a bit too long. Until I look away. When I look back, she's disappeared without my hearing her go. Mice's never grown up. She isn't a child and she isn't an adult, she lingers somewhere in a region where general modes of human conduct are skewed in a Micely manner.

"You were out walking for a long time." She's breathing at the screen again and I almost manage to control a nervous twitch.

"Uh huh," I smile from the other side.

"Pizza doesn't have to have cheese and tomato sauce," Mice continues, pinching a strand of hair and poking it through the dust clumps clogging the screen door.

I wait impatiently, knowing she is working up to something.

"Doke!" Dad lurches past, Mice, jumping to get out of his way, crashes into Okasan's laddered clotheshanger draped with laundry. Dad's briefs fall to the muddy boot-room floor and Mice's feet get caught in the leg-holes.

"Bakatare!" he spits, and bangs the porch door open with one of his crutches.

I cringe instinctively. Then, manage to stand still.

"Good morning to you, too," I smile sweetly.

And in an about-face, with Napoleonic charm, he laughs, tossing his head back to reveal his pumpkin teeth.

"Happy Eastah," he grins. Dad fists a hand into the crumbly reaches of his pants pocket. He draws out two pieces of chewing gum wrapped in tinfoil that is beginning to fleck off. Grins his chin at me to hold out my palm for the dubious offering. Smiling, our father thumps down the porch steps to his golf cart. Crutches in the golf-club holder, he whirs down the gravel track.

Mice glides back to her place at the screen. So silent in her movements after Dad is gone. His underwear still on the floor.

"Pizzas are nice for breakfast."

WHILE I SHOWER, Mice rolls out dough, chops pineapple, raisins, almonds, and canned flakes of ham. Bakes Micely morning pizza for me.

Steam rising from my heated skin, still glowing, my hair drips onto pancake-sized disks. Mice stares at my mouth, watches each grind of my pumpkin teeth, compliments of good old Dad.

"It's yummy," I say, meaning it, lapping up spilled topping from my plate.

"What's good?" pipes Slither, mincing up the stairs.

"Mice's pizza."

"Pizzas are healthy," Mice states.

Slither raises her Noh eyebrows and pats her slender butt. "I can't be too careful. There's all that eating to be done tonight. I'll just have some of the cottage cheese I brought down with me."

"Yes, dahhhling, do eat your cottage cheese," I trill. I snatch my fork and stab a heaping disk, dripping minced fruit and ham goo down my fresh gingham pajamas, my sodden housecoat drying on the shower curtain. I shove the mass into my mouth and chew, chew, smack, chew, squelching between my colossal teeth.

"You're so gross. Why can't you grow up?" Slither smiles sadly.

Mice's serious eyes burst wide and she tips back her head, "Wa! Ha! Ha! Ha! Ha! Ha!"

"Shut up!" PG bellows from the living room. Not enough bedrooms for all of us at home. "Shut UP! SHUT UP!" Frowns furiously as she barges through the kitchen and pounds down the stairs. To sleep in the still-warm pocket left in Slither's bed.

"Easter ni shut up yuwanaino," Okasan calls from the bathroom.

Egged on by Slither's disappointment, I jab my fork through the last three pizzas. Cram my mouth so full that fruit paste, bits of canned ham spurt from my nose. Mice rolls on the floor, clutching her stomach and gurgling in seldom-heard laughter.

"Okaaaaaasan!" Slither screams. "You stop! You're going to ruin the holiday home!"

"SHUT UP!" PG bellows from the basement.

"Ara maaaa," Okasan murmurs. She steps over Mice, still convulsing on the sticky linoleum, and hands me a piece of Kleenex.

MICE'S BREAKFAST HAS SETTLED MY STOMACH. But pizzas are not enough. I must have cucumbers. I rustle in the fridge where I have hidden my stash. Good. No one has found them. Grab two thin, crispy lengths and sit at the kitchen table. Ahhhhhh. Nothing like Japanese cucumbers. In a pinch, I can get by with the English variety, but they are as watery as they are huge. Japanese cucumbers are lean and crunchy sweet, green like summer. I munch them with delight. The creature, inside me, stretches with satisfaction and I can almost hear a sound like moving water.

Okasan mutters at the sink about people who like to cook but who don't clean up after themselves. Sighing profoundly. Mice is outside again, trying to ride her bicycle backwards. Slither blow-dries her hair. None of us offers to help our mother with the dinner preparations, the soaking of azuki beans, the boiling of cabbage leaves, the chopping of celery and carrots for the turkey stuffing. Slither always complains about the giblets and kidney and I always want them.

I join PG, downstairs. I don't particularly want to sleep *with* my sister, but I'm willing to risk the intimacy. Slither's old bedroom is the only place far enough away from the clatter of kitchen and Okasan's chronic sighs. Okasan's turned PG and Mice's room into her own, and my old basement room is storage. When we come home for these family dinners, there aren't enough places to sleep. Luckily, our stays never exceed forty-eight hours and I usually manage to pass one night on the wicker rec-room couch, one night on a fought-over bed.

I thump down the stairs, my white socks getting dirtier and dirtier with each step. I hear Dad whirring back from his inspection of the fields. The thunk-pad, thunk-pad of his crutches on the linoleum. The rattle of bottles in the fridge door.

My small eyes curl with disgust. I push my butt into PG's back until she flops over. But my tense body keeps her from falling back into the pools of sleep.

"What's wrong?" my sister whispers. Her brows squeezed together above her clenched eyes.

"Dad's started snorting already," I hiss. "Can't he wait until after dinner?!"

"Too bad, so sad. It's a holiday so he thinks he can relax and do whatever he wants."

"Well, I guess every goddamn day of his life is a holiday, then!"

"You wouldn't be so fucking disappointed if you didn't expect him to change," PG snaps.

I glare at her floating left eye. "You're starting to sound like Okasan."

PG flips angrily over onto her stomach. Flicks her long hair into my face, stinging. "Face reality. He's addicted to nasal spray and he'll never quit. Happy endings, sad endings. Just shut up, because I need to get some sleep."

And she does. Sleeps like someone whose guts aren't twisting into pretzels. I curl up into a tight ball and slowly hug myself into nothing.

When I wake up, PG is gone and Mice is in her place. Flat on her back, with her arms crossed over her chest. All she needs is a sarcophagus. Breath shallow and even. I stare at her like I cannot when she is awake.

Her unplucked eyebrows are wispy, incongruous with the jut of her nose. Cheekbones sharp like our Okasan, tiny, childlike lips. Her eyelids move with the motion of her eyes, seeing events pass in a kaleidoscope of dreams. And because she can't see me, will never know, I lean over and kiss her gently on the forehead.

Upstairs, Okasan furiously rolls minced beef and rice into floppy cabbage leaves.

"You haven't started stewing them yet?" I yawn, picking sleep out of the corners of my eyes.

Okasan sighs, mutters something about so many children who don't like to help, then smoothes her complaint with a smile.

PG eats a bowl of Raisin Bran without milk. She catches me looking at her and she rolls her eyes, the left one on its own time. She mimics our mother's pained expression and stuffs dry cereal into her sneering mouth. I halfheartedly grab a limp cabbage leaf and slop meat stuffing into the middle. My mendo kusai fingers clumsy, the cabbage tears when I try to roll it. Okasan sighs and clicks her tongue. Nudges me over with her hip and salvages my attempt with a toothpick.

"Potato salada wo tsukutte kurenai kana?" she suggests.

"Sure," I answer. She hands me a bowl of boiled potatoes and I furiously mash them. Add mayonnaise, pickle bits, celery, and tomatoes. Toss in some pickled herring to make it more festive.

Slither toes her way into the kitchen, flapping her hands limply to dry her Passionately Pink fingernails. She leans over my shoulder in a cloud of VO5 hairspray. Opens her mouth for a taste and I spoon some obligingly. Her eyes roll frantically in her foundation-slathered face and she spits the mouthful into the sink where Okasan has her boiled cabbage.

"Okasan! The potato salad's ruined! It's disgusting!" Slither shrieks.

Our mother sighs. Picks out Slither's spat potato and throws it in the garbage. Rinses each of the cabbage leaves contaminated with my sister's saliva and manages, through pinched lips, to sigh again. Slither and I look guiltily at each other for making more work for her.

"It's your fault," Slither hisses. "No one's going to eat that slop."

"I will," I spoon a big glob into my mouth. The flavor is odd and before I can stop myself, the potato flies out of my face and into Okasan's cabbage sink.

Okasan just stands there, shakes her head, shakes her head without making a sound. From the living room, there is the snap of a newspaper being straightened, loud and sudden, like the pop of a gun. We jump, then we are still.

I KICK THE PORCH DOOR OPEN with Okasan's boot. Night again and the stars don't care. A waft of minty tobacco. The porchlight shines a pallor around PG, perched on top of Dad's golf cart. Her knees pulled to her chest, feet making the seat all mucky. She flicks the butt without watching and the ember glows.

"Wanna smoke?" she calls out.

"Hardly," I mutter. Warm vapor breath clouding before me. I cinch my terry robe more tightly around my square body and trudge toward her.

"Is Okasan finished her dinner frenzy? It's fucking almost ten. I don't know why she fucking bothers." PG sighs. Wiggle-butts some room for me to sit beside her, but I don't.

"Why do *you* bother?" I ask. PG swears more than anyone I know. Maybe as a countermeasure for her floating eye.

PG takes a hard drag of her smoke and flicks it away, a high arch into a crust of ice. Flips her long hair away from her face with that upward chin jerk.

"As soon as I figure it out, you'll be the first to know," she smirks. "Besides, you're older. Haven't you figured things out yet?"

"Would I be here if I had?" I snort.

Black Cat's green eyes stare from outside the circle of light. Click of lighter. Curl of more tobacco.

"You smoke too much," I say.

"Too bad, so sad," PG quips.

As it turns out, Mice likes the herring-flavored potato salad and doesn't bother eating anything else. Okasan sits with pinched lips, still trying to force a happy face, taking little sips of her martini. Like James Bond. PG eats slices of the dark meat from the thighs of the turkey like meat is going to be extinct tomorrow.

"You'll be constipated if you don't get some vegetables," Slither advises, concerned. Slither turns to me; her teeth are smooth and even. A polished row, they're lovely enough to be put on a necklace. "My orthodontist could do so much for you."

Mice bursts into a loud giggle, stops herself, glancing at Dad. He ignores her.

"Okasan," Slither beams, "I can do your home permanent if you want. I brought a kit with me. Imported from France."

PG's eyebrows screw even closer together, her left eye looking for an escape route while she forks up more meat. Okasan doesn't bother answering. The martini is icy and her face glows. I cringe, drag the sleeve of my dressy going-out pajamas across a dish of soya sauce. Shit.

The clink of metal forks on cheap ceramic plates. I stare at the turkey carcass. We would have killed for a turkey when we were kids. Slither may be annoying beyond belief, but she always brings something home to roast in the oven. Mice giggles for no good reason and PG pinches the soft meat of her underarm.

"Ouch!" Mice squeaks. Glances up at Dad but he's thumped

to the kitchen. The fridge. The blast and snort. PG slides me a look.

"And how's work, PG?" Slither tries. So hard.

"Work sucks," PG grins. "I'm looking for a new job after the holidays."

"Easter ni sucks te yuwanaino," Okasan mouths slowly, her pupils round and shiny. Dad thumps back and Okasan's cheek gives a little jerk. She lifts her martini-cooled hand to stroke the jumpy place on her face.

"What's this about quitting?" Dad asks.

"Nothing," PG mutters.

"We are not a family of quitters!"

My sisters and I, we hold our forks still. Silence made tick-tock loud. My knife doesn't have a serrated edge. My small eyes dart. The turkey knife does. The silence tick ticks in a compression of time.

Dad snorts. Hacks at the phlegm in the back of his throat. We all unclench our breaths and our lives seep out into the world again. Okasan brings her martini to her lips and kisses the icy liquid.

"Isn't this turkey nice?" Slither smiles. The foundation on her face doesn't hide her tremor. "This turkey is free-range. It's never had any antibiotics."

"Great," I chew.

PG circles her thumb and forefinger, another mouthful of dark meat in her mouth. Okasan nods slowly. She hasn't eaten a bite. Dad points his finger at the turkey. Juts his chin at Mice to cut him a slice. Mice flicks her panicked eyes at each of us in quick succession, but we turn aside our faces.

"What are you waiting for?"

Mice makes a small sound and raises trembling hands. The carving fork and knife clink against the edge of the serving plate and Dad's jaw tightens. Mice hacks at a drumstick, saws desperately through sinew and gristle. Stabs the limb with the two-pronged fork and jerks the meat to Dad's plate. The meat pulls away from bone and slips off the tines, rolls off the plate to splat into our father's lap.

"Bakatare!" Dad roars, and raises his hand. The pattern so ingrained he can't stop.

We cringe to the thud of blood in our heads. Anything more and Okasan will shatter like a pane of glass, we will only slice our hands if we try to salvage her. Don't move. Be still. Okasan's martini stem in her knuckled fist. Black Cat meows from the kitchen. Shudder of wind against the screen door. The thin windows. Black Cat meows from the kitchen. Please, be still.

Then, we all stand. Slither, me, PG, and even Mice. We all stand, around the table, silent. And we are not small. Dad can see that we are grown. We aren't little children and he can't strike us anymore. His eyes scorch our faces, muscles in his jaw clenched into teeth, blood shooting into his forehead, our silent protest to his face. Rage frustrated, he turns to the table itself. Grabs two fistfuls of tablecloth and pulls. Turkey carcass, stewed cabbage rolls, buns, sashimi, sekihan, potato salad, peas and carrots. The hours of work Okasan has spent, wasted on the floor.

Okasan sits. Her martini in her hand.

In her sock feet, Mice flies out the door. Slither grabs a coat, plunges into rubber boots, and chases after her with extra shoes and a jacket. PG's mouth falls open. Bawling, she pounds down the stairs, slamming the door to Slither's old bedroom, and Dad looks bewildered at the carnage around him, dumbfounded.

"Going to bed," he says, and limps slowly down the hallway.

I get a garbage bag and gather all of Okasan's sigh-laden food. Save the turkey for soup or maybe for the cats. Wipe up the floor, wash the dishes, and even put them away. The clock above the sink ticks too loud. PG won't come upstairs. How far can Mice run? The creature inside me must feel the danger, keeps still. *Everything's okay,* I think soothing thoughts. *Don't be scared. See, no one got hit. We're fine.*

The whole time, Okasan sitting in her chair, drink in hand but not drinking. Wide-eyed and smiling. I let her stay there for a while so her heart will calm. And I go to the fridge for a cucumber. Stand in the open cool, stand there and crunch and crunch.

MY SISTERS AND I are all physically grown but people would be hard-pressed to describe us as adults in the house of our parents. Every time we come home, we slip into our childhood roles. No one is exempt. Until death do us part.

Slither comes back after I manage to get Okasan to the spare upstairs room. The coffee I fixed tastes worse than bad. I add more grounds and lukewarm water from the kettle.

"I couldn't catch up with her. So I got in my car, but she started running cross-country. Without her shoes!" Slither slumps onto a chair.

I shake my enormous head. Pour her a cup of mud.

There is a cold emanation and we jump. Mice. In the doorway. Shivering and sweating at the same time, her eyes glittering.

"Good run," she states.

"You'll catch pneumonia!" Slither gasps, runs to the living room for the TV blanket. She wraps Mice and pours her a mug of coffee. Pushes her into a chair. I reach down, lift Mice's icy feet onto my lap. Gently pull off her torn socks and inspect the bottoms of her feet.

"Get the first-aid stuff," I tell Slither.

She comes back quickly, her pretty face wrinkled with worry. And in an instant, I know what she will look like when she is old.

"Give me the tweezers," I order, and Slither hands them to me. Gets out cotton balls, gauze, and iodine. I hold my sister's foot and carefully pick out thistles, straw, bits of tiny gravel. Mice doesn't even wince, just sips her coffee. With the warmth and the removal of the debris from her feet, the blood starts to flow.

"Oh, gross," Slither groans and goes to lie down in the living room.

I sigh. Slither is such a wimp. I can never count on her.

Orange Cat curls around the legs of Mice's chair and she swings her free foot at him. The cat figure-eights out of her reach. Click clacks across the linoleum floor to sit in front of the dried goods cupboard.

A sliver embedded deep into the tough flesh of Mice's heel keeps on slipping out of the bloody tweezers. I wince, grit my teeth, try pulling again.

"You should get a tetanus shot when you go back," I manage.

Mice shrugs. Takes another mouthful of coffee.

I glance up at her face. "Does this hurt?"

"Not at all," Mice smiles.

Footsteps coming from the downstairs. My sister and I turn our heads at the same time.

PG, nonchalant, swings her overnight bag over her shoulder, a cigarette between her lips. Her eyelids are swollen from crying into her pillow and the traveling eye rolls wildly from the strain but she grins razor-sharp.

"Nice fucking Easter. I'm leaving before Okasan has one of her fits."

Mice and I glance at each other.

"Oh yeah," I mutter, wondering if I could feel lower than this, how the bottom falls out from beneath us over and over again.

"If you were smart, you'd leave too. They're both so pathetic. Nice fucking family. I'm not coming back," PG sneers. Tears fill her eyes.

"Don't say that! Where are you going?" Mice's voice rising in panic.

"Happy endings, sad endings," PG chants her childhood refrain, until her lips wobble. She lights her cigarette in the kitchen, an act of disrespect and utter bravado. Takes three quick drags.

"I'll drop a line, kids," she salutes, keys jingling in her hand. The porch door slams behind her and the revving engine of her used MG. A present from a moderately rich ex-lover. Gravel spins from the tires and peppers the siding on the house.

"She's gone now," Mice says softly.

And Mice is right.

Eggs can talk, only most of us choose not to. Words are creatures without skin, without living fluid. There are no allegiances in language. Take, for instance, the word love. I may utter "love" and someone may take this very word and use it against me. Words are tricks I seldom want to play.

What I do trust is the pounding surge of blood streaming through the caverns of my home. Sound, pulsing tidal and eternal. At least I do trust, until the time of the splitting. When something whole is made to fracture in order to grow. The sounds of my six thousand sister eggs begin to fade, their comforting murmurs grow silent. Words are never spoken yet their beautiful siren voices hum living songs in endless harmony. My perfect companions, they grow still, one by one, until I am alone. I did not ask to be alone. I did not ask.

I begin to understand that events yet unimagined will still ripen without consent. So I must imagine the unimaginable. I may be cast from my water home.

No.

I am a creature of water. And I will remain one.

I have an inkling, then, of someone other than the sisters I have lost. I can sense, with my thin outer membrane, a pulsing and heaving that cushions my being. Maybe even a glimmer of intelligent life. I nourish a small hope in my nucleus that intelligent life can exist outside an egg.

SLITHER FALLS ASLEEP on the couch, exhausted. Who knows what she carries for baggage, the whiny child who got clobbered the most. Mice and I sit at the kitchen table. Calico Cat minces in from somewhere and leaves when she sees that Okasan is not in the room. We should go to sleep too. I should go to sleep. There's no use in sitting here. And if we stick around, our mother might get it into her head that her children ought to notice her and give her the love she always wanted but could never receive. Ha! That's a laugh. We can't even love ourselves.

A cucumber would be nice. A crispy, sweet cucumber. But Mice still rests her feet in my lap. And I can at least do this much for her. We sit in the clock-ticking silence, and drink shitty coffee.

How We Came to the Great Prairies:
A Family Drama

I T WAS A WINDLESS DAY. An oddity southeast of what I know now as Lethbridge. The Old Man River churned brown and feeble, barely even bothering to flow, and grasshoppers gasped their last, midair, then shattered like Christmas tree ornaments on the heat-pounded ground. The air so hot that you could hear the pavement warping, the hum of melting tar rising into the air.

The temperature inside our station wagon was unbearable. We might have cooled our bodies by turning on the heater full blast. Past the point of bickering, my sisters and I stuck helplessly to the vinyl, too hot to bother avoiding the gluey smear of skin on skin.

Okasan drove in jerks and starts. The seat of the car pulled close to the steering wheel. Dad sat with two fists clenched on his thighs.

"Migi!" he barked directions. "Hidari! Migi! Koko! Koko! KOKO!"

"No need to yell," Okasan smiled tiredly. Her lips fading.

"Could we stop soon?" Slither whispered. "I feel dizzy."

"Ara!" Okasan glanced in the rearview mirror before returning her bug-eyed gaze to the shimmering road.

"We're not stopping anywhere!"

"It's really hot," Slither whined, as carefully as she could. Our two baby sisters heaped limply against each other in the middle of the seat and they couldn't even moan. They slept, hardly breathing.

"Damare!" Dad shouted.

Slither swung the car door open, leaned out, holding onto the handle. She puked cherries onto the oily pavement like she was lining it with paint. A blur of smell and sound. I thought that she was vomiting blood. Dad reached out, crammed the transmission into park, momentum flinging all of us like wet gunnysacks.

"No more," he uttered. Stepped out of the stinking car and pissed on the land he claimed for his own.

The spread of dusty grass stretched as far as the eye dared to look. A barbed wire fence leaned outward, the posts tipping in the same direction. A faded For Sale sign flaked paint and a sudden gust brought no sound of living people, only trills of unseen birds. And the peeps of gophers.

We lifted our eyes to the forever sky, forest rabbits searching for a canopy of leaf and branches. Okasan's hands hung limply from her arms, only attached by skin. I worried that they might drop off, but her fingers moved a little, so I knew they weren't dead. Our mother stared at the baked ground beneath her feet. Muttered something softly, I couldn't sort out the words for the hum of exhaust lifting off the car, the grasshoppers shattering on the ground around us. I pulled my copy of *Little House on the Prairie* from the inside of my T-shirt and flipped to the section where the Pa and Ma set up camp and made molasses sandwiches. Pa went out to shoot a fat rabbit for dinner.

The station wagon hissed. A piece of plywood had been drilled into the roof for the pile of crates, plastic-wrapped bedding, and some wooden chairs. Slither was snuffling in the sweaty crook of her elbow, the tang of puke still stuck to the back of her throat. PG and Mice could only hold each other's hands and stare. As I watched Dad trampling prairie grass, all I could think was where did we come from? Where are we now?

Okasan dragged our bruised cooler from behind the back seat. Unpacked the glass milk-jar still half-full of tepid barley tea, arranged onigiri on paper plates for lunch. My sisters and I flopped on the ground. We reached with weak hands for the paper cups that Okasan filled.

"Going back to that last town," Dad muttered, and got behind the steering wheel of the car. He drove away, leaving us with no shade at all.

Okasan smiled. "Sabakuni kita ne," she said.

We have come to a desert.

I thought there was too much grass to be a desert. No one said anything, though. What mattered was the heat.

Okasan walked to the edge of the tawny spread and started plucking long stems.

"Anatatachimo tottechodai," she requested, so we left our unwanted lunch to pick grass with her. The dust rose into our nostrils and we sneezed until the heat turned the tickley dust into hardened clots of snot.

"We need more, please don't stop," our mother told us. Okasan squatted by the pile we had made and started to braid the stems together, her fingers shredding, turning the gold-green stems red. She wove with her hands and her blood five canopies of grass.

When she was finished, we lay beneath our individual domes, heads all close together, our legs the spokes of a human wheel. We were synchronized swimmers on the prairie ocean, looking skyward from beneath our shelter. Bits of intense blue meshed into our vision. We were no longer frightened. Gophers came to sniff, nibbled at our feet. We dozed in and out of sleep like ebbing water.

"Pa," I cried. "I'm on fire!"

"Half-pint," he managed. "It's the malaria from the creek. Get your Ma some water . . ."

I woke up.

The sun squatted lower in the forever sky and we heard the crunch of gravel beneath tires.

"Ara!" Okasan exclaimed, pushing the shelter of grass away from her head. "We must have fallen asleep and nothing made for supper!"

We rushed to where we'd left our lunch in the blazing sun. Our rice balls were pecked and scattered into clear, dry pellets. The tepid barley tea hot to the touch. Okasan hurriedly packed everything into the cooler before Dad could see.

The car door slammed and my sisters and I sat closer together. We had all fallen asleep. There was nothing made for supper.

Dad carried the stink of fried chicken. A greasy brown paper bag held against his chest, his free arm swung enthusiastically and he grinned.

Fried chicken was the last thing I wanted to eat. I touched my swollen tongue to my lips; they were coated with dust. I longed for green platters of cold somen noodles, icy soup to slurp into my brittle mouth. But Dad was cheerful. His fast hand reached out before I could duck, and he mussed the top of my head.

"That smells great!" I beamed my gapped teeth.

Slither gulped back sour porridge of cherries and stretched her mouth into a smile-face. "I love fried chicken," she whined.

Okasan lugged my heat-stupid baby sisters beside the car. The sliver of shade was a little wider, though the engine ticked like a bomb. Our mother made PG and Mice swallow pinches of salt before she gave them more tea. Then, they drank until their tummies expanded like balloons. PG frowned, her left eye rolling toward the summer sky, her right eye glaring at nothing I could see. Mice just clung to PG's hand, her still baby-fat legs bowing slightly. Slither had rings of dust around her nose holes, but I didn't laugh. She was pretty no matter what she looked like.

"Picnic!" Dad's hair stood up off his wide forehead, making his large head look even larger.

"Ara," Okasan murmured.

Dad unwrapped the greasy chicken on top of the cooler. Slither gulped with a choking sound. Our father handed out pieces of deep-fried meat, beaming, and I almost stumbled backwards. He was so handsome when he was happy.

"Here," he thrust pieces at each of us, "here, here."

He thrust me a drumstick.

I quick-glanced my mother, but she gave a small shake of head. A drumstick, I thought. A drumstick. A drumstick with all that rubbery hosing along the bone and fat black threads of blood. Bile rose acid-painful and splashed the cavern of my mouth. I swallowed. Tore off big chunks with my colossal teeth and gulped them whole so I wouldn't have to feel the texture between my molars.

Dad laughed. Tossing back his head, revealing the teeth that only I inherited. "Go on! Go on!" he urged, handing me the second drumstick.

My chin wobbled, but I clenched my teeth and bit the insides of my cheeks. Never in front of people and never ever in front of my family. I never cried.

I ate them both. The two disgusting legs, the gristly white threads growing like tapeworms in my stomach.

Slither glanced at me. She knew how awful the drumsticks were, but she could hardly help. She couldn't even help herself. Okasan handed me a cup of tea so I could flood the chewy meat down.

Dad swept his arm toward the spread of land. "I bought the property!" he exclaimed.

"This land right here? What we're sitting on?" Slither asked, incredulous. "This is where we're going to live?!"

The charm dropped off his face and he snatched another piece of chicken from the moist box. "You don't like my choice?" he chewed, spraying some soggy crumbs with the force of his words.

"No, Dad, I-I really like it here. There's lots of room," Slither started sniffling.

"Maaa," Okasan said gently. "Isn't that wonderful."

Dad stared off to the edge of prairie. Sighed. The square of his shoulders settled a few inches lower. "This might be our lucky chance," he muttered, then tossed back his head to laugh. He plunged his hand into the greasy box for another piece of chicken. "Go on, eat!" he exclaimed.

No one asked where he got the money to buy that sorry piece of property. No one dared.

So very late at night. Okasan hasn't come downstairs to stare sadly at us. To wait for words of support and love. I should count this as a gift but all I can do is keep sinking into childhood quicksands. I used to be able to shut out the bad. Why do my defenses fail me now? I should phone someone! There's no use talking to anyone in this madhouse. Calling friends is reasonable if there's a family crisis. Maybe I could phone Genevieve. She has sound intuition. No, she's been asleep for hours by now. Maybe late-night Midori is still up. Watching an old Godzilla movie, eating corn chips and smoking her nasty Camels. Maybe Midori is wondering how my Easter is going and—no, of course not. Why would she be thinking about me? Especially when she has Genevieve. Maybe I should just eat a cucumber. The creature nudges encouragement near my left kidney.

"You make interesting coffee." Mice is solemn, her bandaged feet still in my lap. Slither sleeps on the living room couch, her soft snoring, which she always denies, even and deep and somehow soothing.

"It tastes like shit," I smirk, then pour us some more. We sit together, Mice and I, in the quiet, twitching space of waiting for Okasan. Mice and I sit, uncomfortably comfortable. Wide wide-awake.

"It's funny," I suck up my disgusting dregs. "For the longest time, I couldn't remember whole sections of my childhood. Especially the year we moved here. But now, pieces are coming back. Chunks and scenes come together and—I don't know. I don't want to remember."

"Oh," Mice blinks. Pause. "I remember everything."

"Everything? No one can remember everything!"

"I see it," she taps her head with her chewed fingertip. "Everything's all inside here, and I can see our past like a movie. Over and over again."

I think about the distant blur-memory I have. The body-memory of things my mind blanks out for me. All saved in spools of images trapped inside Mice's mind.

"Oh," I say softly. Can't imagine the weight of our lives etched into her brain. "Oh." I want to say something. But I feel so useless. There is nothing I can say to make things better. There is nothing I can say to make things go away.

"I feel better," Mice blinks. "My feet are sore."

I set her heels on my seat and get painkillers from the washroom cupboard. I hand her two and she obediently dry-swallows them, then, as an afterthought, chases them with tepid coffee. I sit in the empty seat across from Mice and watch her watching the refrigerator. I don't bother trying to make conversation. Her brilliant eyes dart back and forth like she is dreaming, only her eyes are wide open.

"The silence is better." Mice blinks, the first since she started watching her movie on the door of the humming refrigerator.

"You cried so much when you were little. You cried so much. Everything was so noisy." A hard knot inside my throat. I swallow dryly.

Mice turns from the refrigerator and stares into my eyes. I grit my teeth to endure the intensity of her gaze.

"Okasan was working, you know," I babble. "She told me once, when I accused her of neglecting us. We were living in a one-bedroom house. Dad and Okasan went out to work, strawberry picking, house cleaning, anything. Slither had to go too, in the summer holidays, and I couldn't—I didn't—"

"How could you?" Mice's eyes burning into my face. "You were still a baby too," she says softly. Then she lets me go.

An egg is an egg, fertilization a concept without substance. Science is a trickery of words designed by measure. An egg doesn't think about life or death. Life and death are simply curtains to the same room. An egg doesn't aspire to become fertilized, fertile or otherwise. I do not care to be and I do not care not to be. But not caring does little to protect me. The last thing I want is to be cast out in a world filled with empty spaces and brittle edges.

I will remain a creature of water.

Planets in faraway wombs collide and the universe sighs in her sleep. The warm thud of blood slows, no longer oceanic salt but sweet as morning dew. This change pleases me and a new world seeps into existence.

Choice is a false word, too polar. I prefer choices, a myriad of paths that spiral outward into streams, sky, soul, body. When I choose to become a kappa child, I diverge from human choice. No longer a potential egg, I coalesce with an aching shudder. Cool, wet slideglide of membrane and water. Glisten gleam and s-t-r-e-t-c-h curl of webbed fingers, hands unfurling like a fern toward the sun. Green as dappled forests, the whisper of bamboo leaves wet with morning dew. Licktaste on tip of tongue. My webbed feet, the fluid skin between my toes, the itch of limbs grow growing.

Yes, ah yes.

Too Much Chicken

AD HAD BOUGHT A BUCKET OF TWENTY PIECES. After we forced ourselves to eat the limbs he doled out, Dad ate all that was left so nothing would be wasted. The cheap country grease ballooned his stomach so he lay down in the widening wedge of shadow beside the tired station wagon. Okasan pushed back the strands of hair that straggled out of her back knot but the rising wind wouldn't let them still. She dropped her hands beside her hips.

"Okasan," Slither whimpered, "Okasan, I want to go back to British Columbia."

Okasan didn't answer, her eyes looking inside to a faraway place. I yanked Slither's forearm and herded my younger sisters before me.

"Come on," I hissed. "Let's go exploring."

PG frowned, but in an interested way. She grabbed Mice's T-shirt to drag her with us. Mice looked longingly back at our mother, but she didn't call out. Mice was four years old and she still didn't talk.

Okasan didn't wave.

Slither twisted out of my grip and crossed her skinny arms. "I don't want to explore. There might be wild animals. There might be snakes!"

"Rattlesnakes," PG muttered.

I dug my elbow into her scrawny ribs.

"What?!" Slither shrieked.

"Shut up! You want to wake up Dad?" My small eyes darted.

"I'm not going any farther!" Slither balked. "You can't make me. I'm the oldest."

"You've got dirt rings around your nose holes."

"I don't!" she gasped, touching the tip of her fingers to the rims of her nostrils. When she felt crusty rings caked on her skin, she desperately picked with her fingernails. "I hate this place," she wobbled.

"Rattlesnakes," PG chanted. "Badgers, coyotes, jackrabbits." PG's favorite TV show was Mutual of Omaha's *Wild Kingdom*.

Mice squatted, grubbing in the grass, looking for wild animals. She hooted softly in excitement.

"Why don't I read to you from my book?" I reached into the neck of my T-shirt and pulled out my sweaty copy of *Little House on the Prairie*.

"You keep your book inside your shirt? That's disgusting!" Slither wrinkled up her nose.

"It doesn't fit in my back pocket."

"I'm not going to sit on the grass," Slither continued. "There might be bugs."

I trampled the grass with my heavy feet. Stomped, trod a circle to make a small matted floor. Mice sat right in the middle with her legs sticking straight out. PG sat behind her, back to back, facing away from us. Slither sighed, blowing upward to her bangs. The dirt was picked clean off her nose, now ringed with tender pink skin. She crouched down on her haunches, making sure her butt touched nothing.

I opened the cover of my book, soft from numerous readings, damp from the heat of my body.

"The Ingalls family were from the east so they went west. We're from British Columbia, so we were in the west, but we moved east to get to the same place, funny, huh?" I beamed. Gapped teeth I could bare only to my family.

"No," PG frowned with the back of her head.

"Why don't you just read?" Slither sighed.

"All right."

WHEN I HAD FINISHED reading two chapters, Mice was asleep with long grass clamped between her teeth. PG pulled at the dusty stems but Mice's jaws were wedged tight. The grass just broke off and Mice was left with a mouthful of short stems.

"I don't get it," Slither said. "Why does that Laura girl want to see a papoose so bad? I bet there were a lot of flies in that wagon. It's kinda sad that the dog got swept away in the river. Do you think salt pork is like bacon?"

I scowled. "It's about being pioneers. See, we're like that right now, get it? It's not about salt pork!"

"Did Laura's pa hit the ma?" PG muttered.

"He never hit her! Ever! He played the violin!" I exclaimed. Though something gnawed inside. I hadn't noticed before, but now that I read it out loud, Ma seemed so much weaker than I'd imagined. *Oh, Charles,* she said. *Whatever you think, Charles.*

"Anyway, they all liked each other and got along. Except for Laura and her older sister who was a goody two-shoes."

"I like Mary most of all," Slither said. "At least she was clean."

I looked down at my tie-dyed T-shirt smeared with chicken grease, fingerprints, armpit stains spreading toward the middle of my chest. I snapped my book shut and stuck it back down my front.

"What are you girls doing?"

Slither frowned so hard her eyes disappeared and Mice jolted awake with shock, stems of grass falling from between her lips. My heart thudded inside my mouth and I swallowed it back down.

Okasan there so suddenly, out of air. Her limp hands trailed at the ends of her wrists.

"Just reading, Ma," I gulped.

"Whatever are you talking about?"

"I mean, Okasan!"

"You're a strange child," Okasan smiled. "Come on back. Your father's feeling better."

She walked toward the car, leaving no footprints in the grass.

"Hurry up!" Dad yelled. "Who said you could go for a walk?"

"Sorry," Slither murmured. "We're sorry."

"I must have dozed off," Okasan apologized.

Mice picked a drumstick bone off the ground, sucking on the gristly bulb. PG smacked it out of her mouth. Mice opened her eyes wide, but didn't make a sound. I elbowed PG in her scrawny ribs and she stepped on my foot.

"Never mind," Dad muttered. "Get in the car."

"We're sorry," Slither repeated.

"Just get in the car!"

Okasan put her arm around Slither's cringing shoulders. "Can you help me get the cooler packed?"

I breathed out. Silently. I picked up paper cups, stacked them, and gathered balls of cheap tinfoil. PG grabbed the front of Mice's shirt and dragged her inside the wagon.

Dad sat on the hood of the car. The sun was starting to set and the orange lit his face.

He could pass for an Indian, I thought.

"What are you staring at?" he asked, not turning to face me.

I gulped.

"Answer me."

"I like it here," I managed.

He turned his enormous head and looked into my face. My big head, my small eyes, so much like his own. He smiled, revealing his gapped teeth, and I wondered at how smiling could change his face.

"You understand," he nodded. And I smiled in return, though I didn't know what he meant.

"Let's go." He jumped off the hood.

The wind was picking up. I watched in wonder as a huge tumbleweed bounced over the station wagon and rolled across the land that was supposed to be ours. I couldn't remember Laura mentioning tumbleweeds. Maybe they didn't have them in the States. Strange how their Pa just parked their wagon anywhere he felt like and called that place his. Maybe Dad did the same thing. Maybe everyone did.

"Get inside. Now."

Still hot in the car. Slither's puke lingered. Okasan was behind the steering wheel again, in her place like an ox in harness.

"We can go any time," Dad prodded.

Gee up, I thought.

Okasan resignedly raised her hands to drive.

"How much further?" Slither spilled out.

Dad swung his huge head around to glare at her. Slither pulled back into the hot vinyl. "Nothing," she said quickly. When Dad faced the front again, she raised her forearm to cover her face. PG's lazy left eye rolled violently. Mice crouched on the floor, picking up old cherry pits and sucking on the dried bits of fruit that clung to the seed.

"Maybe we can get a dog," I whispered.

Mice looked up from the dirty carpeting.

"We could name it Jack, just like the Ingalls."

"Dogs smell bad," Slither still had her forearm over her eyes.

"A dog'll protect us and be our companion," I expanded. "We wouldn't have to be scared of stuff."

"Scary things aren't scary if you're not scared of them," PG chanted.

"Woof!" Mice barked.

We stared at our youngest sister.

"Okasan!" we called out. "Okasan! Mice talked!"

"Ara!" Our mother gave an excited jab on the brake and Dad sucked his teeth in annoyance. She glanced at him in apology and kept on driving.

"What did she say, then?" Dad relented.

"She said 'Woof!'" Slither exclaimed.

"Bakatare!" Dad leaned back and lightly cuffed the top of Slither's head. "That's not talking! That's barking!" He laughed and laughed.

"Hey, pup," I chucked Mice under her chin with my worn running shoe. "Hey, little pooch."

"There's a story about a dog, a human, and a kappa," Dad said.

"Yes?"

We waited. Would he tell us? Were we good enough?

There is a story.

A kappa, a human, and a dog warm themselves by a fire in the chill of fallen evening. The world has ended, like worlds often do. But this catastrophe disconcerts the dog and he wants to blame someone.

"Welllll," he whines, "the cats were sneaky. I wouldn't put it past them to have done this awful thing." He gnaws his jowly lower lip for emphasis.

The kappa waves one webbed hand, a sideways motion, not bothering to answer.

"Wellll," the dog whines, "doesn't my say have any weight? Sure, just ignore Dog. Dog likes to talk out loud to no one in particular!" And he sits up and howls and howls.

The kappa dips webbed fingers into the bowl of its head and flicks a handful of water at the annoying animal.

"Yipe!" Dog leaps up and shakes himself excessively. "What did you go and do that for?"

"Hush!" the human admonishes. "Don't you hear how the quiet rings like music? A few centuries of silence is exactly what we need after the din and clatter we've lived."

"The earth wants sleep," the kappa nods. And lowers onto its belly, arms and legs drawn close to the body like a hibernating frog.

The human, too, lies down. Curls on the left side, facing the heat of the fire.

"Well," Dog whines, "I don't think now is a good time to be sleeping. I think we should be out looking for our own kind." He pants, nervous. "I guess that means Dog's leaving, then. Don't anybody try and stop me."

But the two are already sleeping, dreaming.

"HA! HA! HA!" Slither laughed. I glared at her idiotic noise.

"What are you laughing at?" Dad still. Quiet.

"Nothing," Slither wobbled. "I really like your story."

PG joined Mice on the floor of the car, in the corner farthest away. I edged to the farthest window.

"It's not a funny story," he said softly.

"Yes. No. It's not funny. Not funny," Slither nodded. Mucus starting to bubble in her nose.

Dad breathed. The air was thick. "We're not getting a dog," Dad stated.

The station wagon rattled and bounced on the gravel track. I wondered about Dad's story. Was the human a girl or a boy? What about the kappa? Did Dad make up the story or did someone tell him? The dust billowed in two plumes behind us, rose inside the car where rust had worn through the body. Mice pulled her shirt over her head and her baby-round tummy popped over the elastic of her polyester pants. PG coughed. Her tired left eye swam in its socket. I wished I had tape. My head bobbed. I jerked upright. My eyelids drooping with every dip in the road.

The prairie stretched in yellow greenness. Spread as far as the eye could see. The sky expanded, simultaneously heavy and light so that my eyes spun in circles. I pushed the itchy bonnet off my head and scratched the too-tight braids. Mary was dozing, her pretty mouth slack with drool. I wanted to smack her.

"Laura," Ma called from the front of the wagon.

How did she do that?

"Wake up your sister, Half-pint," Pa's eyes twinkled. "We're almost there."

"Wake up," Slither poked my arm with the tip of her forefinger. "We're here."

I scowled.

"Your hair's all standing up. Why don't you do something with it?" Slither didn't offer the comb she kept in her back pocket.

I ran my fingers through my head so the hair stood up even more. And turned my monstrous gaze out the window.

"WHAT'S THAT?" MICE SAYS.

"What!" I jump. The unexpected one lurches inside me, kicks at vital organs. I double over and Mice doesn't notice. I jerk my head toward the stairs in case Okasan is coming down in an unknowable emotional state. "What's what?

"I thought I heard something. From outside?" Mice tilts her head like a small mammal.

I tweak an eye-width's portion of curtain away from the small window and peer into the dim. No cats hanging off the porch screen. There's a green cast to the sky. Must be northern lights. But not much otherwise.

"I don't see anything. You're just jumpy, huh?" I smile in what I hope is a supportive way. Casually draw my hand across my belly.

Mice turns her eyes to me and I stare back as long as I can.

"There's something odd," Mice says, more to herself than for my benefit.

Surprise, surprise! I think sarcastically. But don't say anything out loud. Sarcasm is lost on Mice.

"Those are nice pajamas," Mice continues. Like we've been chatting about clothes all evening.

"Thanks!" I look down at the silky sheen of dark purple. I lift my right arm and inspect the damage sustained at dinner. Shit! Soya sauce dried on the embroidered cuff! I lift the sleeve to my lips and suck the salty stain.

I am not a beautiful Asian. I am not beautiful. There is a difference between petite and short; one is more attractive than the other. Don't get me wrong, I'm not bitter about my lack of physical beauty. My beauty lies beneath a tough surface, like a pomegranate, my Okasan is fond of telling me. Slither thinks all I need is a good orthodontist, a professional makeover, and a haircut done without a pair of toenail scissors. Maybe she's right, but I refuse to succumb.

I am not beautiful, but I am a collector of abandoned shopping carts who has the most expansive collection of pajamas in the western hemisphere.

Clothing does not fit me. My big-boned arms, my daikon legs, my beta-beta feet, and splaying toes. My bratwurst fingers and nonexistent neck. And my head. My poor colossal head, too huge even to dream of a ten-gallon hat. It was excruciating torture when what clothes I'd finally found started threading into tatters. I held out as long as I could until the state of my unraveling would lead to public nudity. Then, I'd sigh, turn my money socks inside out and pick out linted coins to roll into dollar bills.

I spent years cursing the racks in the malls of despair. Jeans designed for long-legged hips. Slacks with no slack. Rugby pants were in for a while but without enough give across the butt. Knickerbockers had potential—portly men in the Baroque period didn't even look half-bad—but they were out in six months. And they haven't come back. Clothing either squeezed material across my square body, exposed my neck-gaping lack of chest, or confounded me with pant hems trailing like a bridal train. I buttoned, squeezed, choked, sweated years snarling at lovely salesclerks, crying in the changing rooms. Until I stumbled across a pajama store closing down on its opening day, because no one was interested.

OPENING/CLOSING SALE! SALE! SALE!

I wasn't a pajama person, and slept only in boxer shorts, but I was amused by the sign. Could almost picture the mouth of the store opening and closing, gasping for clients it would never have.

I thumped inside and three clerks glided up to me, eyes glowing and hair flowing like they were underwater. Glossy as mermaids.

"Welcome to the first and last day of The Pleasure of Pajamas," they purred.

"Just looking," I said curtly, force of habit after years of clothing torment.

The swishy boy with one blue eye and one green eye, and the ginger-skinned woman with exquisite features glided away, discreetly, not a ripple in their wake. The tall, plain-haired woman lingered. Not invading the large space I needed around my person to feel comfortable, but just on the outskirts, gently present. She was plain as Wonderbread, but I couldn't help but take covert glances. Really. There was nothing remotely interesting about her. Still, I didn't march away. And as soon as she opened her lips to talk, I drowned in imagined memories, sweet and evocative. The air that flowed from her mouth was pure as an infant's, like breast-milk, like dew on spring fresh grass, and sun-warmed peaches, peeled by someone you love. I swirled in the sweetness of her breath.

"If I can help you in any way, please don't hesitate to ask. I'm Genevieve," she smiled.

"You've helped me already," I said, then blushed. *Geek,* I thought to myself. *Dork!* I spun around and thumped through the doors, the glassy aquarium behind me. Hurtled through over-thin teen-agers, squalling toddlers tied into strollers pushed by defensive young mothers, older men with arms draped over young women too old to be their daughters, I shoved my way through them all to the comfort of the Cookie Hut. A pimpled girl unblinkingly took my order of a dozen milk-chocolate chunks and gave me one free to make thirteen. I didn't even bother to sit down. Crammed the overrich, buttery sweetness into my mouth. I ate them all, barely chewing, filling the want in the pit of my stomach. But I still felt empty, left with a greasy coating on my tongue and crumbly bits all over my T-shirt. My hands shook with the aftereffects of sugar. Shoelaces untied. I gulped back something that filled my mouth, that made my chin tremor. Crouched down with a gasp. I managed to retie the laces, then I rose slowly, the roar in my ears something more than blood. Took one step, another, looking at no one, marched forward until I stepped into the pajama store once more.

I sidled quickly past racks weighed down by unsold items, ducking up and down rows of pajamas I had no interest in buying. I wanted to look up to see where Genevieve was, but I couldn't risk meeting her eyes. If only I could smell her breath once more! I ran my fingers along some material, and stopped. Cool, liquid silk. I gazed at the clothing my fingers had brushed.

Blue-green the depth of mountain lakes, the colors swirled with a black that would swallow stars. I could plunge into the hues and never surface. I pulled the pajama top from the shelf and shook it, shimmering in my hands like water. Clasped the bottoms and held them against my body. I worried that my sweat-covered hands would dirty the silk, and my bratwurst fingers spasmed. The clothing slithered into a heap at my feet. Red shoes stepped up and a woman crouched in a cloud of sweet air.

"You won't know until you try," she breathed gently, although her hand was firm as she led me to a changing room. I was capable only of tasting the sweet smell of Genevieve's breath.

I pulled my tatty T-shirt over my enormous head. Fast. Unbuckle, unzip, dropped my trousers before I could change my mind. Then, I stood there, the unsunned parts of my body quivering. Teeth chattered.

"It's okay," Genevieve murmured from outside the curtain.

I shook my head. *No,* I mouthed.

"There's nothing to lose," someone whispered.

There wasn't a mirror inside the room, and I had to step outside to see how I looked. But some magic clothed me. Unselfconscious, I stepped from the protection of the cubicle and stood proudly under the glare of spotlights, in front of three hinged mirrors and three mermaids.

"It's you," Genevieve breathed, and I swallowed her words, their intoxicating scent. The pajamas weaving some strange magic. I was found.

THE NICE THING ABOUT PAJAMAS is that they come in matched sets. Like business suits. I hang them in my closet and I can click-clack through hangers to find the outfit that will inform my day. And I don't crawl out of bed and go to work wearing what I wore to sleep. There are flannel pajamas for bedtime, cotton pajamas for daywear, and furry rabbit pajamas for watching rented videos. There are linen pajamas for power lunches and classic silk jobs for weddings and funerals. I have pinstriped, checked, single colors, tie-dyed, long-sleeved, short-sleeved, even heavy woolen-weave imported from countries with no central heating. There are pajamas for every occasion and I'm never at a loss. Not to mention the selection of dressing gowns! Slither has no idea what she's been missing.

Because the first day of the pajama store was its last, every item was fifty percent off or less. I bought seven pairs. When I circled back to the shop at closing time, Genevieve sold me seven more pairs with her sales clerk discount. Unfortunately, Genevieve isn't in the retail business anymore. She was only working herself through massage school. Now she's a bodywork practitioner with a three-week waiting list. When film crews come to the city for their shoot, bigwig stars beg to be put on her list.

Genevieve and Midori. My two friends. When they met they became lovers.

I MET MIDORI THE NIGHT OF THE COUCH.

A work shift from hell, every salvaged cart was strewn with grocery castoffs, slimy strands of green onion, the silky hairs of corn. Blood from ground beef dripped off the metal mesh onto the van floor. After I dropped the load off at Gary's, I drove to the nearest coin car wash. Sprayed out the stink of rotten vegetables and sour meat juices with the handheld wand, then rubbed the interior dry. I rolled down the windows so the soapy air would evaporate.

I was ready for my personal mission.

I know alleys well because of my job and Kensington is where I make the best finds. Most people are leery of taking in outcasts, but I don't have any false pretensions. I'm not above taking over where others have left off. In Kensington, people throw out shelves still filled with books, dishwashers with matching crockery, and full sets of knives. I've found grandfather clocks, hope chests, cockatoos, and poetry.

I spotted the couch from a block away, clearly a good find, the weather'd been great for over a week so it wouldn't be soaked to the springs, smelling like an old dog. But a shadow figure meandering in a looking-at-people's-things kind of way was closer to the treasure couch than I was. I sidled, crab-like, in my sturdy houndstooth pajamas. The open quilted dressing gown flapping. The lean chick glanced up, our eyes met, and we dashed to the sofa like it was a life raft.

"Don't get your hopes up," she sneered. "This baby's mine."

"Huh!" I puffed. "Not likely. You weren't even interested until I made a move." Caught my panting breath. Gulped. She was beautiful.

"What are you staring at?" she demanded, scratching one hand, then the other. Patches of red dry skin. She pulled a cigarette out of nowhere and lit it.

"Listen," I bluffed, "I've come out here tonight for the express purpose of finding a couch. I need a couch. I'm living in a basement suite and if I sit on the floor, I'll get piles!" I made her laugh. I blushed.

"I propose that whoever lasts the longest sitting here gets to take the thing home," she smirked.

"Fine." I made myself comfortable.

"Good." She flicked her butt. "I like your pj's," she nodded approvingly.

I blushed again. "Uh, thanks," I coughed. Ever the charmer. "You live around here?"

"Uh hmmm. You?"

"Up the hill."

"How're you planning to get this monstrosity to your place?" She glanced at my cotton-clad body. My thick forearms. "You look pretty strong but this sofa is at least two feet longer than you."

"I have a van," I bragged.

"Really. What kind?"

"Ummmmm," I hedged, "it's kind of used."

"So what kind of used?"

"Palm," I clipped.

She stared at me blankly.

"A milk van!" I snapped.

"Cool," she breathed, eyes gleaming. "I'll help you move the couch if I can have a ride."

"I thought we were fighting over ownership?"

"I have a couch already," she grinned.

When she sat in the passenger seat, she sighed and stretched out her legs. The milky smell of air, vanilla and honey-sweet. She curled into the moist atmosphere like it was a quilt. "Cool," she breathed again, closed her eyes.

"Your friends sound nice," Mice nods.

"Huh?" I splutter, coffee in my lungs. I hack and hack and the creature inside me curls lower in my body. Have I been talking out loud? Can't I tell?

But Mice is staring at the fridge again; maybe I've imagined her statement. Great! Why not just have a falling-down fit and join the path of my mother before me?

"CanIsleepwithyoutonight?" Mice glances me nervously. Chewing on what's left of a thumbnail. I cringe. It's not that I can't understand how she feels. That hollow ache, alone and vulnerable, like you're teetering on the edge of your mind, nothing to keep you solid except physical reminders of your existence. Pulling out hair, one strand at a time. Chewing fingernails raw and bleeding. Eating your way into reality. But can't she take care of herself? I don't ask anyone to look after me. I've never asked anyone for anything. She's supposed to be an adult.

God, what am I saying? She's my *sister!* She's done nothing to hurt me! But she could hurt me all the same. She's so needy. What if she starts needing as much as Okasan? What if she wants me to save her and I can't? What if she tries to take more than I can give? I don't have anything for her. She has to take care of herself. I take care of myself. And I'm fine.

"Maybe Okasan won't have a fit," I smile hopefully. "It's so late, she must have fallen asleep by now."

"Listen, do you hear something?"

"What!? Will you stop that!" Nervously flick my small eyes around the expansive circumference of my face.

"Oh, nothing. That your stash of cucumbers in the fridge?"

Jesus!

"Yeah, so what? You didn't take any, did you?"

"No, but better be careful, they're so healthy, Slither might start digging into them. Are you pregnant?"

"Jesus god!"

O

O

O O O

O O

OO O

O

Being not an egg is a cause for exploration. I am not threatened with birth so there is no need to remain in the womb. I am free to turn my keen green mind to the world outside. I wish to know more. I slide, slide inside my realm of water. Gently nudge with the curve of my buttocks. The moist give of living flesh, the warmness of blood. Hello, I bubble, I am pleased to meet you.

There is no answer.

But all is not silence and isolation. Because water is never silent. Life surges in waves of tidal magnitude, like the pull of moonlight darkness. Alone isn't alone unless you seek to be.

Birth will not circumscribe my existence and I will not be cast from my wetly home. But that does not mean I have no interest in matters outside. Life is curious, and I am alive. So I crouch, knees to chest, then kick, propel myself upward, bubbles a long stream rising above me. My webbed hands and feet stroke stroking ascent.

I T NEVER OCCURRED TO ME that I was pregnant. My moon cycles weren't cyclic. They came in bursts and spurts, a sudden deluge of blood while waiting in a checkout line, then several months without a drop. So when I didn't bleed for four moons straight, I wasn't concerned. When I started eating more cucumbers than I'd ever eaten in my life, I thought my body was reacting to some sort of deficiency and remedying it in the most appropriate way. I wasn't worried.

But a growing presence started to creep into my unextraordinary life. An unknowable sensation filled the edges of my awareness. Like a sneeze quivering on the tip of my nose, I could almost realize a presence. But not.

I was sitting on the toilet in my basement suite when this overwhelming feeling of someone other than myself hit me like a wave of nausea splashing the back of my throat.

My eyes darted around the cubby space of my washroom. I pressed my thighs together so that flesh met flesh and completely covered my crotch. I'd heard of people who drilled tiny holes into walls. Sad-ass voyeurs who watched strangers sitting on the can. It didn't immediately occur to me that the presence was inside me. I'd been alone in my body for the whole of my life. But the sensation made me sweat cold drops down my spine, sliding between the healthy mounds of my ass.

I was scared. Mind jumping. Paranoia. No, someone inside my basement suite, maybe Midori, trying to be funny, or one of my sisters. But none of my sisters knew where I lived. Too many hours of unmonitored TV. Too many vampire-neck-sucking-rip-the-face-off-alien-abduction-satanic-rituals-sex-slayings. Schizophrenia. Doesn't run in the family. Too much time in the dark. Isolation madness.

And something prodded carefully, inside my body. Below my navel and slightly to the left. A round pressure like the curve of tiny buttocks or perhaps a rounded shoulder.

Oh my god.

No way.

No fucking way. I pulled up my plaid pajama bottoms and washed my wide, salty face in the chipped sink. Maybe I could trim my bangs, my scrub of hair. Humming to hear myself, some strange song I heard on the oldies station:

"Secret Asian man,

Secret Asian man . . ."

I got the handy toenail scissors from the cabinet when there was a pressroll against my kidneys, cresting into my esophagus. I almost gagged. Clatter of metal on enamel. Terrified, I grabbed my keys and wallet, pounded up the stairs. I didn't bother with my dressing gown, just raced to my Palm van and tore to the nearest drugstore.

I burst through the door and skidded to a stop while five people turned to stare at my entrance. Grabbed a basket and nonchalantly walked between the rows, just another person picking up personal hygiene supplies: toothpaste, a scrubby brush for my coarse feet, dental floss—no put that back, food never caught between my teeth, nothing to catch between—Band-Aids, toilet cleanser, batteries for my vibrator, no-name carbonated peach drink. Finally, I meander over to the pregnancy test section.

"Holy shit!" I exclaimed out loud.

"Pretty expensive, aren't they?" a woman nodded sympathetically.

"Do the cheaper ones work too?"

"Wouldn't count on it, love. The midrange ones should be all right, though." She pointed with a long finger. "I've used this brand before and it was accurate."

"Were you pregnant?" I asked, curious.

"No, thank the goddess!" she laughed, and clicked away on spiky shoes.

I knocked the box into the basket with a nervous finger, not wanting to hold the package in case contamination made me more likely to be pregnant. There was a young man at the till and he dragged the items from my basket. I burned red-sweating with mortification, but he was so used to hygienic gloves and condoms that he didn't even glance at the pregnancy-test box. He just wiped his hand on his pants after I handed him my anxiety-damp bankcard.

When I got home, I stumbled down my basement-suite stairs and threw the bag onto the kitchen table. Ripped off the plastic wrapping and read the directions with shaking hands. Just pee on stick. Wait to see if it turns pink. Pretty straightforward. I thrust down my pajama bottoms and penguin-waddled across to my washroom, scattering the box and directions paper behind me. I crouched over the toilet, thighs quaking, and dribbled warm urine all over my hand.

"Shit!"

I'd inundated the entire stick-thing as well. I shook it off like a thermometer and set it on the bathroom counter. Stared at the little square box on the stick until I started to see purple stars rising.

"Pathetic," I muttered, and washed my hands. I left the telltale test on the rim of the sink and bare-ass–waddled back into the kitchen for the batteries I'd bought at the store. Got my vibrator out of the dishrack and popped them in. Anxious, I thought. Uptight. Mustn't lose control or start down the path of Okasan-like Wts. An orgasm will help. An orgasm always makes a body feel better. I flapped my plaid bottoms off and left them in the hallway. Curled up on my futon, on my left side, and flicked the switch. A cheap vibrator; anyone would have been hard-pressed to call it tastefully quiet. I had always planned to buy something a little less clamorous, a little more artistically pleasing, but I had gotten attached to the noise and the fluorescent green.

On the crest of coming, a series of jabs on top of my bladder. Like an annoyed elbow or knee. The pressure built, a balloon being filled by water to the point of no return.

"Oh! Oh! Oh!" I yelled. Yelped. Came and peed simultaneously.

What was there to do? I buttoned into fresh cotton pajamas and stared at the state of my bed. Could I salvage my life?

"Looks like someone has a bun in their oven!"

"Jesus god!"

Midori was waving the pregnancy stick-thing like a birthday sparkler. "You didn't lock your door again, either," she added.

MIDORI POURED ME another cup of ocha and shook her head. Rubbed hand over hand, like a raccoon, dry skin flaking onto the table.

"This doesn't sound ideal." She shook her head.

"Look, I'm feeling bad enough already. I need some support here."

Midori raised her cocky eyebrows and flicked out her Camels. She tapped a cigarette onto the kitchen table and thoughtfully lit it with an Elvis Presley lighter. Rubbed the bottom of the lighter against the cracked skin of her hands.

"How many months are you?" She blew out smoke.

"I haven't had a period for four months," I muttered.

"Four months!?"

I shrugged my shoulders and pasted a sick grin on my face.

"Have you been to the doctor?" Midori looked concerned. Of all people, Midori was the last person I wanted to find out about the pregnancy. What would she think?

"Isn't there some sort of cutoff date if you want an abortion?" she asked.

"Abortion?"

"You're not thinking of *having* it, are you?"

"I haven't thought that far yet," I muttered. "I'm still trying to process this."

"There's not much time for processing. You made a mistake, that's all. People make mistakes all of the time. You should definitely go the doctor." Midori stubbed out her butt.

"Shut up about mistakes right now, okay? You're making me feel even more anxious."

"It's not like you actively chose to have a baby," Midori gently said. I'd never seen that side of her before. "You didn't decide to become a parent. Will you go and talk to your doctor?"

"I think I need to be on my own for a while." I looked away.

"All right, but try not to mull on this too long, okay? Call me if you need anything," Midori said, then gave me an awkward hug, half a pat on the back and half a clutch. I was touched.

"By the way," I called as she shoved on her combat boots, "I would rather have this information kept private."

"Who the hell would I tell?" She raised one eyebrow. Scratching one hand, then the other. True, I thought. She was the perpetual loner, an offhand friend who sometimes slept in my van when her eczema flared up. Midori of the sarcastic mouth and Mona Lisa lips. She pounded up the stairs without saying good-bye.

After Midori left me in my concrete basement kitchen, the temperature dropped at least ten degrees. The sun had dipped behind the frozen peaks of the Rockies. I couldn't actually see the sunset from my subterranean home, but I could *feel* it in the most unpleasant way. I shuddered. I loved the security of basements. The knowledge that earth, stones, and the roots of plants surrounded my walls. But the cold and the darkness were sorry companions when doubts plagued the mind. I shouldered into my winter housecoat and stuffed my feet into boots. Grabbed keys, wool-lined gloves.

My warm breath crystallized into silvery shards. The winter air sucked heat from my nostrils as I trudged to my van in the back alley. By the time I'd finished unplugging the block-heater, started the engine, and finished scraping the windshield, I was shivering and coughing from ice in my lungs. Checked my diving watch. 5:37 P.M.

Midori was right. I didn't want a child. I never aspired to have a child. I was definitely not fit to raise one. So why the dilemma? Why did I feel this gnawing sense of I-don't-know-what churning my wide-waisted gut, making my head swell huge with unturnoffable pressure. Like when I was seven and I would lie in bed and try to think about infinity until my brain was spinning and I'd fall, thumping to the cold cement floor. I couldn't turn off my head because of what was in my body.

A baby? Of all things! In me?

I shivered. No point in staying in the basement dark when thoughts turned enclosed spaces into claustrophobia. I ground the frozen stick shift into first and drove out of the alley. The streets were empty, everyone home for warm suppers and an early night. No one drove around aimlessly when it was minus thirty-seven. I had two days off before my workweek resumed but even the cold couldn't keep me inside.

Breath stopped clouding in front of my face as the van slowly warmed. My nose started running. I dragged a glove over the wetness and halfheartedly thought about finding an empty garage and asphyxiating myself. Snorted at my television melodrama. My headlights caught an errant gleam behind a bus shelter. I jabbed the brakes so I wouldn't slide on treacherous black ice, flicked on the hazards as I pulled to the curb. A lovely aspect of my work was that the job was never done. I swung open the rear doors and flipped down my homemade ramp, ran down the steep plane. Every cart retrieved was a tiny satisfaction. I smiled while I pushed the saved up the incline. I bungeed my ward snugly to the bolts, then stood with my hands on my hips.

Four months. Hmmmm. Wouldn't I be *showing*? I untied the drawstrings of my comfort cotton pajamas and dropped them into two circular puddles around my ankles. Peered suspiciously at my abdominal area.

"Hello!" I yelled. "Hello in there!"

"*H*EAR THAT?" MICE ASKS.

"What?! What?!" I jump to my feet, almost knocking over my cup of coffee.

"I don't know," Mice whispers.

"Will you stop that?! You're making me a nervous wreck!"

"Don't yell at me," Mice cringes.

My hands curl into knuckled rocks, a thudding in my temples, then I manage to release. Breathe in. Breathe out. There, not so hard. I'm not angry, not angry at all.

"Sorry for shouting," I say curtly. Mice just stares with her brilliant eyes. "What do you keep on hearing?"

"Something. Something like a sound but not. I hear, but don't. You know?" Mice tilts her head.

"No, I don't know," I sigh. "You want me to go outside and check?"

"No," Mice shakes her head. "Don't go out there."

Sudden surge of hope. "What if it's PG?"

"It's not PG."

I sigh again.

"We stay here," Mice whispers.

The Prairie Didn't End

A SCAB OF HOUSES marred the spread, old grain elevators and a few paved streets with stores. I stared out the dusty window, my mouth open. Main Street, a sign read. A couple of pickup trucks and huge cars were parked diagonally up to the sidewalk. There was a drugstore and liquor store combined, a Stedman's everything store, a Lucky Dollar grocery, and a motel that looked like a row of old boxcars with siding. Kitchenettes, a sign boasted. A few people on the sidewalk. Men with baseball caps and GWG jeans. Faded white circles in the back pockets worn by tins of snuff. A woman dragged a small blond kid by the wrist, lugging a bag of groceries in her other arm. They all turned and stared as our car drove by. On the other side of Main Street, a Baptist church, a United church, an Anglican church, a no-name bank, and a hotel with a hand-painted sign that read "Beer Here." Off the main street were a few paved roads that turned into gravel after a block. The houses were single-story with barred basement windows. Too dry to waste water on flowers, most of the brittle lawns had little sticks with painted wooden daisy heads and plywood butterfly decorations.

We were going to live here? What was wrong with Laura Ingalls Wilder? Where was the adventure? The romance? No one even had horses! A ratty dog limped across the road and Okasan slammed on the brakes. People stared. A man with MF on his cap took it off to scratch the top of his head. His sun-worn tan ended where his cap did and the top part of his forehead was a startling white, the rest of his face a reddish brown.

"Didja see that guy's head?" I turned to Slither. She had her mouth wedged up tight. Her eyes looked like an old woman's.

It doesn't pay, I thought, to believe everything you read. The book burned wet against my chest.

Okasan circled Main Street once more, but there was nowhere else to go. The only choices were the Beer Here Hotel or the boxcar motel. Okasan parked the wagon and we crawled out from the trapped heat. A tall man rushed out of the motel office. He walked on the balls of his feet so his skinny head bobbed up and down. He looked like he was walking uphill even though the ground was flat. I stared at his head, but it was all white, not two-colored like the man on the street's.

"How's it going?" he nodded. He talked funny, opening his mouth barely wide enough for the words to get out. Maybe he was afraid important personal stuff might spill out.

"How much, one room?" Dad glared.

The motel man counted our heads, pausing at PG's rolling eye, my exploding excuse for hair, a wink for Slither's perfect features. I dropped my mouth open and panted. Scratching my wet pit. Slither pinched my upper arm and PG snickered. Mice plunked onto the dusty ground, her legs sticking straight out. The motel man wrinkled his nose.

"It'll cost extra for a cot. $37.50 plus tax."

Dad considered. The motel man stared at my big head some more. I picked my nose, as far as my fat finger would go.

"You take a cheque," Dad stated.

Okasan squirmed.

"Ya got some ID on your person?"

"What for? You don't believe me?" Dad edged in closer. The rest of us backed away.

The motel man pulled a big, red and white handkerchief from

his back pocket and mopped at his shiny, pale face. "Uh, it's just standard. You're not a local. I've gotta look after my business." He shrugged and smiled at the same time, his mouth pinched like an anus.

"We live here now. You take my cheque!" Even though he was a good foot shorter, Dad loomed over the tall man.

"Of course! Of course!" He mopped at his face. "Wouldn't want to be unneighborly! Welcome to these parts. Haven't seen a new face in ages. Where'll you be putting down your roots?"

"Over there," Dad pointed. Mollified. Toward where the sun was setting.

"Yup, the old Rodney farm. Been a while since anyone's lived there. Was a shame how the missus died. Must have been an accident, though. Old Man Rodney wasn't ever the same after she passed on. He followed not long after. I hope you make a good go of the place. I always thought it was terrible what was done to you people."

Which ones? I thought. Which ones does he think we are?

"What you say?" Dad took a quick step toward the gulping man.

Okasan raised one hand but it dropped heavily beside her body.

"No offense intended," Motel Man stammered. "I figured you folks to be Japanese."

"We are CANADIAN!" Dad roared.

"No need," Okasan nervously plucked Dad's sleeve. "No need to shout," she murmured.

Swinging arc of arm. Smack. A hand-shaped stain on my mother's cheek, the color of pain and humiliation.

The growing wind rattled the thin siding staple-gunned into the boxcar motel, swirling dust, leaving black circles around our nostrils, our mouths, trickling mud from our matted foreheads to our chins.

How did the wind make the air hotter instead of cooler? We rushed into our room, although PG stood outside the door for a moment, and sniffed. I sniffed too. Nothing but musty, old cigarette air and dried-up beer. PG sniffed once more, then decided the room was okay and joined us. Her rolling left eye stilled for a moment when she spotted a small TV in the corner. She trotted over and pulled the knob, but only black and white flecks jittered on the screen. No sound. Mice came up close and pressed her ear to the gritty glass. Her mouth tipped upward into a smile.

The wind rattled, clattered, slid into the room bringing sand and dust and no relief. Okasan stood in the center of the boxcar. She pushed back the straggle of hair that fell into her face, leaving a dirty streak on her forehead.

"Souda!" she exclaimed. She ran to the washroom, came back with two rolls of toilet paper. She balled pieces up and stuffed them into the cracks in the walls, in the seams around the door and window.

Yeah, I thought. They did that in Laura's new cabin. Chinking, they called it. Chinking, my insides curling metallic. How weird, I had thought the first time I read it.

Okasan wadded and stuffed as many cracks as she could while Dad carried two sky-blue vinyl suitcases into the room. Billowing more clouds of dust when he opened the door. We watched our mother trying to stop dust from coming in, watched our father bring dust with him. Then, Okasan ran out of toilet paper.

PG sat on the crusty carpet. She pulled her sneakers off her feet; her sockless ankles were circled brown with soil and sweat.

"Look!" she snickered. "Homemade socks!"

Mice chortled over.

"Is anyone still hungry?" Okasan asked. "There's some fruit in the cooler."

"We ate already," Dad said. "Supper's over."

"'. . . the dishes washed, nothing left but a piece of squash!'" I sang like Mr. Edwards in Laura's book. Arms raised over my head, leaping upward in a jig. Joyfully exuberant. My little sisters stared at me in wonder. I clamped my hands over my mouth.

Okasan took a step but Dad reached me first. My shoulders bunched up, tight and trembling.

He chuffed me gently on my chin. Smiled.

I beamed my gapped teeth in the warmth of his expression. "It's from my book," I glowed. "My pioneer book. Like us," I explained.

"Oooooooh," Slither groaned, holding her arms over her stomach. "I have to go to the bathroom."

The warmth dropped from Dad's face and I swung mean eyes to my older sister. I wondered why she did that. Said the thing instead of doing. But before I could say a word, a coil of intestine drained into my bowel and squeezed. I dashed to the washroom in front of my sister, banging the door in her face, just in time to explode into the toilet bowl.

"Oh! Oh!" I heard Slither gasping from the other side of the door. Then a wet blat. She started bawling.

PG rattled the doorknob. "The chicken!" she hissed. "The chicken!"

I stared at the empty paper dispenser. Turned to look atop the tank of the toilet but no extra rolls there either. Fudge trickling down my stocky thighs, I opened the door, butt raised, and PG rushed in to take the seat.

"Okasan. We need toilet paper," I called. Careful not to yell.

"Ara." She sounded muffled.

Mice whimpered. Scratched the door like a dog asking to be let out. Okasan knocked tentatively and when I opened, Mice crawled inside. PG butt-walked herself off the seat and joined me, standing. Okasan's hand thrust a bunch of toilet paper she'd taken out from the cracks in the walls. I split it evenly and we wiped with the gritty wads, scoring tiny scratches on our tender skin, our puckered anuses.

Slither was sobbing, soiled panties and polyester pants all stinky-shit goo. She didn't see Dad standing right behind her, his huge head turning redder, his fingers squeezing into knuckles.

"Let's get cleaned up, hmmm?" Okasan said, all soft. Her rough hand curled gently around Slither's sweaty skull. Okasan smiled at Dad as we crowded into the stinking washroom. "You can take a rest on the bed, it was such a long drive."

Dad grunted. Turned to flop onto a faded flower bedspread, hands clasped behind his head.

Okasan shut the door and Slither bawled in earnest. Her forearm covering her eyes, her nose making yellow bubbles of snot. Okasan sighed. Her lips turned down at the end, gravity pulled. She grabbed the material at the hips of Slither's pants and gave two quick jerks.

"Kick those pants and panties off," she muttered. And started wiping the crap from Slither's legs.

"Ow!" she squealed. "Ow! Ow!"

"Shut up in there!" Dad shouted.

Slither shoved her fist in her mouth to stop herself.

What a mess, I thought. She is such a mess. I perched my butt over the edge of the copper-stained bathtub and ran some cold water. I splashed the cool liquid over my privates and the cold wet kissed my scored skin.

"Good idea," PG muttered. Kicked off her daisy shorts and stepped into the tub. She plugged the drain and water started to fill.

"Yes, good thinking," Okasan murmured. "My clever children." Mice crawled into the tub with her clothes on. The dust in the cloth came out in the water, making it a murky tan. But it felt good all the same.

"I have to go again!" Slither blubbered.

Okasan pushed my eldest sister onto the seat and we all listened to her bowels burst. Okasan started to giggle.

"There's a story about a kappa who liked outhouses."

There is a girl.

Strong, brave, very clever and beautiful, the girl lives in a wealthy village, the only daughter of warriors who have turned to rice farming. She sits on the wooden veranda, waving the hot afternoon into evening with a small fan. The crows are lamenting as they return to the mountains, a sadness in their voices which echoes in the still hothumid air.

The girl had eaten many pieces of watermelon during the hottest part of the day, and now finds herself full of water. In the outhouse, she raises her kimono as she has always done, when a cool hand strokes her buttock.

"Sukebe!" she exclaims. Jumping outside. She sees the shadow of a small figure running toward the river.

Early in the morning, in the darkness before dawn, the girl has to go to the outhouse once more. She tilts her head to one side, a bright glint in her dark eyes. She retrieves her short sword and takes it with her. Again, when she raises her kimono, she feels a cold touch upon her buttock. Without uttering a word, she swings her sword and takes the arm off at the elbow. The figure runs off, but more slowly than the night before.

The brave girl looks down at the hand. The fingers still move, green as bamboo. There is skin between the fingers, skin like a frog's.

Ahhh, she thinks. Kappa. She picks up the twitching arm and carries it inside.

At morning meal, she lays the limb upon the table.

"What's that?" her parents ask.

"A kappa touched my bottom so I chopped off the creature's arm."

"Araaaa! Evil will befall us now," her parents moan.

"No, I don't think so," their daughter answers.

That night, she sleeps with the arm beside her pillow. Near dawn, she hears a voice outside her sliding door.

"Please give me my arm back," a pitiful voice begs.

The girl ignores the sound and rolls over to sleep some more.

The next night, the same thing happens and the girl still ignores the sad, little voice.

The third night, again predawn, the voice calls out, "Please miss. I apologize for my rudeness. Please forgive me and return my arm to me and I will never touch you or any of your family for all time to come."

The girl is pleased with the kappa's apology and opens the sliding door. A small yellow-green kappa sits, kneeling on the veranda. The creature lowers its head to the floor, careful to keep the water in its bowl from spilling.

"Whatever will you do with your arm?" the girl asks.

"Kappa know how to reattach limbs that have been severed or broken," the creature explains. "If I can replace my arm before the green has faded, I will be able to use it again."

The girl's eyes glow. "You will teach me this skill," she says, "if I return your arm."

"Yes, gladly," the kappa answers.

The girl unwraps the arm she has kept in a cloth and hands it back to the creature. The kappa raises the arm to forehead and chants a few words. And before the girl's eyes, gives an expert twist, the limb back in the socket.

"Ahhh," sighs the girl. "So that is how."

"Thank-you for your graciousness," the kappa bows again. And bounds from the room.

The girl becomes a famous bonesetter and many people come to benefit from her skills. The kappa is never seen again.

SLITHER JOINED US IN THE TUB. With the dust rinsed off, the smears of sweat and puke dissolved in water, her skin shone like fresh ginger.

"Is the girl a princess?" she asked, her mouth open. "Is this a true story?" Slither's body twisting at the waist to face our mother, her slender legs folded beneath her body.

I clasped knees to chest to cover my torso. Boy, I thought, that kappa sure got a bad deal. Just touched the girl's butt twice, then gave up kappa secrets to get the arm back. I stared at Slither's graceful sway in the twist of her spine. The ginger-skin glow on her buttocks. Gave it a little poke.

Slither squealed. Glared at my nonchalant gaze.

Mice was facedown in the water so long PG grabbed the back of her neck and pulled her out. Mice came up with a gasp; frowning, PG pounded on her back until Okasan made her stop.

"Don't keep your head underwater," Okasan murmured slowly. Like she was long distance, though we were all together.

Quietly, we crept out of the cooling liquid. We shared two of the smaller towels between the four of us so Dad could have the big ones.

We stood around, naked, Mice pulling off her wet things, plopping them back into the bathtub.

"We can't put our clothes on," I whispered. "We'll get dirty again."

"We can't go out there naked!" Slither protested.

"Shhhhht!" PG and I hissed.

"Woof!" Mice agreed.

It was a trap. Clothes or no clothes, we couldn't win.

"Woof!" Mice barked. Emphatically. She was on her hands and knees.

"Brilliant!" I patted her on the head, chucked her beneath the chin. "We can crawl out past the bed and get our clothes from the suitcase. Dad can't see us if he's lying down."

"I'm no dog!" Slither trembled.

"Too bad," PG chimed. "So sad." Her left eye rolled disbelievingly at the ceiling.

"No, not dogs!" I looked for an idea on the walls of the bathroom. "Like soldiers! In combat! We have to get past enemy lines!"

PG jabbed her cynical elbow in my wide gut and I trod on her toes.

"I'm no soldier!" Slither sniffed. "They smell bad."

"Fine," I hissed. "Get caught in enemy territory with no clothes. We leave now!"

"Okay," Slither whined. "I'm coming!"

We crawled out, single file, past our father's bed. Okasan, the whole time, not saying a word, just watching the tan water lap gently against the bathtub's rim.

"About time you got out," Dad uttered.

"Eeeeeee!" Slither shrieked.

"Bakatare!" Dad laughed.

I smiled. Got off my tender knees. When he said *bakatare* like that, my heart filled honey warm. Nobody could say *stupid idiot* better than him.

"Let me put in some clean water," Okasan called from the bathroom. Heard the dirty gurgle down the drain.

The clock radio said 9:34 P.M. It was not full dark. I lurched back to the washroom, retrieved my book from inside my clothing. It smelled of old chicken and sweat. I stroked the cover, then pressed my face against a smoothness softer than my skin.

Slither was actually useful when she wasn't scared stupid. She had all of our nighties laid out in order on the bed closest to the door. She helped Mice dress and even combed the kids' hair. She cast one look at the nest on my head and her lips turned down like Okasan's. I stomped past her. Didn't need her stupid comb. Struggled into nightie, book clamped under my armpit. PG dragged the pillows from the head of the bed and laid them horizontally along the side, so there was more room for us on the surface. The motel man would never bring the cot.

"Wash my back," we heard from behind the bathroom door.

I opened my book to the third chapter.

WHEN I WAS FINISHED, Slither was snoring. PG frowned, ground her teeth in shallow sleep. Mice's eyes were wide open, the whites gleaming in the growing dark.

"Woof!" she said, happily. Quietly.

"Yeah," I agreed in a whisper. "I'm glad the dog came back too. But you see how it is. Pa's a nice man, even, but he was going to shoot Jack dead. You just don't know."

I tucked the sheet around Mice's chin and tousled her head. "Go to sleep, little pup."

MARY STOOD BY THE FIRE, stirring the coals. It's too hot, I wanted to tell her, you're not supposed to be touching it anyway. But she put her finger to her lips and pointed to baby Carrie, sleeping in a basket.

"Where's Ma got to?" I whispered, pushing my nightcap off my head.

"She's gone to Independence."

"When's she coming back?"

"Ma said you're to mind me."

Outside, Jack whimpered and moaned. He scratched to be let in but Mary rushed to stop me.

"He's gone bad," she hissed.

"Stop it, Mary! He's crying!" I tried to push her out of the way. Jack, hearing my voice, whimpered and yelped louder.

The sheet was twisted around my thick waist and my skin felt sticky. Soft groans. I lay still and felt my heart shudder inside the curving cage of my bones.

Slap! Slap! Smack of flesh on flesh.

Thud, smack, slap, thud. Smack, slap, smack, slap, the bed thudding, thumping, creak, squeak—

"Hideo," my mother sighed. "Hideo."

"Uhhhhhhn," our father groaned.

An unwanted warmness curling inside my privates. I blinked and blinked. Didn't know I was holding my breath until I noticed that my sisters weren't breathing either.

How could she? I thought. How could she?

We heard their legs move beneath sheets, a few muted words. Dad started snoring right away. Okasan sighed. Then she slept too.

My sisters and I, our mouths opened, gulped silently in the musky air. We didn't reach for each other. We didn't hold hands. We curled up into individual balls and clung to the only person we could trust.

SEX, OF COURSE, is not the only way to find yourself pregnant. I'm confused and relieved that Mice sees what my doctor can't recognize. Even though I have moments of maternal doubt, nothing to show for this pregnancy but an internal feeling and cravings for cucumbers. Feelings aren't the most reliable of things. And a lot of people like cucumbers.

Now that Mice knows about the delectable gourds, there's no need to be hiding them. I set her poor heels in the after-warmth of my seat and shuffle to the fridge. The bottles rattle in the door and I push aside mysteriously cloudy jars for the stash. I stand in the open cold, my back to Mice, so I won't have to give her any. The snap of crispy green is bittersweet between my teeth. A sensation glides up my belly. The unexpected one tastes cucumber-pleasure with me.

How I came to be pregnant confounds me still, but does nothing to make me less pregnant. Like a colossal joke with no one to appreciate the punchline. PG might have. Funny how I want to share this with her, now that she is gone.

I T WAS TO BE THE NIGHT of the last totally visible lunar eclipse of the twentieth century. A singular event, portentous, symbolic. I was simultaneously depressed and elated. Like planets aligning, I was hoping for some lunar intervention in the daily dregs of my life. The cusp of a new century, *hope* such a small word in the face of global disintegration, I turned to the solar bodies with clenched teeth and fists.

No one was interested.

I phoned my few friends, Midori, Genevieve. Had to remind myself that they were actually my friends.

"So what?" Midori said between what sounded like crunches on corn chips. "What's the big deal? The human notion of this being the end of the twentieth century's arbitrary in the scope of time, anyways."

"Quit eating corn chips on the phone!" Offended at her minimizing my lunar moment.

"Tortillas. They're tortillas."

"Fine, go back to your chips while the universe tilts above your head. I'm going to call someone who cares."

"I'm watching some Godzilla movies. You know, like the one with the three-headed flying dragon and stuff. You can come by," Midori suggested, offhand. She'd never invited me to her place before! My heart beat stupid for a moment, then it sagged. Why risk a perfectly undemanding friendship on an unrequited crush?

"Maybe next time. There's something about this lunar eclipse."

"Suit yourself," she crunched, crackling the plastic bag for another handful. "But don't get all new-age Californian on me, all right?" and hung up without saying good-bye, like always, me feeling somehow incomplete without the closure. Like always.

I tried Genevieve next.

"Lunar eclipse?" she asked. "Does that mean the sun covers the moon, or the moon covers the sun?"

"Neither," I sighed. "There's a full moon, but the earth will come directly between the light of the sun on the moon, so that the moon won't reflect the sunlight for a little while."

"So the moon will go out?" Genevieve giggled, I could almost hear her winding her long, soft hair around her index finger. Something she did when she had to think about something she normally didn't think of.

"So to speak," I muttered.

"Don't be mad. I'm not—sorry, can you hold for a moment? There's someone on the other line."

"Sure." I scowled. I hated people with call waiting. What was wrong with the busy signal? I chewed on the ragged end of my pinky nail. I was weaning myself off my fingers, incapable of going cold turkey.

"Sorry," Genevieve breathed. "It's my grandmother. She's just broken up with her lover and having a bit of a crisis. Could I call you back later?"

"Ahhh, don't worry about it." Lucky Genevieve having a grandma who was bi, I thought. My mother probably didn't even know what it meant! "I should hurry anyway. I have to find someone to watch the eclipse with me. And I'm running out of time."

"Good luck. Have a nice eclipse." Hearing her smile in the breath of her voice.

The evening didn't bode well, but I still pursued my portent. Not knowing that some things are meant to be left alone. Hindsight is fine, but hindsight doesn't stop you from getting kicked in the butt. I considered calling PG or possibly even Slither, but my ear was starting to ache after being pressed to the telephone receiver and I didn't want someone there who carried the same baggage as I did. At least, baggage that was tagged with the same last name and formed from the same genetic pool. So I changed into a fresh pair of pajamas, my special-occasion outfit with tasseled drawstrings rather than an elastic waist. Silk-covered buttons and satiny smooth, cool to the skin. Rich red and almost black. I brushed my pumpkin teeth and brushed my ugly hair.

Went out to cruise, as well as anyone could on a Friday evening in a used dairy van. The vehicle was a gift from my dad, a congratulations gift when I finally got a "steady" job tracking down errant shopping carts. Until then, I'd worked part-time, a long list of uninspiring jobs. Chicken-wing cutter, telephone directory delivery person, furnace cleaner, skate sharpener. When Gary shook my hand and welcomed me to his elite corps, I knew that my life work had begun. I was a member of Gary's Stray Cart Services.

What simple pleasure, finding something that was lost and then returning it. Did it matter that the lost were merely shopping carts? What would happen if no one ever returned them?

More than that, I loved the adrenaline that surged in my veins whenever I spotted a silver glow. The quick-fired shoulder-checks before I slammed on brakes. Hazards flashing. The challenges of retrieval from ravines. Shopping carts dangling from one-hundred-year-old poplars. I marveled at human impertinence and thanked my lucky stars that I'd found my place in this world.

Dad's milk van gift was hardly glamorous but timely all the same. I'd interviewed for the position and lied that I had my own vehicle. I was planning to push them all back by hand. But good old Dad, he traded his complete collection of Elvis on eight-track cassettes for a fourth-hand vehicle with "Palm" flaking off its sides. An engine that should be declared an endangered species. Not what a person could remotely link the words *environmentally friendly* with, but beggars can't be choosers, and choosers have to walk, as my Okasan said. So I rode around in a milk van, with no milk. It kind of sums up my life.

Midori loved to cruise with me in the van.

"Cooool," she'd murmur, flicking Camel butts out the window.

I always wore a cap, so people would think I was actually delivering milk. Or, at least, delivering something. I really couldn't understand why Midori found the van so cool. It never occurred to me to take her words literally, that the temperature was pleasant on her eczema-tortured skin. That the milk-soaked walls exuded an atmospheric ointment, smoothed a rash she was conscious of every waking moment of her life, even while she slept, scratch scratching until she bled. The van a healing salve. She'd flick her Asian eyes at me from a Caucasian face, air stirring her dark brown hair, curling outward at the tips, away from her pointed chin. A Mona Lisa smile from irreverent lips and a mouth that could be fouler than all of the Great Lakes put together.

"Cooool," she'd sigh, and blow me a smoky kiss, then fall asleep while I drove around the city, the taste of sweet cream lingering in the corners of her dreams.

I considered driving to the other end of the city to tempt Midori away from Godzilla and into my van, but I had to find someone who cared about the lunar eclipse as much as I did. So I exited off Crowchild Trail and plugged my way to the city center, to Chinatown, the only area in the city remotely interesting. The regular post–happy-hour crowds in pubs had no place for me. A short, ugly Asian with a bad attitude could never mix in those beer commercials. No matter how fabulous the pajamas. No, there was no sense in wasting my outfit on ale-drinking louts. I whipped past empty parking meters and half-filled lots to swerve alongside a length of curb posted with a Delivery Only sign. My hazards flashing. I never got a ticket. There are some pluses to driving a milk van and I wasn't one to pass them by just because I wasn't delivering anything.

Of course, if you think about it, no one would be delivering milk in Chinatown, because hardly anyone buys milk there. Mostly plastic bottles of soya, cloudy sweet and more readily digested, so much healthier. But I could have been delivering ice cream, I suppose. A delivery truck is a delivery truck, and it carries a certain amount of authority.

All the shops were closed, the sweetness of rotting fruit, souring mustard greens filling a Dumpster. A waft of hot oil. The smell brought back a body-memory so sudden and intense my stomach fisted with longing. I stood on the sidewalk, incapable of movement. The hazards clicked, clicked behind me, the traffic buzz fading to the edges of suburbs. The city was filled with a strange silence. A few people ducked into Hong Kong–style cafes, then, the streets were empty. A light breeze touched my face and as I closed my eyes, I imagined tumbleweeds bouncing gently across the abandoned pavement. Out of the silence, a sound slowly grew. Imperceptibly, irrepressibly, the sound grew stronger, roared, enormous and tidal.

The restaurant I stood before was incredibly rowdy. Exuberant, festive, the sheer noise of it an open invitation. Unable to stop, my lips smiled pumpkin-wide, revealing my teeth for all to see. And before any reason could change my mind, I pushed through the door and stood in the foyer.

There was a wedding banquet in progress. Clatter-din of voices raised with alcohol and celebration. An intoxicated groom in a silver tuxedo was trying to bite hundred-dollar bills, the money clipped onto the bride's red dress. She laughed at the excess, the public display. She was beautiful beyond belief. Guests snapped pictures, cheering, and a foolish laugh spilled from my mouth. I stood in the foyer, wanting to be welcomed into the throng of noise and glee. Wanting to be a part of something that was happening without me.

"Look!" a guest shouted. "Someone couldn't find their tuxedo and they came in fancy silk pajamas!"

Five hundred pairs of eyes turned to look at me, but before the pause between sight and voice could stretch into toe-curling embarrassment, hands were outstretched, clasping my arms, my shoulders, drawing me into the room with dizzying enthusiasm. My back patted with warm palms, drinks held high, and "Ganbui!" I downed them as fast as I could swallow. I just smiled and nodded, embarrassed but pleased. Cognac heating my belly, I was pulled to a table with an extra chair and the courses of food began. First, a cold appetizer. Chilled slices of duck. And tender portions of pork and beef with small dishes of spicy salt for dipping. The second cold plate was jellyfish and crisp rice chips served with a zippy chili oil. I licked my lips to soothe the bite. And dished myself some more. The other guests calling out to each other in Cantonese. They laughed at how I held my chopsticks and I laughed too. Cold followed by hot, the shark fin soup steamed richly, the tiniest sour aftertaste of vinegar. Eagerly, I spooned the broth into my mouth. Before I was finished my soup, a beautiful, fried whole fish shone crisply on a plate adorned with chrysanthemums made of carrots. "Oooooh," I admired, even as deep-fried, shrimp-stuffed crab claws were placed on our table. Rice noodles and tofu with Chinese mushrooms. Abalone and duck covered in a crackling mahogany skin. Oysters on shells adorned with green onion and ginger, lobster coated with a creamy white sauce. So much food and still more brought out on trays by young men with slender arms. I drank and ate like I've never done before, an orgy of eating and drinking. "Ganbui!" The bride, in her red gown, threw me a kiss. Blushing.

My head whirled as I stumbled through the crowded tables, weaving my way around dancing waiters, dodging errant children in flouncy dresses and miniature tuxedos. Stumbled through the washroom door to lean against the rim of the sink. I splashed cool water on my face and down my spine. Between my breasts. When I glanced up at my reflection, I was shocked. I didn't know why until I realized it was the absence of sound.

I couldn't hear a single thing.

My ears weren't suddenly deaf. I could hear the heat register clicking into a quiet whoosh of warm air and water dripping slowly from the tap, staining the white enamel brown. I heard my blood thudding in my head. The small hairs along my spine pricked up, skin pimpling all over my body, shivering down to my bladder. Tears filled my eyes and I swallowed hard. The wedding banquet? What was going on? How could so many people be completely silent? What had happened to them all? And the children.

My heart squeezing, I clasped my arms around my middle to hold everything together. Run. I wanted to run. But running meant I'd have to re-enter a room filled with awful silence. My teeth tried to clatter in my mouth, but that would betray my location. I clenched my jaws. Shook my huge head. No. Don't make me. No.

But the silence remained.

I couldn't stay all night. And no one would save me.

I dropped my arms. Took a small sliding step. Toward the door. But what was behind me?! Anything could be hiding in the bathroom stall. Creeping stealthily on long-clawed feet. I jumped around.

No. No one.

No windows, either. No options. I could leave only through the door I'd entered. I breathed rapidly through my nose. Until I started getting dizzy. I closed my eyes, took a deep breath, then prodded the door open with my foot.

Silence. Heavy and awful. Before I could change my mind I stuck my hand out to test the air on the outside of the washroom. Heart tripping. Adrenaline sour-coating my mouth.

No one grabbed my hand.

I whimpered. Just because nothing touched me didn't mean I was safe. Okay, I thought. Okay, try that childhood game . . . if the furnace stayed on, that meant I wouldn't get hurt, but if the furnace turned off, something bad would happen. The soft furnace roar made a gentle whoosh, then was still.

"Nnnnnnn."

I cast wild eyes around the bathroom, until I realized the sound had come from me. I took a shuddering breath. Drew my hand back to my side. Took another deep breath and pressed my wide face to the open space of the door. A cool draft brushed my skin.

The place was empty.

Cold shuddered again, almost peeing myself. Gulped and

stared. The restaurant was abandoned, gritty plywood floor where a dirty rug had been scraped off. Red and gold wallpaper hanging in shreds, a single silk plant dusty in the growing dusk, the light dim through grease-streaked windows.

"There's a total lunar eclipse tonight."

"Jeezus Christ!" I spun around to the hallway behind me, knowing that there would be red eyes gleaming. I crouched into a low stance, karate-like, but, conflicting information careening wildly in my brain, suddenly thought I needed to look bigger, so I stood tall, barreled out my chest and held my shoulders back, my arms into elbows, fists and knees bent outward. Ape-like and aggressive.

"What are you *doing?*"

Strange, I thought. Stranger . . .

The Stranger was leaning against the wall of the hallway. Wearing a silk red wedding dress, snug on her slender body, and slightly worn on the curve of a middle-aged belly. A black beret covered an oddly shaped head, strands of thin hair hanging long and limp. A heavy leather jacket. In the strange glow of the streetlight, the Stranger's complexion looked almost olive.

"I like your pajamas, by the way," the Stranger added, chin nodding.

I deflated my chest, realized I had been holding my breath when I gasped for air.

"Jesus god," I wheezed. "You scared the shit out of me."

"But I've been here the whole time. I watched you come in, stand at the door, smiling like a pumpkin until I blew you a kiss. Then you ran into the washroom. I was worried you were puking or something. And incidently, Jesus *is* God. Didn't you go to Sunday school?"

"What the hell is going on around here? Where are all the people?" I spun this way and that, the tattered walls, the greasy windows, the Stranger, all suspect.

"Relax, will you? You're not on drugs or anything? I told you, there's going to be a total lunar eclipse tonight." Crossing slender arms like a black and white movie.

"I *know* that! That's why I'm here," I said impatiently. "But the people? The wedding banquet. The food and drink. I must have been eating for over an hour." Looked down at my pajamas for soup stains and grease marks.

My clothes were shiny clean, my tummy no rounder than when I had first stepped out of my van.

The Stranger clucked her tongue, shaking her head from side to side. "Consider the wedding banquet a gift. Don't ask why."

"Don't ask why?! Were they ghosts? Am I imagining things? Maybe I'm imagining you and only talking to myself!" My voice rose.

"Shhhhhh. Nights like this fold over like cloth. Don't worry about it, honey. Sounds like you had a good time."

"I had a great time," I whispered.

The Stranger applauded, hands raised by left cheek, like a person at the opera. "No damage done!"

I sighed. "Do you want to go see the last total lunar eclipse of the twentieth century?" I asked.

"You got a car?"

"So to speak," I answered.

All the body, all the sea.

The fluid motion of life. When I weary, my body feeds me; when I tire, my body quickens. I swim, float, never sink. There has always been time before me and there will always be time after.

The kappa will eat many things but a kappa loves cucumbers. I know this without a cucumber ever having passed the pointed beak of my mouth. The tiny buds on my tongue clamor, the cells fairly leaping, and I nudge and slide in this liquid place for some cucumber flavor. Why not piman, I may be asked, why not leeks or nigari? Not enough that the fruit is green, crisp. The crucial snap of verdant skin. Summer held in the juices welling inside my mouth. That sweet play of dew and the after-bitter edge. I am well pleased with many things, but very few things can please me more than cucumber.

As green as the kappa's love for cucumber, people will be heard to say. Can anything be greener than that?

"I thought you were pregnant," Mice nods. "I noticed this morning. On the porch." As if noticing a pregnancy in someone with no visible symptoms is something she does every other day.

I stand up nervously and rub clumsy hands over my square belly, in that movie-ish, clichéd way.

"Am I showing?" Maybe I am, without my knowing. Maybe I'm not. Maybe I'm mad, and Mice with me.

"Noooo," my sister ponders into her empty coffee mug.

I walk back and forth on the cracked linoleum. The fridge clunks, ticks and groans into readiness. I walk back and forth and rub my not-pregnant middle.

"But . . ." Mice muses.

I grind my gapped teeth until they ache.

". . . you smell, well, like water."

"Oh, of course!" I smack palm to forehead. "Duh! I should have known that would give me away. Of course. I smell like water."

"Huh?" Mice, confused.

"I'm being sarcastic! What the hell do you *mean?*"

"Don't get mad at me!" Mice cowers.

"I'm *sorry!*" I yell, Mice still cowering. God! How could she stand to be so weak! People kick the shit out of wimps and victims.

Surge in my body that tastes bloodsweet, I'm strong and she's a fool. Why couldn't she be strong? Like me. Like my father.

And some cool touch sweeps the knots in the corded muscles along my shoulders, the tendons in my neck. Gone. Peace. Like a drop of water falling from a leaf tip into a still and deep pool. Ripples.

"I'm sorry," I reach out my hands, palms upward. Mice loosens and tentatively places graceful hands on mine. Lightly. Just skin on skin, her warmth realizing my coolness.

"I haven't been myself. Things are really strange. I'm sorry I yelled at you. Don't tell anyone, okay?" I babble.

Mice stares at me in her overlong way.

"It's not a normal pregnancy. Not that I know what a normal pregnancy is," laughing nervously. "No, but really, I might not be, but I know I am?"

"Sometimes, you just know things," Mice nods seriously.

"That's it, exactly!"

"What are you going to do?"

"Nothing *to* do. There doesn't seem to be any growth, my doctor couldn't find a trace. The presence isn't all that much of a burden. The only difference I feel, physically, is a craving for cucumbers, preferably Japanese. And people are commenting on my olive complexion. Ask me if I'm part Spanish or something. Big deal, right? But knowing there's someone in my body, this other-*ness,* that's what really gets to me. And then I start wondering if I'm going crazy."

"I think about that too," Mice nods.

I sigh. Rub my wide tummy with both hands. Mice's sympathy washing over me. I blink rapidly, but not because I have to cry. And feel a nudging from behind my *face.* Like one cool, small hand is leaning against the flesh of my cheek, another gently pushing the moist orb of my eye.

Mice suddenly jerks close. Peers at my face. Then jumps three feet backwards. She scrabbles even farther, mouth open in shock, incoherent words.

I stumble after her and she backs from me like I am a monster.

Spinal fear shuddering up my backbone. I reach out my hand to grab her arm but she wrenches out of my grasp.

"What?!" I shout. "What?!"

Mice clamps hands over her ears, spins away from my face. I try to grip her shoulders to see the answer in her eyes, but she just jerks away. I corner her against the wall and the fridge and clench the material of her sleeves.

"Tell me!" I shake at her refusal. "Tell me!"

But my sister will not see me.

I shake her until I realize what I am doing. Drop my hands, stare at the fury they are capable of.

"Sorry," I mutter. "Sorry." Move away from my baby sister. I cover my face with my palms and shake my heavy head. "What the fuck is the matter with me?"

"Fuck te Easterni yuwanaino," Okasan rotes. The door slamming behind her.

We jump. Hearts pounding.

Okasan steps into the kitchen from *outside* the house.

"Jesus god!" I stumble back from my mother. Mice's hands glued to her ears, she shakes her head no, no. Okasan's hair floats around her head in electrical currents, eyes like falling stars. Her nightie a thin cover over her body. Her bare feet and legs are red with winter.

How did she get outside? Where did she go?

"O-O-ka-sa-san?" My teeth actually chatter.

Okasan so still, the cold from the outside sweet, like when the cats come into the house after their nightly prowl. Her pupils full.

"I think I should sit down," she murmurs, sinks onto a chair.

Mice and I stare. Okasan's faraway eyes.

"Jesus," I hiss. "How long was she outside? How the hell did she leave the house? She never left her room!" I trot to the living room and pull the TV blanket off Slither's curled form. Take it back to my mother and toss the blanket over her without touching her body with my hands.

Mice is beyond words. Her feet tap at the floor. Quick-stepping the linoleum, aching to run outside. She raises one fist to gnaw her knuckles.

"Should we call an ambulance?" I whisper.

"Karadaga samui yo," Okasan smiles weakly, then starts shivering. The blanket slides off her body into a heap.

I touch her bare arm and my hand jerks back. She feels like a corpse.

"Fill the bath!" I get kettles, pots, full with water and turn the burners on high, not enough hot water in the tank for a full tub. Hear Mice turning the faucets, whispering to herself.

Okasan's teeth start to chatter. Her numb fingers useless on her buttons.

"Jeeeeezus," I hiss. Help my mother with her clothes. Ugly, floral blouse; old-woman pants way too old for her age; big, squarish, polyester panties—no, leave them on. Okasan shivering, shaking. I lean over my mother and scoop my sturdy arms beneath her knees and neck.

"Get on the other side," I tell Mice.

Mice looks confused, then runs to the other side.

"You put your arms like me!"

Mice slips her arms beneath Okasan too, and we lift her icy, shaking body and carry her to the tub. I stick my socked foot into the water. A little lukewarm. But her body's so cold it'll feel hot at first.

"Down," I gesture with my chin and we lower our mother into the warm liquid. A breath seeps out from between her clattering teeth, metallic and foreign. Mice and I both jerk our heads away from the smell. But Okasan's chattering becomes less frantic.

Mice manages to find a bowl. She fills it up and pours the water over our mother's chest with such tenderness I can't stand to watch. Stumble to the kitchen and turn off the pots and kettles boiling on the stove.

My hands shaking.

Slither comes into the kitchen with her pointed toe-steps. Hands cupped around her elbows, she shivers.

"Who stole my covers?" she accuses.

"A lot of help you are." I kick the TV blanket, then reach down and pick it up. "Okasan got outside somehow. She was freezing."

"Did Dad—?!"

"No!"

Slither's perfectly shaped eyebrows sag and her mouth turns down. The lipstick is bright only in the cracks of her lips.

"PG is smart," she murmurs softly.

Something stings my eyes. "Get Okasan a new nightie and housecoat. Then help Mice get her out of the bath."

I nudge my sister toward the hall and fold the blanket. Toss it back onto the sofa. While my sisters change my Okasan, I slice some meat from the salvaged turkey and make sandwiches with tons of mayonnaise and crispy bits of cucumber. A pot of Red Rose tea.

WE EAT SANDWICHES TOGETHER. No one says anything about PG having left. We can pretend we are normal as long as no one says anything. Black Cat click-clacks across the kitchen floor. Curls around our ankles for a pinch of turkey meat. Mice swings her foot beneath the table, but misses. Okasan bends down to let the cat take bites out of her sandwich, and without blinking an eye, brings the sandwich to her mouth, biting right where the cat has. Slither shudders.

"PG's not coming back," Mice says sadly. Stirs a lump of mayonnaise, instead of milk, into her tea.

"Yes she will, don't say things like that," Slither protests.

Okasan just makes her sad smile-face.

"She said that she'd drop us a line." I try sounding optimistic, and beam my gap-toothed grin. Give up the effort. "Anyway," I sigh, changing the subject, "what were you doing outside, Okasan? How did you get out? From your window?"

"Nani?" She is perplexed.

"You came into the kitchen from *outside*." I stare at her. "And we never saw or heard you leave the house."

"Zutto oheya ni ita wa," Okasan smiles gently at my expression.

Mice and I stare at each other, stare back at our mother sitting so calmly in front of us. How can she think that she's been in her room the whole time? How does she think she ended up in the kitchen? Who is she trying to kid?

"What's going on? You two look funny," Slither nervously bites her lower lip, brushes her glossy hair behind a perfect ear.

"Uhhh, nothing. Maybe she was just sleepwalking? Maybe we all need to get some sleep. It's almost sunrise." I bluff, then actually yawn wide enough to swallow my head. "Maybe you can sleep in Okasan's room, in case she gets cold again," I nod at Slither emphatically. Her lips turn down but she follows our mother to the spare bedroom where she always sleeps now. Apart from Dad.

"Want to sleep with me?" I offer.

Mice beams. And we go downstairs together.

My sister falls asleep as soon as she lies down, her arms creeping up to cross over her chest like an Egyptian mummy. The sun starts rising again. A dim, green light. Mice's nose juts. Her eyelids already running in a dream.

I roll over, face the wall so the dawn will not keep me from sleep. But it's still hard to fall into that pool. Where is PG now? Did she really mean what she said about not coming back? I should have tried to phone her a couple of hours after she left. I check my diving watch, 6:30 A.M. I sneak out of the sheets and trudge up the stairs. White Cat meows nasally for breakfast so I prod his belly with my toes. Black Cat and Orange Cat know not to bother trying.

PG's phone number is written neatly in black marker, on the inside of the cupboard next to the phone. All of our numbers are there. Just ours, and Janice, the next-door neighbor's. That's all.

I dial PG's number, my heart fluttering. An answering flutter of feet further down. The phone just rings and rings, the answering machine turned off. I drop the earpiece back in the cradle with a small *ping*. Pick it up again to dial Midori's number. Who knows? On her off days, she sometimes stays up until morning and sleeps all day, batlike, her cycles permanently altered because of her job as a breadmaker.

"Hello," a breathy voice.

"Oh!" I say, startled. "Sorry, Genevieve. I must have dialed the wrong number. Sorry to wake you. I was calling Midori."

Genevieve giggles sleepily. "You didn't dial the wrong number," she sighs happily over the distance. Something twists inside my gut.

"What's up?" Midori, sounding wide-awake. I can hear the jangle of a belt buckle being done up. Or undone. I smile weakly although no one is there to see me.

"Nothing. Really. There's been a bit of a crisis, here, but I'll tell you about it when I get back to the city."

"You okay?" Midori asks. Her voice concerned.

I shake my head. "Yeah, I'll call you at a decent hour." And I hang up without saying good-bye.

Lay myself on the living room couch, beneath the TV blanket. I let Orange Cat sleep on my chest for warmth.

MIDORI WAS BOUND to meet Genevieve, of course. I never introduced them to each other because I preferred the simplicity of one-on-one to the possible messiness of a group of three. And my instincts were right. I don't begrudge them their happiness. But there seems to be less left for me.

"Do you feel sick to your stomach?" Genevieve asked, stroking my head with her warm hand. My head in her cozy lap. "You look a little green around the gills."

"Not at all," I sighed. Crunched on an obscenely expensive Japanese cucumber.

"You might want to go to the doctor, don't you think? That way, you can know for sure. Why don't I phone and make an appointment?" Genevieve eased my head from her lap and onto a pillow while I sipped from the fading sweetness of her breath.

"Sure," I called but she had already gone to the kitchen, flipped through my meager booklet of numbers, was chatting with the receptionist. Me noticing for the first time that gentle sweetness wielded a lot of power.

Clump, clump, clump of Docs coming down my stairs.

"Door was unlocked again, dope," Midori's greeting as she brought a tide of cold from outside. I shivered, watched as she shrugged off her jacket and bent over to untie her boots. The long, lean line of her back, her tight butt.

"Should be locked all the time, especially a basement suite. . . ." Genevieve had come back from the kitchen, smiling.

"Midori, Genevieve, Genevieve, Midori," I waved from my tatty couch, not bothering to get up.

"Hi," Genevieve extended a dimpled hand and when the sweetness of her breathing floated to surround my loner friend, I watched tough-girl Midori blush from her collarbones up neck, cheekbones, and remarkably, to her cow-licked hairline.

"Wow," I commented sarcastically. A sinking weight near my heart.

"Nice," Genevieve giggled.

Midori cleared her throat, stuffed both hands in the back pockets of her torn jeans, and nodded. Realizing that it couldn't really count as an acceptable greeting, she removed her right hand from pocket and held onto Genevieve's fingers without shaking them up and down.

"Pleased too," she muttered, heat smoldering her neck and face.

"Flame *on!*" I yelled, swallowing a sudden ache in my throat. "Quick, get the fire extinguisher! She's burning up! She's burning up! Ahhhrrrgh!" Midori liked her. That's good, I thought to myself. They're perfect for each other.

Thump thump of Midori pounding across the floor and jumping on top of my prone body, me snorting so hard I could barely breathe, "Shut UP!" she hissed. "You're such a jerk!" whispered into my ear, then she nonchalantly stood up. Dug into her leather jacket for a cigarette and a light, leaned her butt on the arm of the couch, legs casually extended.

Genevieve giggled again. And graciously granted Midori her disguise.

"I made an appointment for you in half an hour. They had a cancellation."

"What! I don't want to go right *now!* What if I'm really pregnant? I don't want to know!"

"Silly," Genevieve murmured. "Best find out sooner, it's late enough already, then we can decide what to do."

"Finally," Midori nodded. "Someone with some sense!"

"All *right!* But," I gulped, "will you two come with me?"

"Of course!" Genevieve rushed to hug me and Midori's tough mouth softened into a vulnerable smile.

Well, I thought, that's that.

BRAT-NOISY-RUNNING-NOSES and bag-eyed mothers clinging to screeching bundles of winter sickness, I sagged in my seat, horrified. Not that I ever envisioned motherhood as a land of Gerber cherubs, breastmilk flowing like ambrosia and honey. But the reality of the doctor's waiting room was ugly in a way that I couldn't normalize. And my friends were no help, making moony eyes at each other, knees brushing knees in a transparent enactment of leg-kissing. They were pathetic. I sighed. Reached for a Japanese cucumber I had tucked into the breastpocket of my flannel pajamas. Ate it as surreptitiously as I could, crunchy as it was. Funny thing. People willing to overlook an ugly patient in pajamas in a doctor's office. Because, obviously, she's sick.

Midori's quick elbow in my solid ribs. I jumped to my splay-footed stance.

"Your turn." Her tender brown eyes saying what her mouth wasn't.

"You want us to go in with you?" Genevieve asked, brushing a long strand of hair, earnestly leaning forward, already there with me.

"Yeah, could you—no, I should go. Maybe? No."

The receptionist called me again. Midori and Genevieve, patiently looking up at me.

Breathed in deeply. "I think I'll go in by myself."

DR. SULERI SHUT THE FILE WITH A FIRM HAND.

"So you might be pregnant." A statement, not a judgment call.

"I have reason to believe so, yes." Nervous and thinking that formal language might somehow protect me from looking stupid.

"When did you last menstruate?"

"Ahh, over four months ago?"

She didn't say anything, only raised one eloquent eyebrow.

I cringed. "I didn't come in earlier because my period skips all the time. I'm not regular."

The eyebrow wasn't impressed.

"I mean, I didn't think anything was *wrong* until I felt—"

"Being pregnant doesn't necessitate there being something wrong," Dr. Suleri corrected. "What did you feel?"

"Like something was moving, kicking me," I muttered.

Dr. Suleri glanced at the squarish body she was familiar with: I wasn't so stupid that I didn't go in for a yearly physical. Her sharp eyes seeing what I had already noticed, that my body looked no different than it did when I thought I wasn't pregnant.

"Have you had any other symptoms, such as frequent urination, tenderness of breasts, nausea, dizziness, water retention, fatigue?"

"Uh, no."

"Hmmmm," she said. "We need to take a urine sample, of course. But I'll do a quick examination while you're here already." She handed me the paper sheet and told me to undress. Left the room.

I dropped my pj bottoms, unbuttoned my feeling-sick flannels, and rubbed a nervous hand over my not-very-pregnant–looking belly. It was square and wide like always. Not basketball-protruding like I thought pregnancy was. I clambered onto the too-high examination table and pulled the paper over my body platter.

Dr. Suleri tapped quietly and stepped through the door.

"I'm going to lift the sheet and externally examine the size of your uterus," she explained, like always, before actually doing anything. "Then, I will be conducting an internal examination to feel your uterus, ovaries, and fallopian tubes."

I nodded.

She placed her warm hand on my belly and pressed, like I do when I'm choosing bread in the bakery section. Soft-pressed right above my pubic bone and arced the flesh above the bones of my hips, upward.

"Hmmmmm," Dr. Suleri thoughtfully breathed. "Your uterus doesn't seem to have grown. If you were four months pregnant, it would have grown to a little below the level of your navel. Hmmmmmm. Have you had any symptoms other than this sensation of movement and not menstruating?"

"Yes!" Feeling defensive. Intensely unsympathetic to hypochondria in any shape or form. "I did a home pregnancy test and it was positive."

"Hmmmm, they're not one-hundred–percent accurate, of course. I need you to scoot down a bit lower so I can insert the speculum to see your cervix." Icy metal against blood-warm vaginal walls, I shudder-winced like a wimp. Could never get used to this foreign contact no matter how many physicals I had, year after year.

"Ouch," I cringed. Double-cringing for being a cringer.

"Sorry, is it the angle?"

"It's pinching on my left." She adjusted the gadget, the pinching pain lessening.

"Almost done. The color of your cervix hasn't changed at all. I'm taking a culture and a pap. There. Finished." My vaginal muscles instinctively clenched, expelling the alien metal contraption in a clatter to the cold floor.

"Oops," I giggled, mentally rolling my eyes at myself. Giggling!

Dr. Suleri looked up from between my raised knees, one eyebrow raised. "You'll feel me slip two fingers inside to examine you internally. You may feel a little discomfort." Dr. Suleri gently pressed from the inside of me. "Well, your uterus doesn't feel like it has grown. When you're pregnant, it feels like it has filled up, fattened. Hmmmm, nothing seems to be developing in the tubes or ovaries. Let me try to listen for a fetal heartbeat with the Doppler." Still sitting on her stool with three wheels, Dr. Suleri rolled across the floor to the cabinets. She peeled off the gloves and dropped them into the waste. Rolled back with a black, tape recorder–like gadget that had a coiled cord attached to a microphone. Mental images of a fetus singing karaoke from inside the womb. Seventies love songs. I giggled again. Goddamn! I never giggled!

Dr. Suleri looked concerned. She squeezed gel onto the "mike" head and some onto my wide belly. Cool slick. Low rush of moving sound. Deep and darkly loud. I was amazed.

"Is that the fetal heartbeat?"

"No, that's the sound of your heart. A fetal heartbeat would be much faster." She moved the mike all over my belly, but always the same oceanic roar of my blood. Nothing else. She clicked the instrument off.

"I can't locate or detect one." Dr. Suleri handed me a Kleenex. "But that doesn't absolutely prove whether you are or are not pregnant. I'll have you provide a urine sample and we'll see if the results are positive or negative and work from there, okay?" She handed me a small cup and smiled gently.

"Okay."

STEAM DRIBBLE ALL OVER MY HAND, AGAIN. The nurse took the urine cup away. Back in a moment with the results, he said. A fluid of my body. I went back into the examination room.

Dr. Suleri tapped on the door and stuck her face in.

"May I see you in my office?"

I gulped, followed her. First time in the room, no photos on the desk, just a huge poster of a cucumber-green frog on a dewy leaf. Framed. A single iris in a slender vase.

I plunked into a chair and nervously chewed the dry bits of skin on my lower lip.

"Well, your test is negative," Dr. Suleri stated.

And I breathed a sigh of relief, instinctive, but quickly followed by confusion. The news was what I wanted to hear. I heard it gladly. But somehow, my body told me something else.

"You still believe you are pregnant." She was sharp.

"I don't know." Rubbed my hand over forehead and through my uncombed hair. "Physically, I don't feel any different. Except for having cravings for Japanese cucumbers, but I don't think that proves I'm pregnant. I just *feel* like I am. Not that I think I *know* what it feels like to be pregnant, but there's this sensation of not being alone in my body. This presence. And not only that, it kicks and prods and pushes from the *inside!*"

Dr. Suleri looked concerned. I started to blush, thinking of what I'd said. Scientific proof otherwise.

"I know none of this sounds rational. But sometimes, you just know things," I said lamely.

"Do you know the approximate date of sexual intercourse that has led to this pregnancy?"

"Welllll," I squirmed a little in my seat, Dr. Suleri leaning forward. "Uhmm, I hadn't been intimate with anyone, other than my vibrator, for seven years, except for a little over four months ago. The night of the last visible total lunar eclipse of the twentieth century. And . . ." I squirmed, rolled my eyes to the ceiling, hoping that possible answers might be written there. Anything that would convince my kind doctor that I wasn't mad.

"And," she encouraged.

". . . and, well, the evening was quite unusual. It was the last total lunar eclipse, you see? I mean, things go strange, and they *did!* We were intimate for this brief intense moment, but . . ."

"But?" Dr. Suleri gently repeated.

"But it wasn't exactly sexual intercourse."

I may be alone in this watery place, yet I am never alone. Light streams muted colors, speckles my shiny skin. Beneath the skin itself, my cells resound. There is a memory of the body, memory held within ancient cells, always ever-present. My cells tell me what has passed and what may pass before.

I swim, here, in this liquid home and listen to the poetry of galaxies twined into double-helix strands.

MIDAFTERNOON WHEN I WAKE UP, I'm surprised that Dad has left me alone on the sofa looking so lazy. The winter-dim sun practically setting, I could try and pretend it is still night and keep on sleeping. But work the next day. PG is gone. Mice has to get back to what she calls Edmonpuke. And who would consider staying another day as a possible option?

The smell of warm misoshiru, hot rice, and fried eggs, the yolks liquid gold beneath a thin sheen of white. A cozy smell and the night before is the night before, not right now. PG is not here but there is no reason she should be.

"You slept well," Okasan smiles when I wander into the kitchen, picking at the crust dried around my eyes.

Slither files her almond-shaped fingernails at the table, a cup of black coffee and two thin slices of dark rye Melba Toast, plain.

Mice, walking up the stairs from the basement, glances around the kitchen. When she sees that one of Dad's boots and both crutches are gone, she breathes less shallowly.

"Otosanwa tambowo check shini itta yo."

"Oh," Mice dumps misoshiru, rice, and egg all into one big bowl and mashes with a spoon.

"I couldn't sleep at all last night," Slither moans. "Okasan kept thrashing around muttering, 'Sawaru na. Sawaru na.' She kept saying something about a steak knife!"

"Did you have bad dreams?" I ask carefully, scared that too much interest might encourage her to inspire a delayed fit.

"Not at all," she chirps, and offers us some more rice.

Mice and I exchange looks. This is odd. Mom with a great opportunity to be sick passing it by? I shrug. Accept any blessings. Maybe we're meant to leave well enough alone. We slurp our soup, Slither munching her petrified pieces of dead bread. None of us offer our mother help with the dishes and when we are finished eating, Mice and I take her bicycle downstairs to dismantle into tiny enough pieces that it will fit into her suitcase. To fool the Greyhound bus people.

The rec room isn't much of one, but Okasan's committed to the concept, a rec room being a signifier of middle-class comfort, so a blue shag rug covers one portion of the floor and the leftover brown stuff from the extra bedroom covers the rest. A plastic coffee table and a black and white television on a piece of wood held up by bricks. Huge, real oil paintings bought in a strip mall for $19.95. And a wicker two-seater with Snoopy pillows. Comfy.

"What are you going to do?" Mice stares in her overlong way.

"About Okasan's Outside Mystery? PG taking off? Dad's violence? What?!"

"Your pregnancy."

"Oh, that," I mutter, my hands greasy from the bicycle chain. I rub them into the rug. "Not much I can do. You got any ideas?"

Mice stares and stares all unblinking until the hair on my neck starts standing up.

"No," she finally says.

Jesus! What goes on in there! Then I remember. "Hey!"

Mice whistles tunelessly. Reefing on the handlebars.

"What did you see last night before Okasan came in?" I demand.

Mice whistles a little louder, twisting the handlebars with intense concentration.

"When my eye felt funny. You saw something."

Mice turns away, shakes her head.

"Tell me, come on. Tell me!"

Mice covers her ears with her hands, shaking and shaking her head, her back to me.

I sigh. Know better than to press her, I'll pay for it with collect long-distance phone calls, her breathing and breathing on the phone for two hours straight, just so she doesn't have to breathe alone.

"Never mind." What does it matter anyway? Knowing things never changed much in our family.

"Itwasgreen," she blurts quickly, then pretends she hasn't said a thing.

Oh?

SLITHER WAVES GOOD-BYE from her red Trans Am, automatic. Yuck. Fuck. Not only is her car the best example of what small-town people think of as cool when they're in junior high school, but it isn't even a standard. At least my milk truck has character. At least there is room enough in emergency situations. I could probably camp out in my van for days on end, maybe even set up a tiny kitchen.

I pop open the back doors, check on the shopping carts I salvaged on the highway home. The mysteries of relocation. Re-bungee them up to the hooks I drilled into the walls so they don't rattle-slide all over my driving. Hang my bag of leftover cucumbers on an extra hook. No, better have them next to me in the front seat.

Mice has already left, picked up at the UFA gas station when she could have driven partway with me, but she actually likes bus rides. Go figure. Slither cautiously steers away, seat pulled so close to the windshield she can turn on the signal lights with her knee.

Okasan stands waving from the small knoll beside the house, our quick dispersal not even waiting for Dad to return from his fields. We will not see each other until the next holiday contortion. I salute and barrel down the long drive. I look back once, in the rearview mirror, and I'm forced into a grin. How capable he is of surprising. Dad bumps across the fallow in his golf cart, the crutches crammed into the back rack, steering with his knees. One hand desperately holds nasal spray to his nostril, the other hand, behind him, pulls a bright orange kite through the pale blue sky.

AN UGLY TIME OF YEAR and a boring drive back to my place. The shopping carts clatter and bang. My head hurts from not enough sleep. Even strange Mice would be a welcome companion, but she's long gone, Greyhound dreaming, a bicycle in her suitcase. Why does she bother bringing it down in the first place? I sigh. Wish for night.

"It's all your fault," I mutter halfheartedly to my middle region. The tiniest flutter against the bones of my ribs. I snort. Reach for a cucumber and resign myself to memories of the past.

We Stayed in the Motel Boxcar
for Three Days

DAD EXPLORED THE TOWN and the local countryside, walking, so that he wouldn't waste gasoline. Okasan refused to leave the room and Slither and I made dashing runs to the Lucky Dollar for eggs and apples. PG sent to the motel man for more toilet paper. Okasan was smart. She'd brought three sacks of rice so she could feed us properly with fried eggs on meshi.

"Don't say *meshi*," she scolded, her mouth turning down at the tips. "That's what low-class people say. And we're not low class," she muttered, almost furiously.

I didn't care. I loved eggs, the whites fried crispy crunch, the yolks so soft that they poured into the hot rice. I circled soya sauce three times and mashed it all together. PG hated the gooey yellow and ate only the whites. Mice plucked the discarded yolks off the tabletop and popped them into her mouth, whole. Sometimes, her small lips couldn't keep all of the yellow from spurting out when she bit down. Slither didn't eat any at all. She ate rice, plain, then an apple.

"Eggs make you fat," she said, looking at my stocky body. "And they also come out of the chicken's bum bum."

"Bum, bum!" I mimicked, flapping my arms, my hands tucked into my armpits. "Bum, bum!"

"Okasan!" Slither whined.

"They don't come out of their butts!" I sneered. Faltered. How many holes did the chicken have? I knew I had three, but then, maybe birds were made differently? I shrugged. The shell protected the innards well enough.

I loved eggs, but my teeth ached for something stiffer to chew. I licked my salty upper arm and gnawed on the firm flesh hard enough to leave bruises. Almost like beef, I thought. Went to the fridge and savored the coolness. Dad was still exploring the new territory. I stood there, eyes shut in pleasure, the chilly air resting on heated skin. Eggs for lunch, eggs for dinner. Eggs. Which came first? Chicken? Eggs! The eggs came out of chickens, and chickens came out of eggs! Okasan was lying on the far bed, her back toward me. She got tired of telling me to stay out of the fridge and her arm was over her head. PG and Mice were at the window. PG caught sun-drunk bluebottle flies and tied Slither's long hair around insect necks. They flew their little pets in circles until their brittle heads fell off. Then, my little sisters laughed at the legs that kept twitching. Slither locked herself in the bathroom. Maybe she would pluck so many different hairs from her body, she would actually turn into the snake she was.

Okasan's breathing wasn't a sleep breath, but a leave-me-alone kind of movement. The kids were busy. No witnesses. It was obvious Dad wasn't able to buy fried chicken for a long, long time, but that didn't mean I couldn't make meat of my own. I opened the carton, heart thudding in my chest, eye-glanced around the room and carefully picked out the two biggest. I made a pouch with the front of my T-shirt, and settled my loot inside. My book stuck to the meat of my stomach, but gravity pulled it to the dirty carpet. I shifted the remaining eggs so they were realigned inside the carton. Shoved them back into the refrigerator, my heart pounding, my small eyes darting.

Now what? Had to keep them warm. Against my body? That was what birds did. But I couldn't sit on them all day and night, and the danger of crushing them was obvious. What would Laura do? She never had to hatch eggs for meat. Pa went and shot everything they needed. Maybe I could get a gun.

The station wagon! The heat trapped inside was perfect! The days were so hot and long, the interior stayed warm all night, warmer than a chicken. The eggs would hatch even faster than usual and everyone would be amazed. Chicks appearing like magic, and no one would complain about missing eggs when there was meat to take their place.

Hunched over, I held potential in a cradle of arms. Drumsticks were vile but chicken breast marinated in sweet soya sauce and ginger! My mouth dribbled with saliva. The dry parking lot was empty. The motel man, his back toward me, sat in a lawnchair with his hands in his lap. His feet in a faded wading pool. He jiggled up and down in his seat.

I scurried to our vehicle. The blast of heat inside was like a furnace. I didn't dare open my mouth or breathe. The dangers of scorching my insides were too real.

Where to put them? Couldn't just lay them on the floor. Dad mustn't find them. A half-squashed box of tissues. I plucked dusty sheets of Kleenex and tore them into strips. I spit on the paper, gobs stretching slowly, then sinking into soft tissue. The thread of spit bounced back to my lips like elastic. I formed the soft, damp paper into a nest and let it bake dry on the scorching vinyl. When I was done, there was a perfect white nest, just big enough for my lovely eggs. Sweat dribbled down the sides of my wide cheeks. My ratty bangs clotted my forehead. I kissed my treasures once, then slid the nest beneath the front passenger's seat next to an eight-track cassette and a fossilized piece of chewed gum.

"That's funny," Okasan said, when she opened the carton for supper. "I was sure there were more left than this."

Dad looked up from his bowl, a grain of rice on his cheek. A muscle jerked in his jaw. He sniffed loudly, hacked at the back of his throat with a throaty grunt. Out of the corner of my eye, I saw Okasan nudging my forgotten book beneath the refrigerator.

"I have to go to the bathr—" Slither blurted, stopped by Dad's chopsticks smacking down on her slender fingers. Her mouth dropping to bawl.

"Not a sound," he said quietly. Eating from his bowl with quick wrist action. "So," he muttered, "what's this about eggs?"

"It must just seem that way," Okasan smiled.

"Don't talk foolish kitchen talk." Dad held out his empty bowl. "Get me my egg." His voice sounded nasal. Stuffed up full of phlegm. Maybe he'd catch a cold and die.

I slouched lower in my sticky seat. My blood pecked against the inside of my enormous head like chicks against brittle shell.

"I have an announcement." Dad cleared his throat.

My sisters and I lowered our rice bowls with the chopsticks lying sideways across the top. We looked up and sat without moving. Okasan took the small skillet off the burner and wiped her hands on a tea towel.

"I will grow Japanese rice!" Dad proclaimed.

"Ha! Ha! Ha! Ha!" Slither laughed joyfully. Mice ducked beneath the table. PG got up with her tumbler for more water, casually striding to the sink. My small eyes dodged around. I only had time enough to lean back in my chair as far as possible.

"You're so funny, Dad!"

He jerked out of his chair, grabbed the back of Slither's T-shirt, and tossed her outside before she could figure out he was mad. The door locked. I could hear her howling in the dust-heat tornado.

Fool! I thought. If Slither just kept her mouth shut. You'd think she'd have better sense, she was the oldest! I chewed my thumbnail, then rotated back to the pinkie.

What could Dad be thinking?! We were on the prairies. Everyone knew that the prairies meant undulating fields of golden wheat, the color of Mary Ingalls' hair.

"Japanese rice," Dad continued. "I will be the first to grow Japanese rice in Alberta!"

"What about wild rice?" I smiled carefully. I kept an eye open. We had lived in British Columbia, for goodness sake, surrounded by goat's-milk hippies on hash cookies. "Wild rice might be better."

And I was tossed outside with Slither, snuffling into the sticky fold of her elbow. Click.

We knew better than to try and find shelter. We could only wait until we were good enough for the door to open. So awful, the wind. But my sister slowly stopped her sniveling now that she had company. We crouched down, backs to the blast of dust, and sat out the storm of our father's anger.

No one knew what compelled our father to try and grow Japanese rice in Alberta. No one knew what we were doing in box-cars disguised as a motel. No one knew how long we had to stay there. No one knew.

What we did know was that no one would save us.

"You want to play a game?" Slither sniffed, her long hair matted with dirt, heat, and the salt of her tears. A painful, wobbly cry caught in my throat. She was beautiful. I nodded my head so I wouldn't have to open my mouth and betray my voice.

She leaned forward. Our heads touched, stickily. Her child-breath sweet with apples. "I stick out my tongue, and you stick out yours," she breathed.

I pushed my tongue out between my lips and watched tip of tongue touch tip of tongue, our flesh warm, but cool with saliva evaporating in the wind. We squealed, jerking our faces back, giggling. We leaned forward again, tip to tip, that surprise of cool-wet and the tickling pleasure of flesh. Giggling, giggling with joy. Just a silly game. The wind caught our voices and whisked them past the row of dusty rooms.

O F COURSE WE GOT TO GO BACK INSIDE. Not the answer to our non-Christian prayers but who wanted to end up like the Match Girl, all frozen with match-light dreams that blew out until she was dead? And why did they think kids would want to watch that story during Christmas holidays? At least inside meant you weren't outside. Maybe Okasan thought like that too.

I pull into the alley and park my milk van as close to the fence as possible. The keys in my housecoat pocket. My heart beats a sudden stop when I approach the door of my suite. Maybe PG has come to see me. Maybe she's standing around, stamping her feet to keep them warm and swearing at my absence with her smoke-mint breath. Maybe she has snuck inside, boiling water for a cup of orange pekoe.

But of course not. She doesn't even know where I live.

My basement suite is cold, but it is home. Tomorrow I will have to search and rescue misplaced shopping carts, buy a few groceries, and return overdue books to the library. Tomorrow will not be today. Tomorrow will not be last night. There is no reason for PG to be around because I never see her unless we meet at the house of our parents. So of course I will not miss her.

I place my lovely cucumbers in the fridge and toss my overnight bag into my room. Glance at the phone, no, no beeping messages. I lift the earpiece, chew my pinkie, then tap out PG's number. A recording; it's been disconnected. That was fast, I think blearily. Sag onto my bed. Okay then.

I look down on the dried-mud mess of my winter housecoat. Laundry. Stick hands in my pockets for used tissue or garbage that'll turn into stucco. There's a small business card in my right pocket and I pull it out. Lilac with loopy writing. It's been scented with a floral spray.

"New Look," it reads. And in smaller print, "Complete Makeovers by Candace."

I snort, crumple Slither's expression of sibling emotion. I consider a shower, then consider it not. I consider a book, then consider it not. I consider a snack, then consider it not, but a plucking hunger and a well-placed kick against my ribcage send me scurrying back to the kitchen.

"Ow!" I rub my side. "No need to get pushy! You could try a gentle nudge sometimes!" I grab a cucumber and sprinkle it with salt. Lie down on my nubby couch while I chew and chomp and sigh.

Hard to know what to believe and what not to believe in this world, but I've become tolerant of incredible stories. What with being pregnant for over who knows how long and not showing, no fetal heartbeat, no doctor's confirmation, no nothing, I'd be hard-pressed to be otherwise. Other than tolerant, that is.

Not that being more tolerant helps me in understanding my family. Some family. Okasan says the past is best forgotten to make room for the future, but if her life's any example, I wouldn't say her approach is the best.

"But what do I know, hey?" I yell to middle. There is an answering nudge in my inner ear.

"You do know how disconcerting you are, don't you?" I mutter.

A dull ache, exuding near my heart. There must be a gland, or an extra organ, the sadness gland triggered by longings for things that cannot be. Or things we fear to hope for.

I press my face into the raised weals of my couch. The corduroy buttons are hanging on their last threads and there are buttock-shaped sags but I love the way the upholstery smells, a small comfort.

I don't know where PG has gone. I don't know why my friends are lovers. I don't know what to do with my poor Okasan. I just don't know. What I do know is that the Stranger started something that's spiraling beyond my control. The waters are uneasy and I'm scared.

Yet, I want to see the Stranger once more.

How strange, this life.

Exponentially infinite, timeless. I hover on the brink, peer curiously. I wonder what must be peering from inside of me. Hmmm. I settle my slim buttocks in a blood-warm niche, elbows on my legs, wet palms cupping my chin. Sit and watch the outer, cozy within my inner. A myriad of visions pass in exquisite bodies of color. The thrumming surge of sound constant, a source of great comfort. Why does unrest grow within me?

I turn from the parade of lights and plunge more deeply into my home. A descent into the known. Ease the troubling sensations which prod my green mind.

But something calls. Distraught and incoherent, trembling with a longing so keen, I am almost sliced. I can't turn away. Something so harmed, so maimed, must be saved. Or destroyed. I plunge through a great hollow, a cavern of wind and sound. Swim with all my strength to make this passage.

And there. A tiny seed, withered, but still throbbing with life. This, the source where the surge and flow of my home begin and ends. How can it possibly be? That this dying continues living? I reach out my webbed hand and cup the brittle shell. "Green," I utter. And so it is.

I T WAS THE LAST TOTAL ECLIPSE of the twentieth century.

"Trust me. This is an incredible idea. Colossal. No one has ever thought of it before and no one ever will," the Stranger exclaimed, waving a clutch purse in an arc of excitement. The almost setting sun cast a dirty brightness inside my van.

"Everything's already been done, usually by someone who's better at it than we are," I muttered sourly. Starting to wonder if my fixated notion of seeing the total lunar eclipse with someone who cared as much as I did was a pathetically poor idea. Hindsight never saved me.

Stranger tipped back, head against seat and barked, laughed at my tone. Reached into the clutch purse and pulled out a flask of sake.

"Wanna slurp?"

"Could you put that away, please? I don't like to drink and drive."

"Ahhh, don't be a party pooper! I thought you were a fun guy. And who's going to stop a milk van anyway?" Stranger unscrewed the bottle and gulped three times.

"It's an ethical thing," I frowned. "And I'm not a *guy.*"

"Guy, girl, so what?" Stranger scoffed. "Do I look like someone who cares?"

"Apparently not," I muttered. The evening was well beyond my control. And I had no one to blame but myself.

"Hey," a strangely formed hand gently touched my clenched shoulder. "I'm really glad I bumped into you tonight. I was feeling sad. And sadness can be awfully dense. Especially when the moon goes out," the Stranger shivered.

"Yeah," I breathed, and consciously relaxed my muscles. Flashed my companion my famous gap-toothed smile. "Could I have the tiniest slurp of your cheap sake?"

"Absolutely," Stranger postured, then burst into a spray of giggles.

I shook my head, grinning. I wouldn't double-guess the unexpected. If that was at all possible.

I EASED INTO THE GRAVEL parking area beside the Calgary International Airport. The stretch kept especially for people who want to watch planes landing and taking off. There were two trucks and a minivan parked there already, the windows fogged with heavy petting, bodily secretions. Not even full dark and people were at it already, Friday randy, and with a twinge of hormonal jealousy, I clicked my tongue in mock disgust.

"How the hell are we going to get past the fence? I don't suppose you have a pair of heavy wire clippers in that magic clutch purse of yours?" I whispered. Not that anyone could hear us, but the volume of my voice was criminal-hushed even within the safety of my milk van.

"We'll go over it," Stranger whispered back, with an attempt at some foreign accent. Breath sweet with the bite of sake.

"Yeah, right," I hissed. "Look at all that barbed wire on top. You'll rip your stockings," I said sarcastically.

"Ta daaaaaa!" The leather jacket presented.

"Shhhhhhhh!" I crouched lower in my seat. "You have a leather jacket, big deal."

"Duhhhh! Haven't you ever scaled barbed wire before? We climb up the chain-link part of the fence, throw the jacket over the barbs on top, then climb over the jacket."

"Won't you ruin it?"

"Nah. The leather'll look even tougher. A great story to impress babes with."

"Sure," I muttered, rolling my eyes.

"So are you ready to do this or are your pajamas all talk and no show?"

"Eeeee!" I squeaked, thunderous roar of a jet landing, reverse thrusters. "This is crazy!"

"Don't you just love it?" the Stranger winked, kissed me full on my ugly lips, and hopped out of the van.

"Fuck!" I gasped, prehistoric roar of a jet blowing off the surface of the planet. I gulped muggy air, slight fall chill rich with the smell of rotting leaves. "Fuck, this is crazy! We're going to get killed or sent to jail!" My short-legged trot no match for my lunar companion's long-legged leaps, despite the retro wedgie shoes. "Wait up!"

A spray of giggles. I chased after the sound through still-green grass, the rows of colored vector lights glowing beautifully bright. Stretching far before us. Higher-pitched whine of a Cessna dipping in for a landing, we hit the ground in stretched-out baseball fashion, rubbing our hands and chins raw. Spat out dirt, bits of grass. Swearing, giggling like junior high school.

"Do you think they saw us? Reported us?"

"Who cares?" Stood up and brushed off the front of the red wedding dress. "For someone who wears cool pajamas, you sure act like a wimp."

"Huh! Listen, I may be fixated on seeing an incredible celestial moment, but that doesn't mean I want to go to jail for it. And if I were to go to jail, it would be for a better reason than for being caught running around an airstrip with a retro-dressed person of questionable gender and racial origin."

Stranger pealed a spray of giggles, a fine mist of saliva, a particular scent drifting to my face.

"Does it matter? I bet you haven't had this much excitement for years!"

"Well," grudgingly, "that may well be, but I don't know anything about you. Maybe you're not someone I should be having fun *with*."

"Little late now, pumpkin," Stranger leaned in close and I was almost dizzy with the sudden odor of algae. "But I'll tell you a secret," whispered moistly in my ear, "appearances are deceiving and chance meetings might not be chance." The Stranger flicked a wet tongue so quick and fine I didn't realize until I was spinal shivering.

"Listen, the earth is shuddering. Take off your clothes. We have to be naked when the three celestial bodies align." The Stranger spoke seriously. Eyes so close I couldn't discern their color, only that they were darkly keen, bright. Smell of rich, green moistness slow-drowning my senses. I took off my clothes.

I was horribly self-conscious. In my pajamas, I was saved from my body, covered and protected and even bizarrely interesting. But without them, I was a short and dumpy Asian with bad teeth, daikon legs, stocky feet. A neckless wonder with cone-shaped pseudo breasts. It took great self-control to keep myself from covering inadequate parts of my body with my hands. But Stranger was undressing more slowly than my panic fling of clothes. Bending with smooth hips, the slow pull of shoe buckle, how could undressing be so erotic? In seventies shoes? The rollllllling of stockings down hairless legs.

"Can you unzip me?" Whispered.

A shiver spread across my skin, half in cold and half in anticipation. I gulped. Tugged with trembling fingers, down the curve of back, spine. I pushed the two edges of the material forward, over the slender bones of shoulders, and the sleeveless dress fell from childish arms to a heap on the ground.

Funny, I thought. The rising glow of moon so peach-full, the airstrip lights running vertically, the Stranger looked almost greenish, skin hairless and moist. Without clothes, the Stranger looked smaller than I had imagined. Could have thought possible.

When the Stranger turned to face me, I could only gaze with wonder. No nipples. Nor a bellybutton.

"It's not polite to stare," the Stranger said crisply, then smiled, so I wouldn't feel uncouth.

"I'm sorry," I blinked. And looked down at our feet. Feet. There was something odd. . . .

"It's almost time."

I breathed a sigh of relief. Something that was meant to happen since I had come into this frightening world was about to happen. This lunar alignment was a beginning. A moment set in motion.

I slowly stretched my hands to clasp cool shoulders.

"We must sumo tori."

"What!?"

"You know, sumo. Wrestle. Japanese-style."

"I know what sumo is for god's sake! Are you crazy? We came out here to watch the last total lunar eclipse on an airstrip while we sumo tori? Naked?" Embarrassed that I had misread signals. Rejected, even. Sumo! Jesus god! I bent down to retrieve my crumpled silk pajama bottoms. When both hands touched the ground, the Stranger rushed me in a sudden flurry of speed and agility and at the last moment, I dug my peasant feet into the rough tarmac and our bodies collided in a shower of stars.

The Stranger was remarkably strong. We clasped our arms around each other, me shocked at how cool-tiny the Stranger's body had become, no larger than that of a five-year-old child, but gigantic in strength, and eyes so old and intense I shuddered in their gaze. I wouldn't give up. I was a country girl and had spent years in my father's futile rice paddies. Trying to churn chalky fossilized clay into fertile mud, my farmer body wasn't about to lose a wrestling match with this slender, green creature. We gripped tight, neither of us moving, my breath panting. The Stranger feinted with a foot, tried to trip me backwards with the other, I heaved my legs away, dragging downward with my weight. Whoever touched the ground first would lose. The trick was falling slower than your opponent. Clasping still, I spun with the weight of my colossal head, tilting the scales of matter, the Stranger held beneath me, the air thick, but heavy enough to hold us. Our bodies rotated, spun like solar creatures, time spreading in slow motion. Blood roaring in my heart, my ears. And above our heads, even as we fell to the pull of earth, the throaty scream of DC-10 engines. Burning heat, the stink of fuel stung our throats. The screech of giant tires slammed into tarmac burning rubber into smoke and sound, the back roar of engines, thrusters reversed, blasted senseless thunderous. The sun, the earth, the moon, aligned, we kiai, loud enough to shatter trees, kiai.

Stranger hit the ground before I did, the beret knocked off a strangely shaped head, something cool-wet spilled, covered me in liquid sweetness. I thought that she came. Came in waves of pleasure. Hearts pounding. The celestial bodies slow moving across the fabric-space of time. Arms clasped around each other, still.

"You win," Stranger winked. Eyes so close. Intensely dark with a color I couldn't name. I could only gasp for air. Stranger nimbly clambered over my exhausted body and nudged between my legs. Blissfully, I let them part. Mouth. Wetness. Cool as a dappled pond in a grove of trees. The Stranger blew.

The dry grass prickled beneath me. I couldn't say where the stars lay. They glittered and spun, constellations chasing planets toward the horizon. Time spiraled and inflated, how could I know? A moon rising to seek the darkness, the earth just a mote in the breath of the universe. I wanted to laugh, to weep, to keep this moment forever.

Eyes dark and liquid enough to drown in.

"Wait," I almost managed to whisper, incapable of speech.

Skin moist, green. My fingertips stroked a slender arm, softly elastic like the skin of frogs, like tiger salamanders.

"Wait," I almost cried. Scent of algae a rich cloud around us. The stars shuddered in the dome of night and the earth fell so fast my heart was left behind.

Those eyes filled with unbearable promise. They blinked once. And the creature was gone.

I WAKE UP COLD AND SHIVERING. That's the thing about living alone. No one's going to toss a blanket over you if you fall asleep on the couch. Mind you, no one will tell you to stop eating with your mouth open, either, I cheer myself up. Wipe drool oV my chin with the back of my hand.

The dark-dim might be morning or the evening of the same day, how can I tell? Freezing. The other creature is a hibernating ball near my still-warm heart. I should phone in to work, check the schedule. Do the week's pajama laundry. Buy more cucumbers at Bernie's market. But I don't. I ought to take a bath, but I make a dash for my bed and burrow beneath three quilts. I'm tired. All this thinking. Would love to turn off my brain or change the channel. But there's no stopping the memories, they come and drown me.

Dad Had No Idea How to Grow Japanese Rice

H E HAD NO IDEA how to grow anything at all. We had lived in a poor area of Osaka, where the eternal roar of subway trains lulled Slither and me to sleep and where Dad was a nighttime parking attendant for a department store. When the store closed, he delivered flyers for noodle shops. He never went drinking with his colleagues on the weekends, never went to topless hostess bars to toss back shots of overpriced scotch, hooting and pinching, singing enka songs off-tune to the raucous laughter of other patrons. He couldn't drink a drop of alcohol without turning blue, then vomiting for three days in a row. And Okasan's few neighborhood friends would always say how lucky she was for not having a husband who drank. Yes, she would softly smile, still pretty with her cat-eye glasses, so lucky. The nasal spray didn't happen until the dry, dry prairies for some strange reason filled my father's head so mucus-full he couldn't breathe without it. Nasal spray. His cavities filled with memories lost, or maybe the unattainable future.

Dad didn't know how to grow Japanese rice. Forget about the fact that you couldn't grow it in Alberta anyway. No water. The too-short growing season. Old Man River flowing sluggish brown north of us and the Milk River, chocolate, winding too far south. All he knew was that we needed water to make the flooded soft mud of his childhood thought-place, years disremembered and half a world away.

Luckily, we arrived in high summer, too late for any active pursuit of the growing season. So we left our father to hunt down a used John Deere tractor while my mother, sisters, and I tried to make some semblance of a home.

Dad left us in front of the old Rodney farmhouse. The prairie spread we'd thought flat and unpeopled had small nooks of poplared houses in pockets of land. Dad helped us unload the station wagon, everything left in piles on the driveway, then he drove off in twin plumes of dust. The sun was directly above us and we cast no shadows. Okasan's face so pale, I knew she would never tan. Like the translucent skin of grubs or maggots, she would stay pale or dry up and die. I shuddered. My book clammy against my stomach. We stood in the middle of our belongings and all we could do was stare at what was now our home.

The house had a face. There were two tiny windows peering malevolently and a door-nose right in between. A tiny porch in front of the door the gritting mouth. The triangle roof was steep, pointing to a sky that never ended and we tipped back our heads, our mouths sagging. A tinier window in the crotch of the roof, cracks around the frame, scarred the house's forehead.

The sigh that came out of Okasan's mouth broke into shudders. Mice spun to her, arms outstretched, but PG grabbed the neck of her T-shirt and Mice gagged. PG had sense. I was glad she stopped our baby sister. Okasan was so boneless, she might fall to pieces if anyone touched her. Slither prodded her foot against a stack of boxes, picking at small semicircles of dirt trapped beneath her fingernails.

"Well then," Okasan shook herself. "Let's get settled before your father gets back. He'll be so surprised." She grabbed a cardboard box and marched forward. The dry grass crackled beneath her feet and hoppers clattered away on brittle wings. Mice, barking, chased after them.

"Come on, then!" I shoved Slither. Grabbing a suitcase, shoved her once more.

"Don't push!" she whined, picking up the smallest box.

"Come on, PG. You can help too."

There was no answer.

I turned around, glaring at my lazy little sister. But she was rigid. Hands fisted. Her left eye roved madly, looking for escape, and the right eye stared directly at face of the house. Muttered something over and over. I crunched over to her. Frowning.

"It's not the nicest, but it's shelter, huh? Laura Ingalls lived in a dirt house, once, so we should count ourselves lucky."

PG didn't even look at me or answer back. She kept muttering her charm, over and over, "Scarythingsaren'tscaryifyou'renotscare dofthem."

The hair rose on the back of my sticky neck all shivery and weak. I scowled. "Get over it. You'll be living here for the next thirteen years!" And I left her out there to face her own monsters.

BY THE TIME EVERYTHING was moved in, floors, counters, cupboards wiped well enough to put things away, the afternoon was falling into evening. Crates, a green Formica kitchen table and four mismatched chairs. Powder-blue suitcases scored with scratches and shoeprints. Cardboard boxes with plates and coffee mugs printed with plumbing company logos. Dad had bought two sagging beds that were going to be thrown out from the motel man.

PG wouldn't come inside until it started getting dark. Once in the house, she kept spinning around to see who was behind her until she was so dizzy she lay down on one of the beds in the living room. She made Mice lie with her, back to back, so no one could sneak up.

No running water. A sink in the kitchen with no faucet, and the bathroom had a bathtub with no water source. Not a toilet to be seen.

Slither started blubbering. I went outside to squat next to the rusted drum cans, a little apart from the house.

Heard the roar of dust coming up the drive, I crab-walked, still squatting, drips of hot urine splattering my thigh meat.

Dad was back. A blue port-a-potty tied to the top of the wagon.

"Where'd you get that, Dad?" I called out. I clamped my hand over my mouth to take it back, but too late.

"Ha!" Dad laughed. My heart stopped pounding. "Looks like you need this! Your dad's always thinking ahead!" He snorted some phlegm and spat the ball into the dust. "I remembered driving past two of these in the campground. They don't need two," he grunted. Lowering one end of the potty from the back of the car.

Well, I thought. Maybe Dad was just like Pa parking his wagon wherever he wanted. Maybe it was like Pa chopping down trees by the river. He didn't ask for anyone's permission. It wasn't stealing. No one called it that. I hoped. I left Dad tick, ticking into hard ground with a pickax.

After the kitchen was put away, Okasan stood in the doorway of the living room. One of the house eye-windows let in the sunset light. There was an unhealthy red glow on the walls. "It'll take a little while for us to use the other rooms," Okasan said. She was right. There were ugly stains on the ceilings. Walls with foot-sized holes and nails sticking, points up, from the floor. "We'll all sleep cozy together for a little while."

Cozy, I thought. We'd get to listen to Dad doing it to Okasan, much like Laura and her sister must have. She never mentioned it in the book, though. Maybe her parents were quieter than ours. But I couldn't imagine any child sleeping through those intense graspings and clutching sighs. I glared at the beds, my baby sisters still sleeping back to back, my short fingers twisting with each other.

Smack! Metallic taste in my cheeks, a high-pitched whine in the canals of my ears. The pain washed up and stung my eyes. I blinked furiously so no drops would fall.

"What are you sneering at?"

How was this always such a surprise? Why couldn't I get used to it? I gulped something hard and dry in my mouth.

"Ahh—"

"Well?" Dad, streaked with dirt, his small eyes staring into my stupid mouth.

"Maybe she's tired and needs to sleep?" Okasan suggested.

I nodded furiously. My chin wobbled, so I nodded harder. Okasan curled her cracked hand around the huge curve of my head. I closed my eyes.

"You spoil them," Dad spit. Jerked a handful of toilet paper from a roll and blew with a trumpet blast. "If they aren't tough, they won't make it in this world."

Make what? I thought. Whose world?

Mice woke, wandered over and absently patted my grubby hand.

"I have to pee!" Slither blurted.

Dad's eyes swung to her. I exhaled. Slither took two steps back, then, two steps forward so she wouldn't look like she was trying to run away. She anxiously crossed her legs, her face turning red.

"There's a washroom. Use it." Dad blew his nose once more, then went outside. We could hear the tick, tick of the pickax again.

"Okasan," Slither moaned. "Okasan, I can't go in an outhouse. It'll make me sick. All those flies. Maggots."

"Don't forget the kappa," I jeered. "They like pretty girls. When you go at night, it'll touch your butt."

"Shut up!" Slither shrieked.

"Shush, your father will hear," Okasan said. "And there are no kappa here." She was grim. "If you don't pass shikko, the poisons will stay inside and you'll rot from the inside out."

"Ohhh," Slither groaned. She tottered out the door, glanced around to look for our father, then ran, hunched over, to the blue outhouse.

Okasan made a funny noise and I jerked my head around.

Her hand covered her mouth. She was laughing.

I smiled to see this side of my mother and I stepped toward her to stand in the sweetness. Mice tugged my hand and I looked down. Her dirty hair was matted with sleep but her eyes were alert. Hackles rising, she growled low in her throat. Her small teeth bared.

PG slowly moved toward us like she was deep underwater. She raised her finger and pointed toward the kitchen.

"There's a white woman standing behind you," PG slurred, not just her left eye, but her right eye swirling too.

"It's not polite to point at people," Okasan murmured, putting on her company face before turning to the unwanted guest.

I sneered. Great. A nosy neighbor come to get gossip for the townspeople.

I turned around.

An icy draft skated cold fingers up my arms and across my shoulders. The hair prickly all along my spine and my knees tipped toward each other. Okasan's brows were raised, her mouth slightly open, Mice growling even deeper.

There was no one there.

"Shut up, PG. That's not funny!"

Okasan spun around and her pale face turned tofu-white. She shook her head, a sideways jerk, then placed her hands on her hips.

"Shut up te yuwanaino," Okasan reprimanded. "And it's not nice to play tricks like that," she scolded PG. "We have to live in this house. Don't scare your baby sister."

"She's right there!" PG jabbed, her brown tan face turning ashen. "She's wearing a dress. She's counting her fingers!"

"Old Lady Rodney," I whispered.

Mice barked furiously and ran to where PG still pointed. PG gasped, and tried to grab the back of Mice's shirt, but missed. Mice ran through the kitchen, all the way to the back door, barking, growling, snapping at the air.

PG screamed.

"Stop!" Okasan's voice was terrible. I didn't know who she was telling to stop. But something stopped. Because PG's right eye stopped spinning and she ran to Okasan, throwing her scrawny arms around our mother's waist. Bawling.

Okasan lifted PG up and my sister wrapped her arms and legs around our mother like a monkey. She snuffled into her neck, her eyes wedged shut.

"Scary things aren't scary if you're not scared of them," she muttered and muttered. Gulping. After-shudders of tears. "Scarything saren'tscaryifyou'renotscared ofthem," she chanted until she fell asleep once more. Okasan held her tight, murmuring into her hair. We backed away from the kitchen and I held Mice's wrist in my hand, pulling her closer. Okasan lowered PG to the kids' bed and pushed back the sweaty bangs that clung on her forehead. PG frowned in her sleep. Ground her teeth. Okasan shook her head. She marched into the kitchen, banging cupboard doors open shut, couldn't remember where she'd put things. She came up with a box of salt. Frowning, she poured a small amount into the bowl of one hand, then, she tossed some grains into the air. Went back into the living room to sprinkle some onto my sleeping sister, a frightening look in my mother's eyes. Then she sprinkled what was left onto me and Mice, Slither too when she came back from the outhouse.

"What are you doing?" Slither ducked. Trying to brush the crystals out of her long hair. Mice laughed, spun in circles, pretending it was snow. Okasan brushed the last grains over her own head and muttered, hands held together.

"Who're you praying to?" Slither continued. "I thought you were Buddhist? What happened?"

"Shut up!" I hissed.

"No one tells me anything," Slither sulked. "How're we supposed to take a bath and brush our teeth?"

I stared at our mother. Would the salt be enough to protect us?

Outside, Dad tick, ticked the pickax in the fossilized ground. So suddenly dark, now. Why was he digging in the dark? What was the hole for? What if bones came up?

"Your father is digging a well," Okasan said.

Oh! I was excited again. Just like Pa Ingalls! I quickly leafed through my book to the well section. Yes! Poison gas in the bottom of the well! Maybe Dad didn't know the candle trick to check for dangerous vapors.

"For serious?" Slither looked hopefully up into Okasan's face. "Will we be able to take a shower?"

"No, but once your father finds water, we will have baths." Okasan looked absently around for something. I thought she was looking for Mice, but when Mice ducked into Okasan's hand, Okasan pushed her away.

"But no bath tonight," our mother sighed. She poured tepid mugi-cha into a plastic bowl and dropped in a hand towel. She wrung it out and wiped our dust-ringed faces with tea. She wiped not roughly, but not gentle either.

A sudden gust of prairie wind shuddered the thin panes of glass in the window, and we jumped. Dad stepping through the door, pickax over his shoulder. His hair stood on end and his teeth were rimmed with dust.

"What a wind," Okasan murmured. "You must be tired."

"This is a land for pioneers!" Dad beamed.

Yes, I smiled back, rubbing my book from the outside of my T-shirt.

"We struggle and fight. For water. For success. For life!" Dad laughed, so handsome. My eyes glowed. Dad set the pickax next to the door and spun around, wrapped his arm loosely around my neck and ruffled my exploding hair.

"A head just like mine," Dad muttered, low and warm and my heart almost burst. "Come. I have a story about water to tell you."

A kappa lives in a tiny pool of water in a deep, deep forest. No longer youthful, the creature has been lonely for many seasons of rain and light. Seldom has passed another being and the saying is, a kappa who cannot play tricks is a kappa who loses water. So the creature decides to venture to untraveled lands.

It is well known that a kappa must be near water in order to survive, must always be able to replenish the bowl-shaped head with the vital liquid, so the poor kappa is very worried. Luckily, there are large platters of forest leaves which cup pockets of dew, and the kappa can tip them into its head and be replenished.

After several days, the kappa comes upon a human hut and a small spread of field near the dark edge of forest. A hut of thin sticks, the garden patch rudely made. There is no well, no brook to keep the place watered with sound. The kappa is not pleased.

Then, a small noise seeps from inside the tattered home. The sound is pale, thin, like a flute held to a breeze. It is a very sad sound, indeed. The kappa creeps closer, moving lizard-slow, pausing to let skin adapt to shades of grass, then dust. The creature presses against the rude sticks of the hut and peers one large, iridescent eye into the striped darkness inside.

There lays a bundle of rags next to the firepit. Bony limbs extended. The kappa shivers, draws a webbed hand over eyes to unsee what is seen. Movement, in the corner of the room. An over-thin child with an enormous head sits facing the bundle of clothes. The child moans softly, with dry, dry lips.

The kappa moves with the eye-blink swiftness of its kind inside the hut. Draws a webbed hand over the child's eyes so the child can unsee what it saw, then kappa clasps warm fingers with a moist, cool grip and leads the young human outside.

What should be done? Should the child be drowned so its suffering can end and so another beginning can be born? Should there be a sumo match, as kappa oft initiated with the humans they encountered? The kappa sits on haunches and gazes, with intently bright eyes, at the strangely shaped young human.

"Mizu," the child croaks between cracked lips.

"Ahhhh," the kappa sighs. Of course.

The creature reaches with one webbed hand and cups some of the precious water from the bowl of its head. Without spilling a drop, the kappa holds the life source to the young human's mouth. The child's dry lips soak up the liquid like desert sand.

I WAKE UP SMILING FOR NO REASON. I could be smiling all my smiles in my sleep for all I know. There is a yellow stain the shape of Madagascar on my ceiling. If the people above me keep on leaking water, the whole world might be revealed. I could learn to read my fortune from the markings. I could quit my job and become a professional reader of bedroom ceiling stains, have my own advertisement on late-night television.

I'd love to skip work, and I'm surprised. When my vocation has been such a source of satisfaction. Where does this unrest come from? I would happily skip work today but then, how would I pay for my cucumbers tomorrow?

I jump into the shower, don't bother with shampoo or soap, just an excuse to raise my body temperature. In the moistness of the stall, the creature turns over and over with ecstatic somersaults. And it comes to me. Maybe PG just moved to a different apartment and has a new number. There's nothing saying that she's left the city!

I run to my phone, feet slipping on linoleum, and dial directory assistance.

"Sorry, there is nothing listed under that name."

"Well," I'm desperate, "would it tell you if it's unlisted?"

"Sorry, unlisted numbers don't even come up."

"Oh. Thank-you."

Drop the receiver back onto the cradle. Shiver. I'm cold again, all that water and heat wasted, and no time for another shower. I rub hard with a towel. And pick my warmest flannel pajamas, the color of green garbage bags.

Peevish feet pummel my stomach from the inside.

"Yes! I'm hungry too! What are you going to do about it though, huh?! When have you ever fed us?" Out of habit, I grab my backpack that has emergency books for boring situations. I haven't been reading much since meeting the Stranger. Okasan says that books make for good companions, but they can't hug you back. That's true, but then, being family doesn't mean they can hug you either. And to top it off, they aren't even good companions. Put it this way: A book will never ask for a hug you don't want to give.

I grab my bag of Japanese cucumbers from the fridge. Peer inside. There's only five left. Two English cucumbers in the vegetable drawer and seven of the bread-and-butter kind in the fruit drawer. I'll have to stop by the Korean market for more.

I bite into the green, bumpy fruit and the water, sweet-bitter, floods my mouth. Energy flows through veins, fast and wet. Ahhhhh. Is this how a vampire feels when it feeds on blood? Shut up! The creature kicks. Quit thinking and eat more!

Crunching, I trot up my basement steps, struggling into my quilted work housecoat.

Warmish this morning. What a surprise. There's a glow in the tips of poplars and the pointed, bloody fingers of peonies are forcing through winter-packed soil. Hello, spring. You surprise me every year. I bob my great head in greeting and there is an answering bow from somewhere in my left buttock. I shrug my quilted housecoat off my shoulders.

"Could you just stay in the uterus, please?" I call out and hop into my milk van. The engine turns over and I roll down my window. The air is green as leaves.

Lucky for me I work by myself. Well, unlucky for me, because I'm not always happy having myself for company. But better than the clutter-mess of working with other people. What if they wanted things from me without my ever knowing? Dealing with my own expectations is hard enough.

There is a quick kick in my right buttock. A strange sensation to have your ass kicked from the inside.

"All right! I acknowledge you! I'm not really alone," I sigh. Sigh again. "I might be more accepting if you could talk to me," I mutter.

Blat of CB. My boss comes on.

"Breaker, breaker one-nine, you copy?"

I roll my eyes. Gary was overjoyed to find out I had a still-working CB and waved away my request for a pager like everyone else.

"Yes, Gary, copy! Which quadrant am I on today?"

"Breaker one-nine, you're in the core, I repeat, you're in the core. Watch yourself in there, soldier. Return to headquarters at 1800 hours. Over."

"Get real, Gary! Out!" God! Some people should never watch movies.

What a beautiful job. The one and only shopping cart collection agency in the whole of the city. There are seven of us trackers and we go all over the urban sprawl to collect the abandoned, the lost, the vandalized. Truck them to the large garage turned warehouse and get them sorted. Then we deliver them back to their respective stores. For a while, there was talk about closing down shop, Gary was worried when the superstores attached coin-operated locks onto individual carts. He thought that customers would return them for the sake of their hard-earned money. But the stores'll have to make ten-dollar-deposit locks before people return shopping carts. No one cares about a dollar any more.

My profession's not exactly a brain job, but who wants one? I want to use my brain for myself, not some corporation. Slither is always mentioning college or beauty school, like she did. How she'd make some phone calls for me and get me a good situation, I would make more money and could put a down payment on a condominium. Just like that! Condominium!

I like my job. I like my library card. I have enough money for cucumbers and movies and I put a little cash aside in an empty one-gallon kimchee jar for something special. I haven't decided what, yet. I must admit, sometimes I do choose pajamas that are just a bit hoity-toity in price, but you only live once. Some people worry about being in an accident and found wearing tatty underwear. I only want to be found in a pair of pajamas, preferably a nice silk job.

What a crummy day to be assigned the core. Spring so fine and green and the river babbling like it does this time of year. God, what Dad wouldn't do for a river like this one! Too bad, so sad, as PG would say. Too fucking bad.

All of the trackers have their own methodology. Their own special tricks to garner elusive carts. They can be found in the oddest of places. Up a tree. On top of a roof. Dangling off a bridge. They're treated in the most disrespectful ways, and we're the wardens to salvage them. Some of the trackers drive their trucks, what have you, slowly up and down alleys, hanging out the window for that errant gleam of silver. Of course, they can't watch both sides that way. Midori used to come with me when I was feeling tired and her eczema flared up. She wouldn't let me roll down the windows, but she'd track with her keen eyes and we'd wind up the carts lickety-split. But it's hard to do the driving search on my own, easier to get out and walk, especially in the downtown core and all the crowded alleys. Garbage and cardboard can hide a whole clang of them and I could easily drive by. No, most days, I walk my search. Park at one end of a street and walk down the block and return up the other side, pushing any stray carts I've located.

GETTING DARKER THAN DUSK, my tired-ache legs and feet almost stumbling in exhaustion. I'm hungry too. The other one gave up the pummeling complaints long ago, must be curled, asleep, in bitter resignation. My cucumber snacks long gone. I have seventeen carts in my van. My diving watch gleams 6:17 P.M. Shit. Night turned and I didn't even notice. I stumble to the van and get on the CB.

"Hello. Calling from downtown. I've just finished and I'll be late coming in."

"Thank god, soldier! We were going to file you as missing in action!"

I breathe heavily through my nostrils.

"You're breaking up! Repeat. You're breaking up!"

"Ahhh!"

"Are you okay?" Gary asks, like a normal person.

"It's late. I'm hungry. I don't want to play today."

"Oh." Gary sounds sad.

I roll my eyes and inhale. "Sergeant!"

"Yes, soldier!"

"Request permission to return to base with the carts, the cargo, at 1000 hours tomorrow morning sir!"

"Permission granted," Gary says sternly. "You've done good today, soldier. I'm proud of you. Over."

"Over and out." I smile. Blink. I'm so hungry my eyes swim. Cucumbers. I'm out of Japanese cucumbers. Raise my shaking hands to the steering wheel and reverse slowly out of the unlit alley.

I make the Korean market just as the shopkeeper is locking the door.

"Please!" I bang.

Bernie looks up and sees me, the one who's been buying over one hundred dollars worth of cucumbers every month. She smiles, and opens the door.

"Working overtime?"

"Yeah," I sigh. The spiced miso, fish-broth smells flooding my empty stomach.

"I just got a fresh shipment, direct from California," Bernie winks.

"Wow," is all I can manage.

Bernie deftly packs two bags chock-full and weighs them on the scale. My hands are shaking when I hand over my bills. Bernie frowns.

"When was the last time you ate a meal?"

I puzzle over what she means by "a meal." When I don't answer for three full minutes, Bernie takes my money, gives me change, then locks the door again, only with me on the inside. She flips the sign to Closed and pushes me to the backroom.

A microwave oven and a high-tech rice cooker in a tiny kitchen area. A kettle and teapot. Two tea bowls. There's an overturned wooden crate with a piece of plywood on top. Two rice tins for chairs. On the crate table is a large bowl of steamy rice, a rich broth with oxtails and dark greens, and a plate of cucumber kimchee.

"Eat," Bernie says, handing me silver chopsticks. I sink into the tin chair and accept a smaller bowl of rice she's filled for me. Take the bowl with two hands and wordlessly nod my thanks. My thin chopsticks wobble, but I somehow manage, the cucumber spice-licks the inside of my mouth. I gobble shamelessly and Bernie grins.

When my empty stomach starts to fill and the compulsion is appeased, I eat more slowly.

"Did you cook this?" I ask, in wonder.

Bernie laughs, shakes her head. "No, my father is the cook in the house. The girls like to work outside. Grandfather likes to cook."

We eat until we are full, then share cups of tea.

"Can I ask a personal question?" Bernie asks. I glance up. How old is she? I never really looked to see. Thirty-five? Forty? Her hair, sinking out of an enforced perm. Maybe she's Christian, I think. A lot of Asian Canadian Christians have permed hair. Or else she was a headbanger, a woman still in touch with a heavy metal adolescence.

"Sure," I shrug. Now that I'm full, I feel slightly embarrassed.

"Are you in the family way?"

"What?!"

"Sorry," Bernie looks concerned. "It is very personal."

I shake my head. "No, no. I don't care. How can you tell?"

"The cucumbers," Bernie grins. "When there's a pregnancy, there's often a craving. I craved kale during mine."

"Kale? What's that?"

"It's a leafy plant, chopped up and cooked with a ham hock. And some lean sausage. At least, that's how I like it. People eat it in Germany."

"Kale," I shake my head. "Where'd you ever taste that to crave it?"

"I read it in a book," Bernie grins with one side of her mouth.

"So, how old's your kid?" I ask. Never figured Bernie to be a mom.

"Three. His name is Gabriel," she beams, dreamy. Yup, I think, must be a Christian. "My father, Gabriel's grandfather, takes care of him while I'm at work."

"Oh," I mutter. A husbandless, Christian single mom. Really, I think. We have nothing in common. And I'm beginning to feel uncomfortable. Who wanted to talk about life stories, anyway?

"Thank-you for the food," I nod, standing up, my cap in my bratwurst fingers.

Bernie waves her chopsticks, then points with them to the back-door.

"Lock it before you leave," she says. And pours herself some more tea.

REALLY, I THINK, quickly driving from the abandoned city center to my suburban basement suite. How can you tell who might actually be a mother in the privacy of their own life? Though I hardly think of myself as one. An unmanifested creature-child hardly counts as a baby. And the Stranger was definitely not a father. Who knows what really happened that night at the airport? And me, left alone, to deal with the consequences.

I LAY NEAR THE BONE-NUMBING TARMAC, the moon, the sun, the earth all shifting away, shuddering in the aftermath of I don't-know-what.

What? I could only think in strange exhausted disjunction. Who—what just—I don't— Gasping. Warm breath clouding into mist, how suddenly cold it was and me naked, chilled senseless, on an airstrip. A thundering roar of another plane catching the runway. Not nearly as exciting all by myself. I started feeling ridiculous.

"Fuck," I groaned, as I rolled over, feeling cramped muscle, bone weakness, like after a long and frenzied bout of dirty sex. Well, what I imagined it would feel like, anyway. On my hands and knees, graceless and achy. Plane winking roar landing. "Fuck," I scrabbled for my pajamas. Clothing scattered across the tarmac and in the grass. My boxer shorts. My top, buttoning all misaligned, who cares, just get it on. Bottoms on backwards. Where were my goddamn socks? Leather jacket. The Stranger had forgotten it. But the red dress was nowhere that I could feel, couldn't discern with my eyes. Looking upward for more dipping planes, I was stunned. The moon was already gone, well past the curvature of earth, in another hemisphere. How long had we been out here? How long had I been lying, butt naked?

Truck engine, not a plane! I flattened out on the grass, like in a war movie, and peered quick-like, all around me. A pickup truck coasted along a side runway. Go on, go on! I prayed. The vehicle stopped some twenty-five meters away and kept its headlights on, the engine running. Someone stepped out of the cab, all cautious, with a high-beam flashlight. Maybe the duty manager doing the nightly check.

"Shit, ohshit," I hissed into the dusty grass, gnashing my teeth in that useless biblical way. I tried gathering up my socks, my shoes, reaching a crab-like toe to nudge them in, all while telepathically trying to convince the investigating person that no one could possibly be here. Fat chance.

"Who's there!" Wild, swinging beam of light. The person backed up cautiously, toward the truck, the open door. "Speak up!"

And I was caught, pinned under a glare. *Fuck.*

I bluffed it.

I sat up on my haunches, in my blood-red silk pajamas, extended my arms, elbows slightly bent, and let my hands hang limply from my wrists in a traditional Japanese ghost–type fashion. Slow-smiled into a maniacal grin with my horrible teeth all revealed.

"Onibabaaaa!"

Slam of frantic door shut, engine revved, and the churn of grass and muck. I snorted, both hands smothering my laughter, pleased with my antics until I clued in. The person probably had a radio and had called security, the tower. Shit! How much time did I have? Distant red–blue circling of light, a spot sweeping its circumference. Apparently, not a whole lot. But odd, the spinning light grew dimmer and dimmer, the night was turning to another place. I would be exposed by the sun! I shoved balled-up socks on my squarish feet, crammed on a hapless shoe. Another patrol car sweeping closer, the cops, royally mounted, on what? Fuck! Clutched a green-wet–smelling leather jacket to my chest and ran hunched over, in a Kafkaesque way. Blood pounding ears. Breath pant panting. I ran with joy and terror across the gray-dawn field.

Luck was with me, or maybe the alignment of sun, earth, moon still worked their magic, but I didn't get caught. A miracle, considering my flatfooted pace. The only thing I left behind was one ugly shoe. Could the cops track me down, Cinderella-like? I hurtled across the chill field, the last sprint to my van, and crashed into the chain-link fence with the momentum. I curled fingers around the cold, thin metal. Scrambling up, my feet sometimes slipping, I held the leather jacket in my blunt teeth. A quick glance over my shoulder, my heart leapt. I tossed the jacket across the barbed wire and crept to the other side.

The coat got caught.

The cops. *Shit!* I wanted that jacket. Wanted it more than anything I'd ever wanted before. Wail of siren. Me all visible on the fence, the predawn glow. I tugged, tugged, left two patches of leather, and toppled backward.

I clutched the scarred jacket to my nose as I made my getaway. The Palm van starting in one go, I escaped in a cloud of black smoke. Merged onto a predawn road with all the other delivery trucks getting ready for another busy day. My thudding heart stopped pounding in my throat. I gulped air and then giggled.

I was ravenous. My gut squeezing, trying to wring the lining into food. Realized I hadn't eaten anything since lunch the day before, a phantom wedding banquet hardly counted as something filling. I rear-checked my mirror, but not a cop in sight, the sun rising. Wow, I thought, cool. Wished that I smoked so the image would be complete.

A twenty-four–hour truck stop. Signaled, and parked beside a double row of other delivery-type vehicles, semi-trailers, and taxis. I squeezed my van between a monster truck and a yellow bus, so little room in between that I had to jump out the backdoor. I didn't give a shit. People could bang out the sides of my vehicle until they were blue in the face. Sauntered into the diner all smug and pumpkin-faced grinning in my post-adventure glow, wearing my new leather jacket. I elbowed in among the pop-drinking butts of other truckers slouching on their stools and ordered the breakfast special. With an extra rasher of bacon, please.

The satisfying munch, chew, grind of burnt toast scraped with butter, and greasy eggs and bacon, salting crisp on my tongue. Sloshing coffee. Followed by a French cruller. Ahhhhh. A breakfast well earned, and wishing that my strange night companion might have been with me despite the ambiguity of our encounter. I sighed and stretched my legs to make more room for my gut. My foot accidentally bumped into another and I flicked a look. "Sorry," I muttered at a man in a Beaver Lumber cap. He just grunted at me without raising his eyes. Huh! Some people needed manners more than coffee.

I glanced down at the leather jacket. Hunger looked after, I curiously patted the pockets, wondering what sorts of things I might find, my imagination and the influence of childhood nights reading under blankets with Mice's flashlight. I rolled my eyes at myself and stuck falsely confident hands into the unzipped depths. In the right, nothing. Not even the usual crumb-lint debris. But the left, I almost recoiled. Long, thin, and strangely bumpy. I bravely gripped the object in my palm. Pulled it out, realizing too late that it was a dildo and all the other customers would see the ugly Asian in the pajamas and leather jacket, one shoe only, holding a dildo in the fluorescent brightness of a twenty-four–hour truck stop.

"Well!" the Beaver Lumber–hat guy boomed and I cringed. Maybe I should run to the washroom?

"Isn't that the freshest-looking Japanese cucumber I've seen around these parts in a long time," the Beaver Lumber cap nodded at me.

"Huh?"

"Your cucumber. Looks right fine."

"Thanks," I mumbled, blushing redly because it *wasn't* a dildo. Go figure.

A Japanese cucumber. Of all things. I didn't know what to do with it, really. Brought the fruit to my nose, the rising green of fresh water. My head spun dizzy with a flash of memories not mine. An unknown ache twisted my heart. Tears filled my eyes and longing rose, not from my stomach, but from the belly of my soul.

Without a conscious thought, the cucumber was crisp-bit between my colossal teeth.

I was addicted.

I JUST FOLLOW THE PATTERNS of every day, like I always have. Such a long time until Thanksgiving, I needn't think about PG until then. No point in missing someone I've never missed before. My sisters and I never meet outside the house of our parents and PG's absence does nothing to change this.

But not quite the same. I hardly go to the library to check out books. I can't remember the last time I turned on my TV. I just duck into Bernie's market, the only store in town with real Japanese cucumbers. Bernie always has a smile and she's been adding an extra cuke, now and then, "For you-know-who!" she winks. I see no one else. And carrying some unmanifested creature inside my body hardly counts as a legitimate companion. But I get an annoyed poke in my right armpit for thinking this too loud.

Phone rings.

Heart to throat.

"What's up with you?" Midori utters without saying hello.

"Oh, hi."

"Oh, hi?! I've made you another tape. I'll bring it over. You must be done with your isolation stint by now," Midori states. I can almost hear her putting on her boots.

"No! No, I'm still not up to seeing people," I croak.

"You sick? Is it your, ahh, pregnancy?" Midori carefully asks.

"No!" Clench my fist. Relax. "Just a lot on my mind."

"Maybe talking would help."

I don't answer. The phone silence weighty.

"You still there?"

"I just can't right now," I manage. "Please."

"If you're sure," Midori says doubtfully.

"Ummmm?"

"Yeah?"

"Ahhhh, you and Genevieve still, you know, seeing each other?"

"Yes," Midori says warmly. "We're talking about moving in together."

I swallow something caught in my throat.

"That's good," I smile. "I'll call real soon, okay?" And hang up before I say good-bye.

I press my face into my nubbly couch and inhale deeply. Why does this have to hurt too? Forget it! Get up! Get out! I drop my listless tan pajamas and change quickly into my no-nonsense navy blues with wooden buttons. Slip into the fleece-lined fancy housecoat because it's the warmest. The sun is shining but the wind slides icy over exposed skin.

I stride briskly. The housecoat flapping. I stare straight ahead so I won't have to deal with guilt for leaving errant shopping carts when I'm not on duty. "Too bad," my feet march out PG's refrain, "So sad," my steps crunch back-alley gravel. "Too bad, so sad. Too bad. So sad."

I didn't ask to be born in this world, but then, I didn't ask not to be.

Water, the source, heart, the well.

And what of kappa love?

This breathing skin so fragile in the mortal world. Life stretches translucent, the distance from water to air. I see with kappa eyes what will come to pass in times long forgotten. I see with kappa eyes what has never come to pass. The forwardbackward spiral which collapses in the ever-present.

What of kappa love?

What of life, without?

*D*R. SULERI HAD SCIENTIFIC REASON to believe that I wasn't pregnant and if I had been in her stethoscope, I would have been hard-pressed to think any differently. The word *pseudocyesis* reverberated loudly in my head and I had to hold it still. She had booked an ultrasound appointment, all the same, she said, just to be absolutely sure. But I knew she was worried that my condition wasn't biological, but psychosomatic. I cringed. Me, hating hypochondria in any form, no excuse for it, never, ever. Me, being thought of as having a hysterical pregnancy.

I was morose and silent as I left the doctor's office. Wrapped my fleece-lined dressing gown more tightly around my suspect middle. Tossed my truck keys to Genevieve and slouched in the passenger's seat. Midori scraped the ice off the windshield, a cigarette hanging from the side of her mouth. When she finished, she burst inside, sat on the empty floor behind us where milk used to be stacked in plastic crates. Legs crossed, leaning against a wall.

"Mind if I smoke?"

I just grunted and Genevieve looked in the rearview mirror to shake her head.

The curl of bitter tobacco.

"Well, then," smiled Genevieve, carefully backing up my

milk van. "We should go somewhere to celebrate. I know I feel hungry!"

Midori did nixing hand signals from the back of the vehicle. I could see her in the mirror on the sun visor, but I pretended not to.

"What do you think, Midori? Feel like some lunch?"

"Maybe another time," she mumbled, trying to wink Genevieve into understanding. My growing irritation at my compassionate friends.

"Lunch is just the thing. People have less energy when their blood sugar is low, don't you know," Genevieve chirped. "My grandmother always says that—"

"That sometimes people don't know when to *shut up!*" I sneered.

Silence that sounded so brittle it was almost shattering.

Thought I'd felt bad before. Midori glowered from behind me, sizzling the back of my head. Burn. I glanced at my kind friend, Genevieve biting her full lower lip and blinking blinking.

"I'm sorry. I'm sorry. I'm just so—it's just that—I know there's no excuse for what I said." I touched Genevieve's shoulder once, then turned again to stare out the window, eyes salty, mouth bitter. Why don't I get rid of my few friends? Might as well have nothing at all!

Silence.

So stupid, I thought. I was so stupid. I wanted to smash my fist through the windshield of the van. Kick in the sides and scream myself into oblivion.

"Turn left here, and park the van," Midori directed.

Humped over a bad cup of coffee in a white mug. I waited for my salad with extra-cucumbers-please to come. Midori and Genevieve sat in the bench across from me, staring. Glancing at each other and shrugging their confusion.

"Please," I muttered, "I know that you're worried. I can't explain."

"Okay," Midori was stern. "You're having difficult times right now. But that doesn't mean you take it out on people who care about you."

Genevieve touched Midori's lean arm.

"It's okay. I know I tend to babble sometimes."

"No, now's not the time to be protective. There are some things friends should never say." Midori gently lifted Genevieve's hand and placed it back in her lap.

I winced. "You're right. I was awful. I *feel* awful. I wish I could cut the words right out of my face."

"Don't say such terrible things!" Genevieve gasped. "Midori, that's enough."

Midori sighed and rubbed hand over hand, dug teeth into an exceptionally itchy spot on the heel of her palm. Nervously flipped a cigarette out of a battered package to take her mind off the eczema.

"What's this all about?" Midori blew Camel, strong and direct.

Genevieve reached her soft hands to hold mine, wrapped tightly around a mug. I hissed out my coil of shoulder-clenching anxiety and loosened my fingers.

"Well, the tests were all negative, right?" My friends nodded. "But that's not the end of it." I gulped weak, bitter-sour coffee thinly disguised with three cuplets of cream and four teaspoons of sugar. "As crazy as I may sound, I'm positive I'm pregnant. I know it in my bones, my belly."

"Go on," Midori nodded, serious.

"Well, I'm at least four months. I'm not sure it's human, and it's not even like I had any sex. We mostly wrestled."

I told them everything. In bursts and pauses, nervously sipping from my empty cup, over and over, until the waitress filled it again and Genevieve put in three creamers, four sugars, so I would keep on telling the whole pathetic story. The lunar eclipse, Chinatown, the restaurant, the Stranger, the airport, naked sumo. I was finally finished and the waitress set down our plates, quarter chicken with fries for Midori, ribs and mashed potatoes for Genevieve, and my salad, with extra-cucumbers-please. The awful silence stretched long and I was getting ready to run out of the restaurant, covering my ears and screaming. My eyes glued to the ugly vat of gravy that came with Midori's dinner.

"Well," Genevieve encouraged, picking up her fork and knife with her delicately dimpled hands. "Well, at least you're eating more sensibly."

Midori and I looked at each other. She snorted. And I almost sprayed out a mouthful of tepid coffee.

"What?" Genevieve smiled. "What's so funny?"

Midori and I guffawed, holding our aching guts, rubbing our arms over our weakly watering eyes. Genevieve smiled, confused, and bit into barbecued ribs.

GENEVIEVE AND MIDORI decided to watch *The Hunger* at the Plaza and kindly invited me along. But even I could recognize when two people might be interested in getting-to-know-you groping followed by a coffee-talk to discuss what had just happened. How significant *was* the groping? Was it mutually pleasurable? Would they grope some more in the future?

Ah, the life of a lonely cynic. But it wasn't only that. I wasn't in the mood to watch a movie about people sucking blood out of each other, even if it wasn't a typical boy/vampire suck virgin-girl/victim. Bloodsucking is bloodsucking, any way you look at it.

Wondered what kinds of adventures my airstrip companion was instigating. Though I doubted that January pellets of snow would inspire any more naked wrestling outdoors.

I felt blue. A specific blueness that no amount of Häagen-Dazs coffee ice cream, jalapeno chips, Twinkies, and a giant bag of black licorice could alleviate. I pulled into a trucker gas station on the way home, bought a double cassette pack of great love songs from the seventies. So I could go home to listen to it in bed. Be as completely and totally pathetic as I could possibly be.

I was crying to "You Take My Breath Away" by Rex Smith when the phone rang.

"How come you never introduced me to her before?" Midori

demanded, without saying hello. "She said she's known you for years!"

I sniffed. Should have known better than to try to win pity points from my tough-girl friend, not so tough now, probably all mushy soft inside, not to mention the state of her men's Calvin Klein underwear.

"Quit sniffling. It's not going to change a damn thing. I always told you to practice safe sex. Shoulda used a condom."

"On *what?!* There was no *penis!* There was no *penetration!* We were wrestling for god's sake. I mean, what kind of world do we live in when we can't even *wrestle* without getting pregnant?!" Wanting to vent and Midori unlucky enough to call. "I don't ask for much in this world. I just mostly leave it alone, you know. Keep a safe space between me and my family, try to be a good person without manipulating other people's lives, go to work, practice sanitary masturbation, pay taxes. I don't have any pets. No major vices. Don't buy on credit. Saving money for a trip to somewhere warm. What went wrong? Why can't I just have a normal life?"

Midori wasn't impressed. Or moved.

"Puh-leaze!" I could hear her roll her beautiful decimate-and-contemplate-later eyes over the phone. "Are you done yet? Maybe I should hang up and phone back after you're done."

"Fine. No, I'm quite done, thank-you very much. How was your date?"

I asked primly, pinching my lips like my Okasan.

"Oh my goddess!" I heard her thump back into her futon, her breath noisy on the cordless phone. Midori sounded giddy. Midori, of all people, and I was happy for her being happy. After all, they were both my friends.

"Hello!" I tapped. "Hello?! Please tell me you are not touching yourself."

She crowed. "You wish! She's incredible! I can't believe what happened to me today. She's not an ex, is she?" Heard her chewing on her lip, scratching her hands at the same time in a sudden bout of anxiety.

"Didn't you ask her?" Smiling coyly, I rolled over my bed, clicked off my tape recorder right in the middle of "There's a Kind of Hush."

"Are you kidding? I don't want her to think I'm neurotic. All hung up about boundaries. Well, is she?"

"Is she what?"

"Is she an ex, goddammnit!?"

"You haven't even said her name once. Are you feeling shy or something? Maybe you're actually embarrassed because you've never been attracted to a white woman before."

"Get real," Midori scoffed. "At least I'm not out fucking green people on the airstrip like Captain Kirk."

Ouch. Midori had definitely not lost her edge.

"All right! Jesus, no need to draw blood! She is not an ex, okay? So relax already. God, some people should never fall in love."

"Who said anything about being in love? I've never been in love. I don't believe in it." Pause. "You don't think I'm in love, do you?"

I snorted. "Well?"

"Well what?" Midori demanded.

"Say her name out loud."

"I don't have to say a goddamn thing."

"What's wrong? You can't do it, can you?"

"Fuck off."

"Go on, say it. Go *on!*"

Long pause of cordless phone fuzz. I knew Midori was feeling the dare, wanting to resist, but at the same time, wondering why she felt like wanting to resist, and, also, having a compulsion to climb the tallest building in King Kong fashion and bellow her name over the sleeping city.

"Genevieve," Midori whispered, hoarse, then actually giggled. Click. Dial tone.

The phone rang immediately.

"Hi Genevieve," I sighed, resigned, blowing hot air up toward my ill-cut bangs.

She gasped. "How did you know?"

"Guess who I was just talking to?"

I could feel her blush sizzle from over seventeen kilometers away. Pictured her twining a long, soft strand of hair around and around her forefinger.

"Oh," she breathed, "was it Midori? I think I like her a lot. She seems like a very warm and generous person."

"And . . . ?"

"And what?"

"And 'She's really cute and a great kisser!'"

Genevieve gasped. "How do you know? Is she an ex?"

I sighed heavily.

"Oh," Genevieve said softly, "I don't have to see her like that. I wouldn't cause you pain for anything."

"Oh Genevieve," I gulped. Swallowed. Then grinned my gap-tooth smile although she couldn't see. "Don't worry! She's not an ex and I'm glad you two hit it off. I'm excited! I'm sighing because you're asking the exact same questions Midori asked ten seconds ago."

Genevieve giggled, twining her hair in her finger. "What did she say about me?"

"What's it worth to you?"

"A catered dinner for two for any occasion."

Well, I thought, despite her slow and breathy way of talking, she was fast with her retorts when she had reason.

"A deal!"

"I'm waiting," Genevieve whispered.

I sighed yet again. Maybe this was bad news, my two only friends falling for each other.

"Midori said that you're incredible and she can't believe what just happened tonight. But listen, I can't tell you everything she says, or tell her what you say to me, there's got to be some ethics around this. All right? This is it for insider information. You two are on your own."

"She really said that about me?" Genevieve sighed, me wishing I were in the same room to enjoy her sighing breath. It was also apparent that she wasn't really listening to what else I was saying. "Wow."

"Yeah, wow. Hello? Get a grip!" Rolling my eyes inside the expanse of my hugely disgusted face. "Ahhhh, never mind. Enjoy. You both deserve it."

"You'll meet someone like that, I know you will. I really feel that there's someone for everyone."

I would have laughed at anyone else. But Genevieve really believed and because of her belief, I could too. Almost.

"Yeah, sure. Hey, I've got to go, okay? Have really nice nasty dreams."

She giggled. "Sweet dreams to you too."

I DREAMT ONE OF THOSE DREAMS where you know you're dreaming while you're dreaming, but events still unfold without you having any power to control them. Like real life.

My family and I sat around the kitchen table, but there were no doors to the room. The walls were lined with long, horizontal mirrors so you knew that people watched from the other side. But so quiet, we could pretend that no one was looking, otherwise, we wouldn't be able to finish eating and leave.

Dad was at the head of the table, Okasan an arm's reach away, and she kept on getting up for more shoyu, to pour seconds for soup, get napkins, fry another egg, make herself a martini, get the salt, salad dressing, stewed daikon, dish the rice into bowls. This continuum of back and forth, back and forth, Dad complaining how she never sat down to eat, could she just sit down and eat, then demanding another dish of salted hakusai. The mirrors weren't mirrors at all. They were sheets of liquid mercury and if Okasan stopped moving, they would shatter to beads and run into our bodies.

And suddenly, the scene changed. We were sitting in a tambo, Dad's rice grown, we were having a picnic, no, night and the full moon floated orange above the horizon. Tsuki-mi. There should have been rice dumplings to eat, but there weren't any. So Dad pulled pieces out of Okasan. Balled them up. Handed them to us to eat and they tasted so good, we ate and ate and ate, Okasan asking us if we liked it, we should have more, enryo nashi. We ate faster, faster, more and more, and I was gasping, couldn't breathe, there was something terrible happening but I couldn't see it and no one else could either and I couldn't stop.

Woke up.

And does a kappa dream? Perhaps.

Perhaps in dreaming, the world grows material. This daily pattern of growth and decay that is called the passage of time. My dreaming eyes see the miracles of whales, mythic goliath beetles, and fish that live on land. Humans with infant eyes dance beneath the sun. My dreaming lips kiss soil, sweet and rich. Perhaps I dream your existence and, you, dreaming, dream my life come true.

A kappa walks as crows rasp their way to mountain homes. The dusk casts purple shadows on the lonely road and the creature does not leap from tree to tree, does not pause to let skin adapt to the colors of soil and grass. The kappa walks safe in the knowledge that human beings fear the coming dark. Just as evening curls to night, the kappa hears a troubling sound in a stand of bamboo. An elegant woman weeps, her face in her hands, crouched in the grove.

The creature watches, perplexed and uncertain. Humans are such strange beings, the kappa finds their unpredictable nature rather distressing. Perhaps, the kappa reasons, humans lost their senses when they lost their water bowl from atop their heads.

The weeping woman weeps and weeps and the kappa wonders at such loss. If the kappa lost as much water, life would surely end! Finally, unable to bear such waste, the kappa creeps forth to touch the weeping woman's sleeve.

"Older sister," the kappa calls. "Why do you cry so?"

The woman does not answer. Her hands covering her face, she only weeps and weeps with mortal pain.

"Older sister," the kappa murmurs, "perhaps I can help you."

The woman utters not a word, only wails, forlorn.

The kappa curls one cool, green arm around her shaking shoulders. And finally, the woman turns, raising her head from her hands and the kappa recoils, scrambles backward on shaking limbs. The weeping woman has no face.

The Sun Seeped Heat

THE TEMPERATURE in the living room rose and I woke, sweaty and cranky. Hotter than an Easy-Bake oven. Mice was already up, staring at me intently even before I'd opened my eyes.

"Get lost, pup," I muttered, rolling over, picking crusty bits stuck to my lashes. PG was still asleep, grinding her baby teeth, frowning. Slither's face was in the pillow she hogged all to herself. Her head was jerking up and down with her shoulders. I turned down my lips. Crying never solved anything.

"Sa!" Okasan called out. "Wash up! We need to clean house. Your father's already outside, working on that well."

There was a faint tick, tick from outside. At least, I thought, he wasn't a lazy man.

Okasan made salty porridge with leftover rice and we slurped down three bowlfuls each. We didn't get eggs. Watched our mother pour more hot water into the pot, biting her lip. I turned my back to the kitchen table and tried chewing on my arm again. I loved the meaty feel between my teeth.

Dad came back inside. His shoulders sagged a little beneath the pickax, the handle clenched with a white-knuckled fist.

"Why don't you children play outside while your father has his breakfast," Okasan jerked with her chin. We sidled past, PG pulling Mice by the neck of her T-shirt.

Play with what? I thought. The sun bleached sky and land into a white blare. The wind swirled miniature tornadoes in the drive. Thought about what Laura and Mary did to amuse themselves on their spread. Who'd be stupid enough to chase gophers in all this heat? I wondered, then turned to spot the darting bodies of PG and Mice giggling past, hands outstretched. They looked like they'd strangle anything they caught. Slither stuck to the sunless side of the plank house. She had sense, even if it was only about her looks.

I shaded my hand over my small eyes. Saw a heap of dirt several feet from the house. I flicked a look over my shoulder, then made my way to Dad's well.

He'd only managed to make a small indent, the size of our washbasin. That was all for soil. The stuff beneath was the color of concrete, with small, shattered rock chips. He had reached the skull of the prairies and it wasn't going to give up any water.

Roaring gravel and plumes of dust. Someone was coming up the driveway! We all gaped, PG facing the vehicle, frozen. Mice's slightly bowed legs stained green on her knees. She barked excitedly and I could see a bit of Slither's face, one eye peering around the corner of the house. As I ran toward the kids, all I could think about was how the Indians came to the Ingalls' house and took all the coffee and tobacco.

The truck bounced down the potholed drive. A truck so enormous there were two rows of seats, like a car, and six tires instead of four. The vehicle barreled up and braked with a spray of gravel and two clouds of dust. My heart thudded in my chest. Okasan stepped out of the door, wiping her hands on her apron, not unlike Ma Ingalls, a pink stain on one cheek. Our mother blinked and blinked in the windy brightness.

A tiny, brown woman with ropy arms, wearing a ratty, white T-shirt and a cap, hopped from the cab of the truck like a beer commercial.

"Hi neighbor!" she yelled over the wind, her voice surprisingly deep and raspy. "Thought you might not be settled yet and heard you had some kids and all, so I brought you some onigiris." She nudged the truck door shut with her shoulder, arms filled with a prairie-sized thermos, a huge Tupperware container, and a basket of apples.

"The name's Janice. Janice Nakamura. Pleased to meet you!" She nodded to Okasan, then deposited the food in Okasan's astonished arms.

"Ara! Konna takusanno—"

"Can't speak a word and no shame about it either," Janice flapped her hand. "I'm Nissei and never set foot anywhere else. Hey," she continued, "I've got a son about the same age as some of your kids." She jerked her head toward the truck and yelled, "Hey! Get your ass out here and introduce yourself to your new friends!"

PG muttered chanting charms and Mice's eyes were puppy-wide. A grown-up woman, a Japanese grown-up woman saying the A-word in front of us! What kind of child could she possibly have?

He was small. Smaller than me in that thin-bone way. Red Smarties lips, pale honey eyes in a brown face. His hair was straight, thick, and black. But unlike any Japanese person's I'd seen before. He scraped the toes of his battered runners through the dust and gravel. Wouldn't look up at all. Just stood, scrape-scraping his shoes, hands crammed in his front pockets.

"Hey, kiddo!" Janice reached to chuck him on the chin, but he scampered away before contact. Glowered at his mother from five feet away.

"This is my son, Gerald. He's got a bit of attitude, especially after his dad and me split up. Personality clash. It happens. Stan went back to the Blood reserve but Gerald didn't want to go with him and he didn't want to stay with me. So now's all he got is attitude. But he's a good guy, aren'tchya! Maybe some new friends'll make things easier. It'd be great if he could play with your kids this summer, keep him outta my hair. I'm looking after the farm on my own now. He can show your kids around." Janice took some paper and a bag of tobacco from her back pocket while she talked. Tapped brown leaves, rolled and licked right in front of Okasan's face. Really! So rude. What Okasan called hinganai. My sisters and I stared with shocked eyes. Okasan's pinched her lips thin.

"Well, thank-you. For the food," Okasan managed. She tugged her lips sideways to make a smile-face.

"Hey, we're neighbors now. Gotta look out for each other!" Janice winked and cuffed our mother on her shoulder. Janice spun around lightly, cigarette dangling from the corner of her mouth, spotted Dad's sorry attempts to break into the ground. "What's that you're digging there? This soil's pretty tough to get through. Might need a backhoe."

"Oh," Okasan cast her eyes down. "Father is digging a well."

"Digging a well?!" Janice laughed loudly, a hoarse croaking sound. We took a step back from the noise and Gerald glared harder. "Can't dig nothing by hand in these parts. Old Man Rodney was a cheapskate, that bastard. He never hooked up his water to the house and the poor missus had to lug it all in by hand. Had to heat everything on the stove. But there is water." Janice, cigarette dangling from her mouth, led Okasan around to the back of the house. All of us kids followed, a row of ducklings.

There was a tiny shed, too small for storage, that no one had bothered to look inside. Janice twisted the nail and small piece of wood that kept the door shut and jerked it back. Moths flew into the bright light of day, evaporated into motes of dust. Cobwebs gleamed dusty, beams of sun breaking through the cracks in the walls. It was a pumphouse.

Janice crouched and lifted a scratched, orange bucket which covered a faucet. Twisted. There was the whir of engine, a glugging cough, and the water spilled onto the ground. Janice grinned up at our astonished faces.

"Not the best-tasting water, but it'll wet your whistle."

Okasan's eyes glowed with quiet joy. My heart almost burst. Mice bent down to lap at the liquid and Janice reached out gently, held her back.

"Best let the water run some. Been holed up for a long time."

I looked up at Janice's lean, brown face and smiled with every one of my teeth. She looked surprised, croaked a laugh, then mussed the top of my mussed-up hair. The scent of sweet tobacco.

Okasan reached out and clasped Janice's rough hand in both of hers.

"Thank-you," she said.

Janice shrugged, embarrassed. "I gotta get back to my chores," she grinned. Nodded her chin at her son. "Why don't you stick around and visit with your new friends?" And without waiting for a reply, she climbed into her giant truck. Revved down the long driveway with a thin arm waving out the open window.

The gravel and dust swirled in miniature tornadoes, then settled back onto baked land that was twitting with birds and cheeping gophers, the burring buzz of insects. The country seemed less frightening.

I glanced at Gerald without staring. From the sides of my eyes, looking away at the same time. With his mother gone, the glower fell out of Gerald's face. Head low, his chin wobbled and he blink-ed and blinked. My sisters and I, even Okasan, looked away so he could see that we hadn't seen. Mice crouched down to sniff a gopher hole and Okasan tried to comb out the wind knots in PG's hair. I walked sideways toward the house on my clumpy feet. And passed Gerald with a small, close-mouthed grin.

"Maaaa!" Okasan exclaimed, when she opened the lid of the Tupperware. "Don't these onigiris look so good!"

We all peered. The rice balls were twice the normal size and there wasn't any seaweed, but we agreed with our mother and nod-ded our heads.

"Let's go inside and have an early lunch!" Okasan curved her arms outward, gathering us in like so many chickens, and Gerald came inside too.

Okasan was light with pleasure. My sisters and I giggled to see her this way.

"What's so funny?" Dad called from the living room.

We glanced at each other. Was it good that there was free water? Was it bad? We glanced at our mother to measure the gauge.

Okasan wrung her hands in her apron. Her hands didn't know either. But she shook her head and smiled firmly.

"Our neighbor has brought us gifts," she said. Patting at the hair escaped from her bun. "Our neighbor, Nakamura-san, has brought us food and shown us where the water is. Isn't that wonderful? Now, you can start farming right away!"

Dad stomped into the kitchen and glared at Gerald with his small eyes. Gerald scampered out of arm's reach and I nodded my head. The boy knew what the score was.

"Oi!" Dad called out. Gerald ducked behind Slither. And Slither let him stay there.

"Now don't scare the new friend," Okasan laughed with her voice.

"So!" Dad smacked his hands together, loud. Okasan jumped. "Where's this water this neighbor man discovered, huh?"

"A woman," Okasan said. "Our neighbor is a woman."

Dad swung his huge head around and glared. Then he stomped out of the house, snorting at phlegm in the depths of his nose. Okasan's shoulders dropped. She was going to get it later because our neighbor wasn't a man.

"Let us eat," Okasan said gaily, drawing up to the table. PG and Mice had to eat in the living room, not enough room for us all, but PG seemed happy to get out of the kitchen. She kept on throwing salt and the floor was crunchy beneath our feet.

I cast a quick look at our uncomfortable guest who hadn't left the corner of the room and I smiled quickly. Without teeth. We all ate into Janice's giant onigiris, surprised at how good they were. After a moment, Gerald scraped his way to the empty seat beside me and ate quietly, with small, neat bites like a cat. No one said anything. There was nothing to say.

AFTER LUNCH, Okasan wiped PG's and Mice's mouths and hands with a warm, gritty cloth. She pulled the cracked shades over the flyspecked windows and nodded at us older kids to go outside. The station wagon was gone. Our shoulders unclenched.

The sun blasted senseless. The wind roared. Slither and I almost reeled, not used to the intensity. Bonnets might help, I thought dimly. Gerald didn't seem to mind at all, only turned to face the roar full on, opening his mouth to gulp air. Slither and I giggled. And he shyly looked directly at our faces. He tipped his head to one side, then started trotting at a deceptively quick pace toward a neighboring field. My sister and I glanced at each other. I shrugged, thudded after Gerald's light steps, Slither mincing more slowly in the tall grass.

Gerald, skinny and small. His quick steps so graceful, I was falling further and further behind. Despite my pride, I had to call out. "Gerald! Wait up!"

He waited. And I thumped to where he stood, panting and sweating in a way pride would never hide.

"Thought you couldn't speak English," he muttered.

"Thought . . . you . . . couldn't . . . speak," I retorted, between gasps.

"Humph," he acquiesced.

We both roofed hands over our eyes, looked for Slither's mincing figure in the wave of fallow grass and dismal sky. No sign of her at all. We shrugged, then kept walking. Through the endless roll of grass and barbed wire. There were sounds beneath the roar of wind. The chik chik chik of locusts, the trill of meadowlarks, and the piercing shrieks of hawks circling on warm updrafts. As we walked, I saw how the land was full of noise and presence. Not empty.

I gasped. The spread of prairie so suddenly a curving edge I could have almost kept on walking without ever noticing. Not a spectacular dip. Not a monumental dip. But a pleasing, surprising dip all the same. The land sudden-rolled downward into a tiny creek, green choked with thirsty grass and snaking back on itself as far as the eye could see.

We heeled our way down, grass dust tickling my nose, making me sneeze. Creeek, creeek, creeeek.

"Frogs," Gerald whispered. But they heard him and fell silent.

We crept close, crouched on the sponginess of well-moistened grass. In the sparkling blades, I saw tiny creatures the size of my thumbnail, more brown than green, still and unblinking. My mouth spread, revealing my ugly pumpkin teeth and I didn't care.

"Wow," I murmured. And Gerald blushed like he'd made it all.

We sat, beside the sweet, greenish water, the air cooler and almost comfortable. Sat so still and silent that the frogs poked their noses from bent blades of grass, looking for delectables. Between batches of algae, long, bent, insectile legs skittered in pools of liquid surface, the water indenting beneath their splayed feet. The consistency of skin. The roaring wind roared, but it also blew the mosquitoes all the way into Saskatchewan. How beautiful the land was. Had been beautiful before Laura Ingalls ever noticed, before her Pa plowed it under. I tipped backward, arms held over my head. The prairie grass bristled and jabbed but I didn't care. The sky floated so high I was sucked upward with the vertigo and didn't want to come back.

"You a boy or a girl?" Gerald inquired.

"You Blood or Japanese?" I retorted.

"Humph," he acquiesced.

Creeeek, creeeek, the frogs resumed.

Close by, a fat bee dropped into a cluster of canola. A bird speck flew by, dipping up and down. My eyes filled diamond bright and the light of summer burst into fragments.

"You're awfully big for a prairie frog," I commented.

A webbed hand reached out and wetly tapped my cheek. Waft of algae drifted by. I sneezed. Wet, trickly sound, water over pebbles. Almost laughter. I rolled over onto my stomach and enormous eyes gleamed moist, bright, a color I couldn't name.

"You fell asleep," Gerald stated. His slender hands clasped behind his head. A green blade of grass bobbed between his lips.

My heart thudded. The shock of waking when I hadn't noticed falling asleep. I gasped and shuddered with a pull deep inside. Below my belly. I almost peed.

"Shhhhh," Gerald whispered. And patted down my exploding

hair. "Shhhh. It's okay." His honey-yellow eyes were sad and old. I could see myself inside them. I jerked upward and sat, back straight, my knees crossed.

"Don't touch my hair," I muttered.

Gerald's expression didn't change. He blinked once, like an owl, then lay back with his hands behind his head.

"You talked while you were sleeping. In Japanese and English."

"So?"

"Who's Laura? A friend of yours?"

"What's it to you?"

Gerald sighed. His red Smarties lips frowned. Desperately, I reached down the front of my clammy T-shirt and pulled out my book. Wiped both sides on my shorts and handed it to him, my chin raised.

Gerald took my book and fanned through the ragged pages, cover silky beneath his fingertips.

"Have you read *Farmer Boy?*"

I shook my head.

Gerald shrugged and passed the book back. "It's not the same as real life, here." He crouched near the water and with a quick motion, cupped his hands around some small thing. He passed the creature into my waiting palms and my fingers closed around the frantic struggle of bent legs leaping against the surface of my skin. The movement was a flutter, a heart inside a curve of ribs. My ugly mouth smiled again, Gerald grinned for the first time, and my belly plunged. He was so beautiful. He stood up and the wind tugged his thick, black hair. The tiny frog still in my hands, I uncupped them so the salt there wouldn't sting. The creature sat for a moment, then leapt, a splash in sweet water.

"I should start heading back," Gerald said. His red Smarties lips. I lurched to my feet and we stepped out of the gully, climbed to the top spread of prairie bed. Full-force, the wind roared and I looked once more at the gift of the creek.

"Come over again?" I managed. Staring at my feet.

"Next time come over to my place," he welcomed.

I bobbed my enormous head. Tucking my book back into my T-shirt, redness seeping into my cheeks. Just the wind and heat, I thought. That's all. The wind blew dried bits of grass that stuck to our clothes and the pieces flew off like confetti.

"Come on," I yelled. And ran full into the wind. Lurching, stumbling, I didn't care. My mouth wide open.

WHEN DO MEMORIES LOSE THEIR POWER? There must be an expiry date. Maybe PG's choice of physical distance isn't such a bad idea. Maybe PG's family baggage is still in heaps in the downstairs bedroom, cluttering the floor until Okasan finally boxes it up. Maybe PG is, even at this moment, soaring in a hot-air balloon, looking for the source of rain. She's deep in the ocean universe, listening to the ancestral echoes of migrating whales, eating sweet shrimp and the soft flesh of oysters. Or she's in the belly of a library, searching archives for the lost secret spells of forgiveness.

Maybe she's dead.

No!

I get out of bed, the quilt and sheet in tangled heaps, and wash crazy ideas from my face. There are carts waiting to be salvaged. I should get out of my burrow and drink some sun. *Eat first!* an annoyed heel jabs into my kidney. I wince, then pee to relieve the ache.

"Stop that!"

A soft flutter against my belly. I'm mollified. Change into optimistic pajamas, bright yellow with green trim. The phone rings. I've got to stop jumping every time. "Sorry," I call out, "you'll have to be patient." The creature is not patient and pummels my empty stomach bag.

"Hello!" I gasp into the receiver.

No answer. Breathing, heavy and sinister.

"Fuck off, loser!" I almost bang the phone back into the cradle. But the breathing intensifies.

"Ohhhh," I mutter. "Hi, Mice."

There's a "hi" quality to her next breath.

"You okay?" I ask.

So, so, says the air.

"You worried about PG?"

No breath. Then a hiss of pain released.

"She's strong. You know she's okay, don't you Mice? She must need space right now. That's why she hasn't called." I tell her things I've been telling myself, though the effect must be the same. I sigh and Mice sighs in return.

"You feel a little better now?" I ask.

No, says her breath. *No, no, no, no, no.*

"I'm still here. I can hear you breathing, don't worry."

And Mice breathes and breathes and breathes. I listen to her for over an hour, until she feels whole enough to breathe without a witness.

Good-bye, her breath says, then she hangs up.

"Good-bye," I say to the dial tone. "Good-bye."

My limbs feel wobbly with need and I stumble to my fridge. The unexpected one doesn't move.

"How can we keep on affording this?" I say into the fridge. Maybe, if I move to California, I could grow Japanese cucumbers in my own yard!

I choose an obscenely large English cucumber, genetically modified written all over it. Cut the thing into long, thin strips and sprinkle on some salt. Cram a piece into my mouth and chew and swallow. Much better. I take the rest of my watery breakfast to my nubbly couch. Washing dishes has been much easier since my pregnancy. Washing dishes was easier for Okasan after Dad set up pipes from the pumphouse to the kitchen. Okasan sighed, "Oh, Hideo," when he finished the work before the fall freeze. Dad glowed and whistled as he went outside. Old Man Rodney might have been a cheap bastard, but not our father. He was a bastard all right, but a poor and generous one.

WHEN I'M DONE WORK for the day, the sun has already set. I smack my worn leather gloves against my thigh, driving the last stretch of road to my cold burrow. It was a mistake to wear my optimistic pajamas. Now they're stained with rotten fruit and engine oil. A horrible day in the newest northwest suburbs where there are no back alleys. Just dead-end streets that curl inward like snail shells and all I've managed to salvage are eleven carts! Gary's curt with me today. He doesn't even call me *soldier*.

I park close to the fence in the alley and drop my keys into my pocket, leave the work cap hanging on a hook inside the van. Bernie's shipment of Japanese cucumbers is late and all she has left are the picked-over oldies, a bit shriveled and starting to curl on the ends. I've been a bit leery but the creature inside gives me a hearty boot and Bernie offers them for fifty percent off. Still, there aren't enough to see me through until the weekend. I give the bag a shake. And my monthly budget is already stretched. I suppose I could dip into my kimchee jar.

There's a rustling in my doorway and I freeze, crouch low, peer with my beady eyes. Burglars! Vandals! Delinquent teens. I scurry behind the spruce tree and peek, trying to discern the movement in the dim-dark light.

Murmur, muttering voices. At least two of them! I creep closer, mincing in the darker shadows, two figures rattling my doorknob, whispering. Then, they turn to each other, their bodies mashed together, kissing like it's the last day on earth.

"Crimony! Find a bed already!"

Midori jumps away and digs in her pocket for a cigarette but Genevieve just pats her mussed-up clothing and smiles and sighs at the same time.

"We've been bad—"

"I don't want to hear the details!" I interrupt.

Genevieve laughs and covers her mouth. "No, silly! Let me finish my sentence! We've been bad, not coming by to see you more often. Look. We brought you some Greek salad because it's got lots of cucumbers."

"Huh," I acknowledge. "Well, you might as well come in while you're here."

We clump down the stairs, into the kitchen.

"How was your Easter? I know you were dreading it." Midori opens the fridge to look for chocolate.

"God! I haven't told you? Dad trashed the table. PG ran off, no one knows where and Okasan had an attack. It was the Easter from hell." I cram chunks of salty feta and juicy cucumber in my mouth. "How was your holiday?" I garble around my bulging cheeks.

"We were going to go on a ski vacation," Genevieve breathes, "but we didn't make it."

"Cozy," I mutter. "Like I said, I don't want to hear the details, okay!"

Hum of refrigerator.

Midori and Genevieve don't stay long. And I don't care.

After they leave, I can't bear my own company. All I can do is double-housecoat myself and go to the dog park. If you walk there without a dog, people leave you alone. And when I walk fast enough, I can almost leave myself behind, a panting breath away.

I walk so fast I never catch up.

Water is the source and water is the end. Kappa lives are seeped in our understanding of this bond. In pools, quiet shaded in the forest deeps. In trickster rivers where children are received. In cold, cavernous lakes from which the mountains grow. Kappa know that kappa life is bound to water.

And when kappa despair, when their green skin grows dry and brittle, when kappa eyes succumb to pain, when kappa parents turn aside their kappa children, when kappa deny water, they rip the tender skin from between their fingers and toes. They rip their water bowl from atop their noble heads. They tear off their turtle shells and expose their flesh to the sun. They turn their eyes away from all things kappa.

They become humans.

I Stood, Waving

AS MY NEW FRIEND, Gerald crawled through the barbed wire between his property and ours. I couldn't see the house from where I stood, but felt good knowing it was there. The evening wind was dying and I could hear Okasan calling for PG.

The roar of tires on the gravel track. Dad. The station wagon was shiny clean where there weren't patches of rust and I was surprised at the difference a good washing made. But when Dad stepped out of the car, there was a held-in tautness in the muscles of his face.

"Get your sisters," he said quietly.

Heart pounding, I ran to the house.

"Ara," Okasan called out when she saw me. "What's wrong?"

I looked wildly about the kitchen. "Dad wants all of us outside."

Mice crawled out from beneath the table, a piece of string in her mouth. For a second, I thought it was a mouse's tail. Slither came down from upstairs cleaning, a bucket of dirty water in her hand. She glared at me for getting away from work. PG crept into the kitchen from outside, casting looks into every corner. "Dad wants to see us," I whispered.

We quickly stepped outside. The wind had died and the quiet was thick. Dad was leaning casually against the bumper of the wagon, something in his hand. He raised it to his nose and we heard a hiss as he inhaled deeply from the spray.

"I was cleaning the car," Dad began, tossing his nasal mist from one hand to the other. A cry almost passed my lips. "And," he continued, "I found something there that shouldn't have been there."

I could feel the stillness in every one of my sisters, as they thought of what they might have dropped by accident. The cherry pits? Slither's long strands of hair?

"Anyone know what I'm talking about?"

"I-I'm s-sorry," Slither stammered. "M-my hair falls all over the place—"

"It's not hair!" Dad barked. Slither shut up.

My gut was a hollow ache. My heart thudded slow and loud in my ears and everything rang with an echo. I could see Okasan moving in slow motion, raising a hand to our father's wrist, him shaking it off, his lips mouthing words like a dream carnival.

"Someone put eggs inside the car."

My sisters glanced puzzled looks at each other, then saw my lowered head. I could feel their relief, then their pity wash over me.

"You," Dad pointed. "Come here. Everyone else go inside."

I could taste salt in my mouth. A sweet salt that made my stomach turn. My legs were stiff and I could barely make them move, although the last thing I could do was disobey.

"Maaa," Okasan whispered, soft and gentle. "The children are not bad. They are children—"

"Get inside."

Okasan left me alone with him.

"What were the eggs doing in the car?"

I gulped. I swallowed. My eyes smarted. I snorted before it became a cry.

Dad took a step closer and I raised both arms to cover my ears, my hands curled around the back of my head.

"Lower your arms."

I lowered them.

"Answer my question. Now."

"I-I p-put the eggs in the car. Because it was warm. I wanted the eggs to hatch. So we could eat chicken. . . ."

There was a long silence while Dad thought about my confession. I stared at the dusty grass stains on my sneakers. Dad slipped his nasal spray into his front pocket.

"Raise your head," he said quietly. And I did.

Smack! The sound exploded in my ears, the thud of brain against skull, the pain last, and I gasped, tears flung through the air.

"That's for taking eggs without asking."

Smack! The other side, my face snapped the other way, brain crashing to the opposite side.

"That's for not knowing eggs have to be fertilized for them to hatch."

Smack!

"That's for forgetting about them."

The tears were pouring. But my mouth would never cry. I stood there, staring straight ahead, my eyes at the faraway place. Pain thudding red in my cheeks, pounding cushions of blood in my head. Then, my father did something he'd never done before. He tenderly gripped my wrist and turned my hand over so my palm faced upward. It didn't matter what he did. My face was dead, so nothing mattered.

He put one dollar into my palm, then curled my numb fingers over the bill so that it wouldn't blow away.

"That's for trying to have a good idea."

THE FIRST SEASON was the worst, because everyone had a tiny seed of hope that Dad's plan of growing Japanese rice might prove fruitful. He traded in the used station wagon for a rusty scrap of metal that tried to pass itself off as a tractor. The original paint was flaking off in big pieces, and where *John Deere* should have been, some wise guy had spray-painted *Joan Dear*. I snorted with pleasure that someone had played a joke on my father, but then, a wave of anger washed over me. Did they think he was so stupid?!

A small flatbed trailer was thrown in with the deal so we didn't have to walk the eight kilometers into town for groceries.

"Let's go!" Dad bared his teeth. "Shopping!"

Okasan pinched her lips together and went to grab her purse. My sisters and I flicked eyelash glances at each other, at the blue-smoke–belching tractor. Where would we sit? On that sorry trailer like we were so many pigs going to market? How could we try to slip into school with no one noticing if we engine-blatted into town in our very own parade? We would get beat up for sure.

I pushed my elder sister forward and chinned her a message, Say something!

"Uh, ummmm," Slither hawed, rubbing her heel into the dry dust.

"Nanda?" Dad grunted.

"Uhhh, maybe it would be easier for Okasan to shop if we kept the kids at home and watched them."

Wow! What a great argument! I beamed my gapped teeth at my sister when Dad wasn't looking. Maybe she wasn't as stupid as I thought.

"Not safe to leave you kids alone," Dad muttered, and that was that.

We chugged and spluttered into town in a way even Mary Ingalls would have found mortifying. People stopped their cars to gape, roll down windows, and ask in a neighborly sort of way if we needed a hand. Dad just stared straight ahead. My sisters and I lowered our heads, "Happy endings, sad endings," PG murmured, Slither sniffling like a baby. She had no pride.

Okasan hated public displays of any kind. She sat with her hands folded in her lap, chin held high, and eyes transparent. We bought our groceries at the Lucky Dollar, then chugged and spluttered the eight kilometers back to our property.

After that, Okasan, who (like Pa Ingalls) hated to be beholden to anybody, and especially to someone who was hinganai, asked Janice if she could borrow her truck once a month to do her shopping.

Sure, said Janice, and in exchange, Gerald started sleeping over some weekends when his mother was taking care of "personal matters."

THERE WAS NO WATER! Well, there was water enough, copper brown and tasting like blood. Enough, at least, for the needs of the household, but no well would ever have the depths to turn Dad's land into a rice-lush, mud-soft tambo.

Dad started by plowing up the fields. The chalky soil all chunky with clay, wedges of sandstone encrusted with tiny seashells. Slither stood, back to the wind, her skinny girl arms hugging her middle. I crouched in the broken seam and ran my bratwurst fingers through pieces of geology. Dad roared by again, dust gritting my eyes. I ran my arm over my muddy tears and spat out a gob of clay. Who would have thought that the prairie was just an ancient ocean? And felt comfort in my recognition. Short-lived. Dad spluttered by again, his nasal spray reaching deep and far into his left nostril. Such a pathetic addiction. If I bashed the bottom of the bottle hard enough, would the plastic tip burst into his brain? Dad lobbed the empty nasal-spray bottle and it bounced off the side of my head.

"Pick up the rocks! The big pieces! Not a picnic." And he billowed away to crack open another row in the brittle ground.

We bent our backs to the slabs of sandstone. The chunks of clay turned rock. Heaved them onto the flatbed that never seemed to fill. The bend of back, childish muscles straining into cramps. All summer long, the days even longer than we remembered or could have dreamt. At least my body was built for the work, at least my girth could turn into gristly muscle, resistant to gravitational deterioration. My ugly salvation. Slither wasn't so lucky, her bones slender to the point of snapping, her fingers blue-bruised, and her collarbones brittle.

"Ow," she moaned, "oweeeeeee," sniffling as she lagged further and further behind on her side of the field, me heaving grunting, sand in my eyes, and the bones of the sea in my mouth.

The roar of the tractor chugging into stillness. Our ears rang.

"Isoge!" Dad roared.

"I'm sorry."

How I hated that. How Slither and Okasan were always apologizing for their weakness, for things that weren't their fault.

"I'm sorry Dad. But I can't anymore." She started blubbering in earnest. Gobs of snot turning into muddy streaks beneath her nose.

So weak, so sad, she didn't deserve this kind of life. But how could she stand there and bawl like that? How could she show him he'd won? I'd smack some pride into her if I thought it would help.

Dad charged down from his pathetic tractor and cuffed Slither across the back of her head. Salt rose like fury in my mouth. Ashamed that I, for one instant, had wanted to strike my sister too.

He smacked her butt, dust billowing from her jeans, and he pointed to the direction of the house, Slither bawling all the way home, fists to her eyes like she was still three years old.

"Tell your Okasan to get out here! You better watch the kids! Make dinner!" Dad bellowed after her.

Me hoping she wasn't wailing so loud that she didn't hear him.

Okasan with a red kerchief on her head. She brought with her a thermos of brown barley tea, the tinkling tiny bits of ice cooling me even before the tea was poured. Dad pulled off dusty gloves and cap and gulped hard, the liquid running down the sides of his mouth. His gapped teeth gleaming whitely in his dust-brown face. Smiling.

I sipped. Prolonging the cool liquid passage through lips, mouth, throat, chest, belly. Savoring the slow chill. It was so good. Okasan smiled her gentle smile, the dimple in her right cheek. Brief.

Dad started up the engine. And we bent to pick what was meant to lie on the earth in the first place.

PG IS GONE AND I FEEL BEREFT. I don't understand this loss. I have never seen her outside our migratory holiday dinners and none of us actually seek each other out with any premeditated intent. We never call up to do lunch, strip a mall, or have a cup of ocha. Our adult lives are impenetrable to each other and for good reason. But now that it's *physically* impossible, I want to see PG in a way I could never have thought or imagined.

Hindsight no sight at all.

Sigh.

There is a nudge in the butt, from inside my body. Thank-you very much. Yes, I will get out of bed. Take off my going-to-sleep pajamas and dress in a going-to-work pair, sturdy, navy blue cotton with metal buttons. I brush my teeth while sitting on the toilet and read an article about cloning in a science journal. If they flaked some cells off of me, could they separate the creature inside of me at a cellular level? Thinking about this will only lead to constipation.

How long has it been since Easter? I really have no clue. I eat cucumbers. I mull. I go to work. I mull. I don't have a calendar in my basement suite. I used to ask, every day at work, if I was scheduled for the following day. At first Gary almost fired me because I annoyed him no end, but now he's used to it and automatically tells me without my asking.

Midori and Genevieve are scarce these days. Love does that. They've been especially scarce since I caught them making out in my doorway. God! Good riddance to ill-mannered friends!

I've learned that the only thing that can get me is caring too much about anything. Fuck it! Go to work. Maybe I need to get out of basement suites. I trudge up my stairs, jangling my van keys. My backpack with the science journal and, of course, my cucumbers.

When I finish work and can't bear the silence of my basement, I walk. Every day, after my shift, and on days off. I pace the city, watching the way sunlight mutates on metallic skyscrapers, how evening shadows of purple stretch across pavement. My short calves and my inadequate flat feet ache after a few hours. Corns grow profuse on my bratwurst toes. But I still walk. As swiftly as I can without my short-legged trot looking ridiculous. My steps are brisk, like I have a destination in mind although I never do. Have a destination. I walk all over the city, the ugly concrete of civilization, and when I run out of cucumber snacks I grab hotdogs from vendors pushing city wieners to gray-skinned suits, eat them walk walking from here to nowhere. Knowing that nowhere is just the earth tilting into tomorrow.

GETTING DARKER THAN DUSK, my tired-ache legs and feet almost stumbling in exhaustion. I'm hungry and the creature should be too, though there's been little movement. I haven't had a cucumber since the morning, that liquid craving less intense. What can this mean?

Seventeen carts in my van. I'll have to look into getting a trailer or something. Like my dad!

I plod to the end of the deserted street where my cozy milk van waits for me. A newspaper flutters with a gust of wind that's channeled down the narrow road, trapped between brick buildings. The paper is caught in a warm updraft that pulls it skyward.

Eye catches. Double blink. That swing sting of hair flung from one side to the other, dark and thick. That walk. Click, clack, gone.

I run, calling out, duck into the alley where I last saw her.

"PG!" I pant. Gasping. "PG! Wait! Wait up!"

Absolutely empty. Just a Dumpster. A broken comb. Glass.

My heart pounding. I was so sure. I run out of the alley, in case my sister is playing a trick on me, look up and down the street, across to the other side. Just a few business suits tired from office slouching, heading home to lukewarm meals. I shake my head.

"Are you okay?"

I simultaneously peep in fear and leap backward. Crouch low in a karate-like stance.

"Relax, dear. I was concerned. You running out of an alley like that. Is anyone bothering you?" An Asian man with a shopping cart half-filled with pop cans and a few wine bottles. Dirty plastic, old newspaper, used Styrofoam cups. Obviously, he's a little touched, not knowing what's worth money and what isn't. I eye the filthy cart. Hope that I won't come across it during one of my shifts.

A huge German shepherd sits quietly beside the man, head tilted, ears directed toward me. The man is so weather-dried, I have no way of guessing his age, somewhere between thirty and sixty.

"Uh, not. I mean, thanks, no one is bothering me," I blush. I back up a bit. Grateful for his concern, but really, how am I to know it isn't just *fake* concern?

"Well, that's good then. You should avoid these alleys at dusk, though. Not the safest place, this area of the city," he nods toward his dog, who whines in return. The shepherd blinking his eyes and wagging his tongue. The slight droop, raise of the ears. "Gracie is more than a source of comfort for me in my retirement. People are a lot less likely to try and harm me if he's around."

"You call him *Gracie?*"

"Yes, he was so graceful even when he was just a little puppy." The man ruffs up Gracie's head in that way people have when their pet dogs are bigger than a bread box.

"What're you retired from?" Curious. My embarrassingly quick assumption he was a junkie-wino.

"I took an early retirement package from the university. Taught there for twenty-five years." He sighs. "Well, I suppose there are worse ways to spend one's life. But I must say, I've been meeting a lot more interesting people ever since I've started my personal city-beautification project."

I blush again. "You're trying to clean up this dump city?"

"Well, I get a lot of exercise. And I think it's a worthwhile aspiration, futile though it may seem." He sighs again. "My thoughts are taking a melancholic turn. Would you like to resume walking?"

I glance once more down the now-dark alley. Shiver. Gracie whines.

"Yeah, I want to get out of here."

"So, you thought you saw your missing sister?" Jules pours me another cup of tea.

My eyes fill, like they always do when something is uncanny. "I was absolutely positive I saw her. But nothing. She looked so real it makes me feel sick that she disappeared. It can't be a good sign." My hackles rise dog-like, along my spine, and Gracie whines from beneath the table. I rub my belly for comfort, but the creature does not answer.

"There, there," Jules murmurs, I think at me, until I realize he is stroking his dog with his foot. Sigh, lucky dog. Sighing again that I should think a dog lucky for being consoled with a foot under a table.

"It may have been her. It may not."

"Thanks," I say dryly, turning down my lips. "That's just so helpful, I think all my problems are solved."

The waitress comes by, takes the metal teapot, returns it full and steaming.

"What I mean is," Jules pinches the last Vietnamese spring roll, "if you want to believe badly enough, you make your need real. A physical articulation. And live your life accordingly. The results of your choice will affect everyone you come into contact with."

"God! I don't think I can stand that kind of responsibility. How can anyone think on those terms and still keep living?" I nervously slop more tea into my cup.

Jules chews his spring roll, stroking his chin, me thinking he must have had a beard one time in his life. Liking him better without.

"Many people don't even think. They enact their lives without understanding the consequences of their choices."

"You're not kidding." I slump in my chair, suddenly full and tired. Gracie sets his chin on top of my foot and his dog warmth there is comforting.

Jules looks up, direct, his gaze so crisp, I turn my head away before he can identify all of my weaknesses. How it's safer to have an ugly face, an even uglier mouth, filled with bite. Because who wants to be vulnerable naked and not have a single person you could trust see you that way? I hot flush up my short neck to my huge, flat face.

Jules just stares. His eyes, bright.

"Jesus," I bluff, "why don't you take a picture!"

Jules smiles gently and leans across the table to cup my cheek with his warm palm. I don't flinch.

He drops a twenty onto the table to cover the bill.

"I enjoyed spending time with you." He stands and Gracie emerges from beneath the table, the place he had his chin on my foot cooling without the comforting weight. "Good night."

"Good night," I call faintly, just a small Asian man disappearing into the street dimness, a huge German shepherd looking back once, tail wagging.

I climb into my van to drive back to my basement shelter.

A ND I DIDN'T KNOW WHY. Why did she want to have someone else's baby? Did she think the baby would be happier with the Ingalls than riding off with the rest of its family? Did she think the baby was more like a doll than a human child? Didn't she know that the mom wouldn't think giving the baby to Laura was such a good idea? I was puzzled.

Gerald Nakamura Coming Singer was incomprehensible. In Laura Ingalls' book-world, Indians meant teepees on the prairies and that was that. Indians didn't equal someone who was both Blood and Japanese Canadian. Indians certainly never meant someone who lived next door on a chicken farm.

"Call me Janice," she croaked and thumped me on my arm, when I called Gerald's mom, Mrs. Nakamura Coming Singer.

I eye-glanced at Gerald's face for signs. Flipping from his face to his mother's, searching for where the ancestry bled into more Japanese and less Indian, but I couldn't tell, and only stared with my pea-sized eyes until Janice noticed.

"Whatchya staring at, kiddo? You never seen a First Nations person before?"

"First Nations?"

"Yeah, kiddo. Don't cut me any of the 'Indian' crap, how they keep on teaching that shit in school, I'll never understand!" She scowled and flicked paper into a cigarette with her tongue.

I giggled with pleasure. A grown-up woman saying *shit* like everyday! I bet no one ever kicked Janice's butt, I thought to myself. I bet Janice could teach Dad a thing or two!

"Uh hum," Gerald coughed. I grinned him a mouthful of gapped teeth and he ducked his head in acknowledgement.

"Have fun, kids. Stay away from the equipment and make sure you get your asses home before sundown!" Janice thumped back to the chicken-stink barn.

Gerald scowled after her. And I breathed a sigh of admiration.

"Your mom's so cool."

"Che!" Gerald clicked his tongue. "I imagine you think so because you don't live with her."

"I imagine I think so because I know so!" I mimicked.

"Che! Did you come over to play or to admire my mom?"

I shrugged my shoulders and followed him toward the twisty creek.

The too-few hours I had away from the blistering non-rice fields of my father's obsession, I spent with Gerald. At any opportunity, I fled eagerly to the squawk and peck of his mother's chicken farm. The animal din was peaceful compared to the time-bomb compressed silences at home. We played in the dry sun, under the seamless sky, the wind blasting our faces.

I could never figure out why Laura Ingalls wanted to see a papoose so bad. Or why her Ma didn't want her to. A baby was a baby. I didn't not want to see a Laura Ingalls Indian, but then, I didn't want to see one either. When I met Janice and Gerald, I had to meet someone I'd never imagined.

When we station-wagoned our way to the prairies, moving east instead of the traditional west, I didn't really think about Indians, First Nations or otherwise. I didn't think.

"WHATCHYA THINKING?" Gerald flicked his lanky hair from the thin bones of his face. His red, red lips. Life Savers, I thought. Smarties.

"Nothing." I lay on the warm spread of prairie, spat out the sweet end of grass I was chewing, and reached for another blade. "Should we go drown gophers?"

"Janice got mad at me for killing the last batch."

"I thought everyone killed gophers." I tongued the blade of grass from one corner of my mouth to the other.

"Janice said we can eat the next one we kill."

"Oh," I gulped.

"I got an idea!" Gerald sat up. "I always wanted to build a dug-out fort. You know, dig out a room then cover the top with sod so no one can see it."

"You kidding? All I ever do is dig at our place. Why would it be any more fun at yours?!"

Gerald laughed his sweet laugh. "Just like you think it's fun changing the water for the chicks!"

"Huh! No way no how I'm digging."

Gerald lay back down and sighed into the sky. "What will you be when you grow up?" he asked.

"Free," I muttered. "This is stupid. We're wasting time before I have to go back to work."

Gerald lazily rolled over onto his stomach and cupped his sharp chin in his palms. "Think of something, then."

"You want to play a game?" I breathed.

"Sure," Gerald bobbed, sitting up again.

I scooted closer and we sat, legs crossed, knees touching knees. The summer sun drying our faces brown. I heard the crrrrik crrrrik of distant frogs carried by the wind.

"See," I said, excited, "we say janken po! And at the po! we either do paper, scissors, or rock with our hands. See," I demonstrated, and shook my clenched fist once, twice, janken and at the po! I held out my spread hand. "That's paper. Scissors is two fingers, and rock is just the fist. Paper beats rock because it can cover it, scissors beats paper because it can cut through, and rock beats scissors because scissors can't cut it. See? We can practice."

"Janken po!" I held out scissors and Gerald held out paper. I pretended to cut through his paper with my two fingers. "I win this time, get it?"

"I think I played this with my grandpa when I was really little!"

"Janken po!" I held out a rock and Gerald paper. "You win this time because paper can cover rock. Okay, you get it now. Let's play for serious."

"How do we play for serious?" Gerald asked. "I don't have any money."

"Ha! Money! Whoever wins the match gets to smack the loser, like this." I held my forefinger and middle finger together and lightly smacked the inside of Gerald's wrist.

"Okay! Serious!" Gerald laughed.

"Janken po!" I flung scissors and Gerald flung paper. I tapped his wrist with my two fingers. "Janken po!" Gerald had rock and I had rock. "Janken po!" I flung scissors and he had rock. Gerald tapped me lightly, like a kiss. "Janken po!" Me paper, Gerald rock. I smacked him. Me scissors, Gerald paper. Smack across his slender wrist. Gerald rock, me paper. Whack! Two weals of pink rising on his thin skin. Gerald scissors, me rock. THwack. God, I thought, beginners were so predictable, they only remember what they lost to so they countered the last move in the next round. Never realizing that the better player knew the beginner would do this on instinct. Without fail. Gerald paper, me scissors. Janken po! Faster and faster. Janken po! Janken po! Me never looking up, just grinning at Gerald's losing throw, every time, the glowing, burning, red, raised flesh of his loser wrist. Fingers flying. THWACK! THWACK! THWACK! THWACK! I glanced up at his face, my grin, my sneer of winning.

Gerald's eyes. Blink liquid. Oh no, oh no. I looked away, horrified.

"I better get home now." Gerald stood up and brushed dust off his bottom before walking slowly back to his house.

I jumped to my feet. A cry in my gut, almost to my throat. I had to yell but I didn't know which words to use, if I was sorry or if I hated him for his weakness.

I didn't say anything at all.

DAD DREAMT A FUTILE DREAM but one he never gave up. Is that respectable? Maybe it was the ultimate challenge, the last immigrant frontier: to do the impossible in a hostile land. Maybe he was just an asshole and couldn't admit he was wrong. Either way, the results are the same for the rest of us now. We drag around the baggage of our lives together. Even when we live apart. Baggage carried, with nowhere to check it in.

For years and years we nurtured a tiny grain of hope that he would finally come to his senses and switch to potatoes, maybe corn. But no. It was Japanese rice or die. The rice never grew and we didn't die, so we lived in the bitter halfway house of rural poverty. Dad could never feed us as a successful farmer so we only got by on him being a bitter hired hand. Doing odd jobs for more prosperous farmers didn't sweeten his temperament and working on his own spread only fueled his fury. We were lucky that Janice kept us in eggs. A blur of Christmases with K-Mart sweatshirts and mint chocolate sticks. When our few friends at school asked us what we got for presents, my sisters and I just looked at each other, told them we didn't celebrate Christmas at our house.

My Okasan says I'm fond of remembering only the worst. But that isn't totally true. I remember good times too.

There was one Christmas when Okasan got us slippers with plastic bottoms. Slither, me, the kids, even Dad. Whoop-de-do, I thought. What I always wanted. I dragged my feet unenthusiastically on the dirty shag rug Okasan had hauled in from somewhere to cover the rotting linoleum. I dragged my slipper-shod feet and nudged past Slither and ZAP! A spark of electricity zinged her elbow.

"Ow!" she winced. "Watch it!"

Huh! Neat!

I slid my feet across the room and circled back with my stubby forefinger extended. ZAP! Right between her eyes.

"Oweeee! Okasan!" Slither called out.

PG and Mice grinned and started dragging their feet too. Slither pinched her lips like our mother and stood in one spot and rubbed rubbed her slippers into the patch of rug beneath her feet. Finger held out warningly to all potential enemies.

"Ha! Ha! Ha! Ha! Ha!" Dad bellowed suddenly and we all flinched at the sound. We turned to stare. Dad all smiling and looking happy. Handsome, I thought. He looks handsome when he smiles.

"Turn off the lights," he grinned. "See what happens."

PG flicked the switch off and we went crazy. Dragging our plastic slippers, rubbing electric, our hair standing. We chased and squealed, the bright snaps of light, zapping, bumping into each other. Tiny lightning fireworks, and Dad. He bumbled around with us. Dragging his formidable feet, we dodged around his bigger body, ZIP! ZAP! We joined forces, my sisters and I.

"Happy endings! Sad endings!" PG yelled. Electrifying our father.

Mice not making a sound. So intent on her mission.

"OW!" Dad bellowed, "OWEEEEEEEEE!" beneath a barrage of tiny voltage.

We squealed, dodged, dragged, and zapped. Firefly bombers attacking the enormous beast.

"AWOOOOOOOOOOOO!" Dad howled madly. And crumpled to the rug, toppled, destroyed. And we kept on sparking our fingers on his inert body. Stood in one spot and ground our slippers on the current-forming rug. Take that! Take that!

"Ara maaaa," Okasan sighed, standing in the doorway of the kitchen.

I STARE AT MY DOUBLE ROW of toes in the reflection of bathwater. A longing to inhabit that upside-down place where I'm the opposite of myself. I haven't eaten cucumbers for several days, maybe a whole week.

"Hello." My voice is hoarse. And there is no answer. No reassuring touch or pointed jab. My body is alone. I slosh from my back to my front so my middle can't confront me.

Maybe the creature is gone. Maybe voided the thing when I passed water.

Maybe it was never there.

So what, I shrug, stepping out of the cooling water. At least I won't have to keep on overextending my produce budget. I stump into the bedroom and pull out a pair of pale yellow linen pajamas. They're a ridiculous choice for work, but I need to feel the prickly touch against my skin.

The basement suite is a mess. I think it's summer. It must be summer. Hardly matters. So hard to go to work anymore, but if I don't, there is nothing else for me to do. And I need the money to pay my bills. If I lost this place, where would I go?

I slide my fingers over the wide spread of my belly, but there is no answer.

Never mind! See, Dr. Suleri was right all along. I'd better pull myself together before I go too far down the paths of my parents. Addiction. Fits. I refuse to inherit these unwanted gifts.

I can go to work.

FRIDAY RUSH HOUR already and still three more hours on my shift. The sun burnt my face while I corralled eleven carts from all over the football stadium. Crowchild Trail is a disaster, two vehicles overheated, stalled in separate lanes. Traffic funneled into a single line of swearing people. The lucky ones with air-conditioning behind closed windows. The procession creeps. I drum my fingers on the huge steering wheel, the other hand on the stick shift. I ought to turn off the engine to save gas. My stick-shift hand drops to my belly, then jerks quickly away.

Nope, still no internal movement. Maybe the creature is well and gone.

"Good riddance to ya!" I call out, testing. Nothing kicks me in return. Well then. Well then, I can just get on with my life.

Creep my van slowly forward, the shopping carts in the back exuding metal heat. Stink of sticky pop and bits of rotting greens. If I threw water on top of them, I could make a steam sauna. Hot. So hot. Creep. Creeping.

Glance up.

Oh my god.

The flip of hair over shoulder. That chin-held-up stride. On the overhead crosswalk and gone.

"PG!" I bellow. Slam into park, keys in hand, dash out of my vehicle. The rush-hour traffic lined up behind me starts a cacophony of honking and cursing. I just dodge between cars and vans, "PG! Wait up! PG!" I can see people mouthing obscenities at me but their lips move strangely, like they are underwater. I'm running fast but everything's ballooning in the unbearable heat. I run with dream-time density, in a distortion of sound. Clamber over city buses and finally reach the stairs. Run them two at a time to get to the top. Panting. My scraggly hair in sweaty clumps and my shoulders heaving for air. PG is not here. Not here.

Of course not.

A wave of dark seeps from the bottom of my eyes toward the top of my head. Bright spots of light burst inside the dark and my knees wobble. Someone pushes me down into a sitting position. Someone else holds a briefcase over my head so that I have some shade.

"Thank-you," I murmur even as someone else slips something cool and damp into my shaking hand. Instinctively, I bring it to my lips. The sweet water scent. Verdant skin. I snap the cucumber between my teeth and the cool, green taste sinks into my tongue.

When I get back to the van, there is a police officer there. I am not charming and I am not forgiven.

Lucky for me, Gary, my boss, has a soft spot for people who are touched, he calls it, and gives me three weeks off, two of them with holiday pay.

I WALK. Alone. All day, every day and well into evenings. Walk the pavement, my small eyes trying to catch up with PG. I am almost run over by a dump truck.

I drive to the country so I can walk there instead.

Never Enough Water

W HAT COULD DAD HAVE BEEN THINKING? There was no goddamn water. None running through our property, no sweet creek filled with the buzz of satiated insects, cricking frogs. No irrigation canals for miles around and the well we were lucky to have had only enough water for drinking and a shared bath every Saturday, the laundry washed in the leftovers.

Having no water wasn't going to stop our father from his rice-growing obsession. He spent a lot of his time stealing the precious liquid from his neighbors. Winters were spent devising foolproof plans. He didn't steal from Janice, because even though she was hinganai, she was still one of us. I didn't care what his reasons were, only thankful that I wouldn't have to die of mortification when he was caught, and Gerald my best and only friend.

Dad's favorite target was the Snyders' a quarter section away. They had a gorgeous windmill, painted glossy blue, in their lush, chemically fertilized field. That shiny, blue windmill must have been a beacon calling Dad, and he muttered and snorted to him-self, tape measure in hand and nasal spray up his nose. He designed blueprint after blueprint of underground pipes. A system that would siphon their precious water into the gaping mouth of his dry rice fields.

"Dig," he'd hiss, the moonful night and stars so loud in the prairie sky they almost clattered. "Dig quietly. Dig faster!"

"Ow," Slither started to moan after a half hour or so. "Oweeeee. I'm getting blisters." And she would. Big, fat blisters all salt-filled and covered with a thin bulge of translucent skin. I wanted to pop them like the sheets of plastic bubbles that sometimes came with the packages from Japan.

"Get away," she moaned, seeing my greedy eyes.

"Damare!" Dad spat, smacked Slither up the back of her head.

She started blubbering, arm covering her eyes like she was still five. Poor Slither. She always got hit. She whined too much, then bawled to top it off. When would she figure out that he won as soon as she cried?

I just turned my back to her and dug, the slow, steady pace of someone who has to dig all night. Slither was no use at all, blubbering, hiccuping, snot hanging from her nose. Dad booted her in the butt and pointed back to the house. Her wailing all the way.

The soil at the Snyders' was almost pleasant to dig through, moist, dark, and easy to turn over. But after crossing the fence, the ground on our side was chalky and concrete ugly. Dad was laying the pipe in the thin trench, then covering it up, trying to make the newly turned soil look like the work of badger or gopher. He caught up to me soon after I had started digging on our side of the fence.

"Chikushyo!" he swore. The shovel bouncing off the ground in a shower of sparks. "Kuso!" His fists clenched into rocks, I slowly backed out of swinging reach, watched him jump up and down. The frustration filled the veins in his head so they almost glowed in the darkness. Please, oh please, pleading that he would suffer a massive stroke. And free us all.

He didn't. After his spasm of anger, he smacked at his pockets until he felt the reassuring shape of his nasal spray, inserted, snorted up into the recesses of his head. "Aaaaaaaa," he sighed, hacked at the back of his throat, the pit of his nose, and gobbed up some phlegm.

I turned my head away in absolute disgust. Got a smack so hard the shovel dropped from my hands.

"No one said you could stop," he hissed, kicking the shovel toward me. I grabbed it without looking at him, my eyes filled with hate.

"Getting the pickax, you keep digging," and he jogged toward the spot of light across the field.

I stopped digging.

The stars were loud. They buzzed with light and the summer breeze cooled the sweat along my hairline. Only then did I notice the sweet sound of the crickets. Breathed in the fresh scent of corn ripening into peaches and cream, summer grass turning into hay.

How beautiful it could be, I thought, and trembled. I don't know why. I plunked down in the sea turned desert, lay in brittle grass. Huge, shiny crickets crawled across my body, paused and played their songs before passing. I stared at the incredible sky, rich, dense, almost dizzying. The stars quivered.

I lay there and thought about my options. There were none. I was ten years old and I didn't have any money. I knew what happened to little kids who ran away—they were either found cut up into little pieces or sold to men more dangerous than my father. Okasan would never leave Dad, she couldn't save herself, let alone her children, and that was that. Going to white outsiders wasn't an option for an Asian immigrant family like us. If you ditched the family, there was absolutely nothing left. When you are ten, something is better than nothing, even if something has a hand faster than the words forming in your head, let alone in your mouth.

I pinched my lips like Okasan and got to my feet so Dad wouldn't come back and catch me disobeying him. Saw a bright, long arc of star falling. Emotionlessly. Didn't wish for anything.

Heard the crunch of dry grass beneath boots, I turned my shoulders to work, and kicked at my useless shovel.

"Whaddya doing?"

"Jeez!" I spun around. "What are you doing up?"

Gerald with wide-awake eyes, his Smarties lips. He was wearing pajamas not because his mother made him, but because he thought it was the proper way to go to bed.

"Can't sleep, Mom's looking after personal matters."

"Oh," I could only say. He crouched a few feet away from me.

"If you're stealing water, you better be more quiet. I could hear you from my house."

"Jeez! I wonder if the Snyders heard us."

"Probably not." He was matter-of-fact. "I'm downwind. But you're still awfully noisy. Especially your sister."

I leaned on my shovel like I'd seen done on TV and flexed prematurely well-developed forearms. Wanting, for some strange reason, to impress my quiet friend. Gerald reached with a slim-boned hand and patted my muscles encouragingly. "You're strong."

Salt seeped to my eyes, I never cried, never, and he wasn't going to make me. Blinked and blinked and the tears pooled inside my mouth, the back of my throat. I furiously bit my lower lip, didn't notice that I'd broken skin until I tasted the metallic edge of blood.

"Don't," Gerald whispered. Awkwardly pulled me close and licked my lip with his small, neat tongue.

I scrambled back, shocked, embarrassed, elated, I don't know what. And not knowing made me furious. Chin pushed out, my head thrust forward, I drew my hands back then shoved with all my farmer strength. Gerald smashing into the ground.

"Hey, sissy boy," I sneered. "I don't let sissy boys touch me. Ever." This hateful coil of ugliness twisting in my gut, the words stinging something inside me, but unable to stop. "Why don't you get your baby butt home."

Gerald scrambled to his feet, his beautiful eyes wet. He carefully brushed the grass bits and soil from his pajamas and my heart clenched. I almost lifted my hand, palm upward—something, say something—but Gerald turned his back and walked away. The breeze picked up bits of grass that still clung to his clothes. The night was over, the stars gone. The horrible sun was rising and the green glow of dawn offered no comfort.

And I was alone.

"Yeah!" I yelled. "Go on! Sissy! Pansy! Go on home to your slut mother!" I screamed until I was hoarse and gasping.

A heavy hand on my shoulder, I almost fell out of myself, squeaked in sudden fear.

"Good for you," my father nodded approvingly. "Shouldn't be friends with weaklings."

Dad was proud of me.

I stumbled. My face caved in. I tipped my head backward and howled, howled to the indifferent sky, my father stunned to see me wailing, just stood and stared. The fat sun rising keen and relentless, I howled until my mouth was parched and cracked. I howled until my voice had left and salt grained my skin.

I dropped the shovel at my father's feet. Walked slowly, wearily back to the house.

I HAVEN'T CRAVED CUCUMBERS for close to two weeks. I feel blessed, really. But all the walking I do makes me hungry and something's happened to my tongue. I can't eat hotdogs like I used to. No chips, no chocolate, no bags of licorice, my tongue curls inward and my lips meld shut. I don't have to buy expensive Japanese cucumbers any more so I spend the extra money on better groceries. Make my way to Bernie's market, the streets slow-moving with church-type people. Maybe Bernie's in church too, though I've never seen anyone else at the counter.

The store is busy with customers getting their weekly reserves of Asian necessities. The bigger chains stock more than they used to, but for cooks who'd never be caught adding hot water to a packet of freeze-dried miso soup, you can get twelve different kinds of seaweed at Bernie's. The long, sticky roots of yama imo, three-liter jars of kimchee, and sweet buns filled with custard cream. Packets of salt-sour shiso seeds, a gourmet's selection of miso, shelves of ground chilis in varying shades of red.

As I step through the door, a small child darts out, eyes gleeful, babyish knees dimpled fat. Without thinking, I grab the back of the child's shirt. The child struggles, arms swinging, hands squeezed into fists. Bernie pants over.

"Gabriel!" she scolds. Gives me a look of simultaneous thanks, frustration, fatigue mixed in with isn't-he-cute.

I smile. The kid *is* cute. Curly hair and big, brown eyes, he's furious at me.

"What have I told you about leaving this store? You promised you'd be good and play in the back." Bernie looks at her watch, then at the growing line of people at the checkout counter.

"Bor-ing!" Gabriel enunciates. Sticking out his tongue. I raise my eyebrows.

"Grandfather will be back soon. I'm sure he'll bring you a present," Bernie wheedles.

Spoilt child. This can't be a good thing.

"I can watch him for a while," I offer. A dull heat rises to my cheeks.

"Really?" Bernie sounds so hopeful. The ends of her perm have completely grown out and she's trimmed her hair straight along the sharp line of her jaw. She doesn't look like a Christian headbanger any more. "Grandfather should be back from his acupuncturist soon. Gabriel's at the age where he needs to run around," Bernie apologizes, proud of him at the same time.

"Excuse me!" A man calls from the lineup. "Is anyone working here?!"

"Go!" I say, giving Bernie a little nudge. She runs to the counter after flinging a bright smile of thanks.

I look down at the child who stares up into my eyes.

"Why are you still wearing your pajamas?" the child asks.

"I wear pajamas everywhere."

"Why?" Gabriel demands.

"Because I can."

"Did you brush your teeth?"

"Of course. Did you?" I ask.

"Yes."

We mull over all of this information.

"I want to go to the river," Gabriel demands.

"Can you swim?" I ask.

"No. Can you?" he says, defiant.

"No. We can't go to the river."

"You're boring," Gabriel says, beginning to struggle again.

"You're a brat." I grip tight to his shirt. If he pulls free, he'll go flying with the momentum.

"What are you doing with this child?" An old man shakes his fist at me. I step back, still gripping Gabriel's shirt.

"Babysitting," I mutter. What a stupid idea that was!

"Grandfather!" Gabriel calls.

I let the brat go with a great sigh of relief. The man's eyes are a bright glare, looking me up and down my pajamas. Gabriel grips his grandfather around the knees dramatically, turning his head over his shoulder to gloat.

"I know Bernie!" I blurt. Then have a thought. What if this old man isn't the real grandfather?

"Bernie!" I call.

"Bernice!" the maybe-grandfather shouts.

Bernie runs over, her face aflush.

"I'm so glad you're back," Bernie smiles. Cupping the back of Gabriel's curls with a tenderness that makes me blink.

"Do you know this stranger?!" Grandfather demands.

"Yes! Of course! My best customer," Bernie beams.

"Hmumph," Grandfather sniffs, tugging Gabriel's hand. "Let's go to the river."

"I loooove you!" Gabriel gushes at his mother and ignores me.

"Say good-bye to my friend," Bernie demands.

"Good-bye," Gabriel mutters. Sticking out the tiniest bit of his tongue.

"'Bye," I answer. And begin to laugh.

The child leaves with his grandfather, the old man casting one more look over his shoulder. Shakes his head.

"Where've you been?" Bernie asks, crossing her arms. "I had to make extra cucumber kimchee because of you!"

"Sorry." I shrug. Turn slightly away. "Maybe you should cut back on the orders." I cup my belly with my hand for a brief moment. Bernie catches the movement and her eyes jump to my profile.

"Hello!" a sixtyish woman calls out. "We could use some service please."

Bernie glances at the lineup, customers tapping their feet, drumming their fingers. She turns back to me and strokes her work-rough hand over my bare forearm. "Are you okay?"

I nod my head, then shake it. Bite my lip.

"Can you believe this?!" the woman says, overloud, to the man standing behind her. "Outrageous! We ought to take our groceries without paying."

"Do you mind?!" Bernie shouts. "Life is hard enough without assholes!"

Bernie!

"I never!" the woman gasps. She drops her basket of groceries and marches past us. "You make me sick," she hisses.

"Well," Bernie purrs, "you could always see me for the antidote."

"Oh!" The woman runs out the door.

Bernie stares down the gaping customers. "Anyone else want to go?" she sneers. There are a few nervous coughs and people suddenly find interesting labels to read, wallets to look into. No one dares leave.

Bernie turns back to me and the tenderness in her eyes makes me blink and blink. "I'm here if you need to talk," she says. She rests her rough hand on mine, before letting it drop.

Her sincerity slices. I nod my head and back out of the store.

PHONE CALL SO EARLY in the morning can only mean bad news. I roll over and cram a pillow on my head, waiting for the answering machine to kick in. It might be PG! Stumble across the predawn room.

"Hello!" I gasp.

"Yeah, good morning, sorry to call at this god-awful hour." Voice so raspy familiar and I can't place it for the life of me. "It's *Janice*. You know, Gerald's mom, the kid you really messed up for five years of his life."

My face burns hot, cold. Gut twisting in embarrassment and denial.

"Listen, I—uh, I didn't—"

"Never mind about that now. I've got your mom over here at my house. There's been some kind of trouble."

My heart drops sudden, nauseous. Hand shaking. Dad finally beat up Okasan so bad she has to be hospitalized. Battered, bleeding, no one there to save her. Okasan finally killed him. A knife. Burned the house down while he bled and now she'll go to jail.

"She says she's been up in a UFO."

Stunned silence.

"Hello! You still there?"

"Yeah," I mutter weakly.

"She says they've been coming and taking her for a long time now and she just realized this morning. Listen honey, I think you oughta get yourself down here and see what this is all about." Can hear Janice exhaling with impatience or worry, I can't tell over the phone.

The immediate slam of concern lingers in my body as soured adrenaline. I am tired and resentful. Four fucking A.M. Fucking UFO, no less.

"Jesus, Janice! Can't you just send her home?"

"Listen, I tell you, there's something strange. Her pupils aren't right. They're spacey, like a goat's. There's a strange smell, too. Something has happened."

"Our dad hits her. Maybe she can stay over at your house tonight?" I wheedle.

"Get your ass home, now," Janice rasps.

"All right! Jesus! Why is it always me that has to nursemaid Okasan? I've got a life too. Why can't Slither ever do anything? She's the oldest." Can't help myself, nothing I can do to stop.

Janice just hangs up on me.

I trudge to my dresser and pull out another pair of pajamas, the silk ones I have on too festive for what is awaiting me. Definitely a flannel day.

IN THE CHILL MORNING, I sit and warm the engine of my Palm truck. There are still no sarcastic kicks, inquisitive nudges. I'm done with prodding, nonverbal messages. I pop in the homemade tape Midori gave me. She'd curled her expressive lip at my seventies love songs double cassette. "Pathetic. If you have to feel sorry for yourself and listen to music that'll make you cry, at least have some taste about it," and the next morning, tossed me a homemade copy of Nina Simone. I fell in love with her voice, her loneliness. Wow, I thought, that Midori.

My life. Okasan. UFO. What next? I try pretending that I'm up early delivering milk to hungry and wailing babies, all across the city. Their mothers overjoyed with my swift efficiency, showering me with praise and affection. Feed me home-baked scones with fresh strawberries, brioche, and café au lait with chocolate sprinkles. But it gets pretty tired after half an hour and hardly makes much sense after I'm outside the city limits and into farm country.

"Hello! Does anybody care?" I call out loud. If I'm going to feel sorry for myself, I might as well go whole hog, as they say around these parts. "Life can get better any time now."

Start to feel foolish. If you don't have many friends, it's not too wise to go down the road detesting yourself. I blow hot breath into my ill-cut bangs. And sneak skeptical glances at the huge Alberta sky, teeming with solar bodies of icy light. Not a UFO in sight.

I pull into Janice's dusty drive when it occurs to me that I could have stopped over at Slither's place and dragged her out of her condominutive. Could have slept in her bucket seat while she drove, ah pleading. Hindsight hasn't saved me yet. Just as well, she's more bother than help and she annoys me so much I swear I pop brain cells in exasperation.

Janice looks much the same, except she's leaner and older. It happens. Age, that is.

"Took your time," as a way of greeting. "Woulda thought you'd have time to change out of your pajamas."

"Sorry. My truck has its limits. How is she?" I peer nervously, around the doorway, maybe Okasan seated all zombie-like, or weeping in post-UFO trauma, who knows?

"I got her settled in Gerald's old room."

I wince. I always try not to think of him. This lingering vestigial organ of guilt in my body cavity. "How is Gerald, by the way?"

"How the hell would I know?" Never one to choose words, let alone mince them.

"Oh." Nothing, really, I could say otherwise. "Uh, maybe I should go check on my mom." Janice just nods me in and jerks her chin up the stairs. Sits at the kitchen table and rolls one of her nasty butts.

She isn't sleeping, but standing in her bare feet and an oversized T-shirt, breathing circles of moisture on the window. She looks so small. I never noticed. Because until now, she's always looked mother-sized.

"Okasan?" I whisper. Something hushing about her posture.

She jumps around. "Oh, it's you," and turns back to the window.

I'm slightly hurt, annoyed, and confused. Isn't she glad to see that one of her kids cares enough to check on her? Doesn't she know it's a long fucking drive? But she's acting odd, not asking anything about me. I must be tired, do I need a coffee, maybe I should lie down and get some rest. She isn't being the nurturing Okasan, and she's not being the other, the martini-escaped-invisible-to-nothing Okasan. She isn't acting like the Okasan I've known the whole of my life. Something is wrong.

"Okasan, you okay?"

"Shhhhh!"

My small eyes widen as far as they possibly can. She's shushed me, definitely, consciously, and without a softening smile, her back to me the whole time.

I yawn colossally, my jaw almost unhinging itself. She is in no condition to talk, and neither am I, really. I crawl into the single bed and nudge around to find a comfortable hollow.

THE SUN, bright and making me too hot, sweaty. The brink of a nightmare. I rapid-eye myself awake. Okasan still standing at the window.

"Jesus, Okasan! Were you standing there the whole time?"

"Jesus te yuwanaino," she rotes, then sighs. "Mo konai wa. Yoru dakeni," she murmurs.

Raising my eyebrows. "Who comes at night?"

"Never mind," she smiles, reassuringly. Making me nervous. What is she hiding? What is Dad doing to her now?

"Breakfast is on!" Janice yells up the stairs, and I can smell the sour, pinched smell of home-cured bacon, the rinds extra thick. Coffee made on the stove and, my god, are those waffles? I scramble out of bed and dash into the washroom to gargle metallic-tasting water. Fouling my breath worse than it was before.

"Wow, Janice! This is great!"

"Where's your mom?" She smacks my greedy fingers and I drop the hot piece of bacon.

"She's been staring out the window all night!" I lower my voice. "There is something very strange going on with her. Has she said anything to you?"

"I think Emiko needs a cup of good coffee, don't you, Emiko!" Janice beams and takes the urn off the stove with a dishtowel.

I glance over my shoulder but Okasan is ignoring me. Ignoring me! She clasps the hot mug and sits down beside me, dumps two spoonfuls of sugar and a dollop of real fresh-from-the-cow cream.

"Ahhh, oishii," Okasan sighs and Janice nods her head in approval.

Despite everything, I am starved. Heap waffles the size of manholes and wedges of bacon onto my plate. Dump maple syrup, then fresh cream over every last bit. Okasan and Janice watch me with raised eyebrows without stopping their own eating. Just watch me cram wedges into my eager mouth. I feel like I haven't eaten for decades.

"Gyogiga warui ko desune," Okasan murmurs.

"Ahh, don't worry about it. A body's gotta eat when a body's hungry. Like to see people enjoying my cooking," Janice answers back.

Wait a minute.

"I thought you didn't understand any Japanese," I mumble around a creamy mouthful.

Janice actually blushes. "Emiko's been teaching me on Saturdays."

"Oh." I gulp down my hot coffee. Imagine that. Janice calling Okasan Emiko. What the hell else would she call her? I think bitchily to myself, Okasan? That would be pretty odd. Snort at my own stupidity, them both looking at me. Mom must have made some leaps of adjustment to become friends with hinganai Janice, that's for sure.

Janice eats like a frugal farmer who has livestock waiting. Finishes way before my city-slicker, greed-filled plate is licked clean and smooth.

"Gotta look after some chores." And thumps outside, smacking her worn leather gloves against her dusty jeans. Pulling an Elephant Brand Fertilizer cap onto her head.

Okasan just chews through her breakfast, mouth tightly pursed—crumbs wouldn't dream of falling from her mouth. Well, it was more like an English tea, time-wise. I saw at my waffle tower. Wondering how I can bring up the subject of UFOs. Abductions.

"So, what's this about you being sucked up into a UFO?" Being tactful not one of my strong points. I cram a forkful and chew in what I think is an encouraging and supportive way.

"Well?" I prod, after a full three minutes of nothing but the sound of food being ground into mush between my teeth. "What's up?"

"Now's not the time," Okasan murmurs. And that's that. She doesn't tell me a single thing. She tidies up Janice's kitchen, puts away dishes and mugs like she's been here a thousand times, then gets her cardigan from the coatrack. Okasan walks home the long way, down the dusty track to the gravel road, then back up her own dusty drive, rather than hop the barbed wire fence. I wait for Janice to come back.

"She didn't tell me a goddamn thing!"

"Not surprised."

"What! Why the hell you ask me to come down then?! I do have a life, you know. What did she tell you?"

"I asked you to come home because she is your mother and she's been through something traumatic." Janice tosses her cap to the hat bar in the boot room. "If she felt like she couldn't be telling her story right now, I don't think I ought to, not without her permission."

"Fine." I hold my hands out in front of me. "I'm outta here. Thanks for breakfast." Don't even bother going over to Okasan's place to say a proper Japanese good-bye. I just spin gravel leaving the drive and swear all the way home.

GET HOME. The rapid blipblipblip of red light on my answering machine. I groan, don't want to deal with messages now. I rewind. Press play.

"—but you may—" Sound of Genevieve's voice. Stop and rewind some more, a message I haven't heard yet.

"—wondering if—" Midori. Rewind.

Beep. "Hey, freak of nature!" Stop.

PG. It is PG. Heart pounds.

Why couldn't I have been home? I press play with a shaking hand.

"Where the hell are you this time of the morning? Sorry I haven't called. But you know me. I can take care of myself, and I have been. Hey, I was just feeling a little blue, you *know?* Too bad, so sad, right? Thought it might cheer me up to chat with you, you being the optimist in the family. Incidentally, that's *sarcasm.* Funny about being away. You should try it some time. The perspective is enlightening, I kid you not. Just a second—"

There's a click and PG exhales. I can almost smell the minty smoke.

"I hope you're doing okay. I worry about you sometimes. I'm moving around a lot so I'll send a proper address when I settle. Who knows. Maybe you could come for a visit. Get your sorry ass out of the prairies." She exhales again and laughs. "Guess what? I'm riding a Virago now, and I'm hotter than I was before. No more sad endings for this girl. Only happy ones." Click. End of message.

I switch off the machine without listening to the rest of the messages. Sit on the edge of my bed. There. She's just fine, so I needn't worry anymore. She's riding a Virago. Didn't that sum up her emotional health? What more could a girl ask for?

But why do I feel so weary?

I nudge myself between the rumpled, heaped-up folds of my blankets and will my anxieties to go away. Doesn't work, only end up giving myself a headache with frustration. There is a roaring in the channels of my ears, like the ocean. The sound so loud, I get dizzy. Frightened, I stuff Kleenex into my ears to keep out the world and curl tiny in the middle of my bed. Tidal waters swirl and I plunge into a restless dream space.

Tissue pulled from my ears. I feel like my brain is being tugged out of my head.

"Fuck!" Midori. Pissed off at me. I groan and cram a pillow over my fat head.

She jerks it away and shakes my shoulder hard.

"Your fucking door was unlocked again!" She is furious. I've never seen her this mad before. "When will you learn to lock it?! How many times do I have to tell you?! It will be too late after you've been raped, okay? Get it?!" Her eyes are wet. I reach out a hand, unsure what to do. Midori.

She snaps her head up, saunters to the bathroom, and locks the door.

Oh, Midori.

My chin wobbles and I clench my teeth. Walk quietly to the bathroom, hear the sound of water running from the tap. I knock softly.

"Midori?"

No answer. I knock twice, more firmly.

"You okay?"

The door swings open beneath my raised knuckles.

"Can't a girl take a bathroom break?" She slouches past me into the living room. Sits on the tatty couch, feet on the coffee table, and switches on the remote. The blah-blah laugh track of a sitcom. I stand awkwardly. Twist my stumpy fingers, not knowing if I should say something, do something? What can I do? Just stand there, squeezing my fingers.

"Jesus!" She rolls her eyes. "Can't a girl get some ocha around here?"

I stop my useless hovering and rush to my kitchen, thankful she's given me a task.

"Just remember to lock your door, okay?" she calls out, casually.

"Yeah. Yeah, I promise."

Kettle on the gas burner, tin of tea from the freezer, I can hear Midori rasping one hand over the other. Digging her teeth into the heel of her palm.

"What's up with you and Genevieve?" I ask lightly.

"I don't know," Midori answers. "She's such a great person. In some ways I think we're perfect for each other. Other times I feel like we have such different expectations."

In the safety of the kitchen, I raise my eyebrows. This is a side of Midori I've never seen. But then, I've never asked a personal question before.

"You got any chips or chocolate?" Midori asks.

"Both. You premenstrual or hungry?"

"Yeah, both, what's it to you? What kind of chocolate?"

I dig through my treats cupboard. "Peanut butter saucers, Hershey's Kisses from last Christmas, a block of fondue chocolate."

"Forget it!" I can hear Midori rolling her eyes. "What about chips, then?"

"Umm. Salt and vinegar. Corn chips—"

"Corn chips!"

"They're old," I warn, pouring them into a plastic bowl. "I haven't been buying junk food for a while."

"S'okay," Midori mumbles. "I just need the salt." Crunching crumbs on the nubbly couch. "So. What's been going on with you?"

I tell her about my mother. PG's message. Like a joke.

Midori raises her eyebrows, her quizzical mouth.

"You can't save people, you know," she says, gently. "And you don't have to. You can just be supportive."

I blush. Defensive. Though I don't know why. I bustle to the kitchen for more tea and Midori lets me change the subject.

Midori and I drink tea. We don't say much and what we do say is not important. But I'm happy in her company. When she leaves I feel lonely.

I'VE ALWAYS HOPED THAT CHILDHOOD could be a book, a sequence of pages that I could flip through, or close. A book that could be put away on a shelf. Even boxed and locked into storage should the need arise. But, of course not. Childhood isn't a book and it doesn't end. My childhood spills into my adult life despite all my attempts at otherwise and the saturation of the past with the present is an ongoing story.

Before the End of that Summer

GERALD WAS PACKED UP, his toys in boxes, pajamas and clothing arranged neatly into one large suitcase. Janice drove him to the airport in the double-decker truck. I watched two plumes of dust rise, lift off the prairie face, and scatter in the wind. Okasan stood behind me, her hands on my shoulders. When she squeezed a little, I pulled out of her clasp and walked around to the back of the house. Slither was washing her hair in the pumphouse, squealing at the coldness. The shampoo wouldn't lather for her because the water was hard. Mice somewhere in the kitchen. I heard Okasan enter the porch, the smack of door pulled by springs. Heard her cracking eggs on the edge of counter. Sizzle of sulfur. Dad was hired out, helping the Snyders harvest their corn. We were all safe until sundown.

I pulled my book from inside my T-shirt. The cover was taped to the spine and the corners were peeling backward, adhesive black and stiff. Held the book to my face and inhaled all that it held. One of my sisters had drawn a mustache on Mary's face and Laura had a bloody nose.

I ripped the cover off. It gave easily, almost like a slice of bread. The damp pages came away from the cracked spine and fluttered heavy as I dropped them into a pile.

"What are you doing?" PG asked, squatting in front of me.

"Get lost," I muttered. I pulled out more pages and tore them in half.

"Don't do this," Laura's bony hand gripped my right shoulder. Her hot breath on my neck. A clammy film spread down my shivering back.

"Get away!" My voice rising. I couldn't help myself. I flung a look behind me. Laura's face. No rosy cheeks. No milky skin. No snapping brown eyes. She was gaunt. The fingers that clutched my shoulders were cracked, nails chipped, wrinkled with malnutrition. And behind her. Mary's listless, colorless eyes. Baby Carrie's legs bowed, scrawny with rickets.

PG's traveling eye roved as she backed away from me.

"Who's going to be there for you if I'm gone?" Laura whispered.

"Shut up!" I shouted. Ripping faster and faster. Baby Carrie whimpered. My heart pounding in my head.

"It's not too late to change your mind."

PG scurried into the house, hands over her ears, chanting, "Scary things aren't scary if you're not scared of them."

I dropped a match onto the paper. The heap smoldered and a noxious, gray smoke rose heavily but the moist pages wouldn't flame. My teeth chattered. Hands shaking. A stick near my feet. I poked the mess so the embers wouldn't go out, until every page was blackened and the print unreadable.

THE CITY IS BEING CHOKED BY SUBURBS. Nose Hill Park is a lovely island in the ocean of vinyl housing, but like the name says, it's only a nose. I want to walk on the prairie's body. So I chug out of the plastic sprawl to the edge of grass.

Why didn't I come to the prairies sooner? The trill of meadowlarks, grasshoppers burring away on paper-dry wings, the rustle of wind through grass, constant and fluid. The oceanic pull embedded in forgotten bedrock. How could it have taken me so long to remember? I walk through field after field, scrunching through barbed wire. The high-pitched peep of gophers warning other gophers to duck. Still wishing for someone to help me through the small spaces between the wires. Snort. At least unpregnancy doesn't manifest itself physically. Not a chance of me getting through a single fence if I were "normally" pregnant, well over ten months now. I'd be waddling, like in a Monty Python movie, people running from me in a panic, screaming, she's going to blow! she's going to blow! I snort again, and feel a gentle prod against my left ear.

"You're back." I should be annoyed. Surprised. But I'm not. Every event in my life has led to this. To normalize the incredible. And really, what other choices are there? If I can't tolerate my own life I might as well be dead.

The sun so direct I barely leave a shadow. The buzzing heat of locusts and the gophers sleeping the midday heat away in earthly tunnels. I think about my cool, damp basement suite with longing. I have no idea how far I have been walking. I always lose count after the ninth set of fences. But it doesn't matter, because I'm not trying to arrive and I'm not trying to leave. Just moving, that's all.

I crouch in the dry sun, crunchy grass. My cottony pajamas fluttering in a Laurence of Arabia way. I sit, even though the dry grass prickles my butt, lie back and stare at the incredible sky. Almost peaceful. The breeze picks up bits of nature and moves them along their way. The shriek of a distant red-tail circling, buzzing din of insects. The blue, blue sky.

"Let's talk. I mean, can we talk now?" I speak, seriously. Hopefully. But not so hopeful as to scare a body away. Trying not to tense my body. Like on the crest of the ultimate orgasm, over-wanting it into disappearing, I have to be careful not to ask too much.

A flutter of movements from my left ear, the hollows behind my nose. Slipping down my throat, the cool curve of buttocks leaning. Rest. A tiny hand reaches up and presses the spot on my tongue where flesh becomes words. I would have thought the touch would make me gag, but the strange sensation is indescribably intimate.

I wait. For words to well from the recesses of my body. Words which would answer my questions, calm my doubts, grant me insight.

Nothing. Nothing but touch.

"Well?" I demand. "Don't I deserve some answers? I didn't ask for an inner life!"

The sun crisp on my black hair, two hawks in ever-widening circles. A bee buzzes into an alfalfa flower. I sigh.

"Well, you could tap out something in Morse code or something. Not that I could decipher it." I sigh once more, then close my eyes. Breeze lifting layers of sun from my heat-drenched body, tugging my gauzy pajamas. I imagine that tiny hands are undressing me and I smile.

When I stop expecting an answer, I am suddenly free.

I pluck grass, even as I lie with my eyes shut, and cover my face with the long dry strands. Not so city-slickered that I don't know the prairie sun will scorch me if I'm not cautious. Nature's not Walt Disney and I'm no fool. The crisscross of light fractures blue bright enough to pattern my eyes beneath their lids. The trill of red-winged blackbirds, there must be some water nearby, I think, as the sun ebbs me into a summer sleep.

THIS IS WHAT I DREAM. A dream when you start off by dreaming that you are sleeping.

I dream that I am sleeping on the moon and I'm surprised, filled with wonder, at how warm the body of the moon is, when she looked so cool. How warm, like the papery hives of wasps, like prairie stones. I want to laugh out loud, but I can't because a mask filtering the lunar air covers my face. One breath and I will shrivel up into a husk of insect nothing. So I lie still, and smile carefully. Shift my hands to push myself into a sitting position and realize they are tied. Heart leap throat. I control my panic and move my feet. Can't. Heart pound pounding, sweat-anxious. I can't struggle because the movement might dislodge the mask. I breathe shallow, quickly, sweat dripping. I watch with dread, as the earth starts to set. Once it is past the horizon, I will never be able to go back. And the thought makes me so lonely I have to gulp my tears so they won't rise to my eyes.

I watch the slow process of earth moving, minute yet inevitable as the end of mortal life. That blue, blue orb, just another celestial body I cannot depend on. Can't help myself, my mouth opens, cries out. And when my tongue touches the mask, it melts like rice paper.

Sweet.

I WAKE, EYES OPEN. No, I'm still asleep, everything dark. I must be dreaming I've woken up. There're spots inside my closed eyelids. No, my eyes are open, the spots are stars!

The earth is still warm beneath my body.

I sit up, stiff, groan, and stretch to my feet. How long have I been sleeping? No way of knowing if the moon is yet to rise or if I've slept through its fall. And something sweet on my lips, I lick with my tongue but the taste is gone.

The cricking of tiny frogs. I was right. There is water nearby. I move toward the sound, strange the way my steps bounce, rise on the air. I'm defying gravity with these soaring leaps. A doubting mind might take the magic away. I bound across the prairie field, drinking from the dry night air like it is water.

The frogs silence, so I must be close and I am, step sudden, wet and ankle deep.

Soaker, I think, and giggle out loud. No use having one wet foot, I take another step and wiggle my bratwurst toes in their sneaker slosh. The wind is strong enough to keep away the maddening whine of mosquitoes. I can enjoy this moment of prairie wet, the wind, the rustle, the fracture of the stars.

Splash.

I blink, the darkness, dim-shape, everything suspect. That splash had weight, no Alberta amphibian. Maybe a muskrat? Duck?

Kappa?

"Hello?" I call out. In a whisper. Feeling slightly ridiculous. What if it's only a duck? When did I become such a chicken? Sudden thought. What if this isn't a little pond, not a tiny pool of water, but a huge dugout? A natural pond unnaturally carved out by a backhoe, tapping into underground caverns that were meant to be left alone? What if the shallows I so casually wade in crumble from stonebed to sand and I tumble into the quiet depths?

What if I don't?

I crouch and dip my bratwurst fingers into cool water. Think about the fountain of youth and the water of life and hope springing eternal.

Somehow, I feel okay. I don't know why, but a stillness spreads, seeps. My feet wet and the stars above me tilt-tilting beyond. The perfect equation of water, cells, and memory. A folding of dimensions. Or wishful thinking.

Splash.

The sound is closer. My heart, warm. I dip fingers in a pool wet with possibilities and something touches me back. I don't know if it is some green, mischievous creature, or just my nightly reflection.

THE PHYSICAL MEMBRANES of childhood are permeable. But those childhood days, how long they stretched, daily, eternally. The turning of the earth was slow, the summers long and our father-mother patterns were as predictable as the seasons. After Gerald moved away and I killed Laura Ingalls, my life settled into childhood stasis.

Why do we measure the passage of time?

There is a small bite in the air although the sun warms skin. I roll down my van window only when I come to a stop at intersections. My empty milk van holds a bubble of quiet. My last load of carts dropped off at Gary's, I can enjoy the late afternoon by myself. The creature inside touches, the merest whisper against my heart, and I hold in my sadness. Glance down at the grime and dust on the front of my navy blue work pajamas. I press my left arm diagonally across my chest to hold in the ache.

I haven't been aching for cucumbers. What minute cravings I have, I've fed with the stumpy fruits of the pickling bread-and-butter variety. Has the hunger has transformed into something else? What a frightening thought! Mutations are so unpredictable, I'd rather have a self-identified hunger than an unconscious compulsion, leading me down a dismal road to ultimate destruction. Maybe I ought to eat more Japanese cucumbers. Encourage the waning desire I have so it becomes full-fledged again. I haven't been to Bernie's market, she must be wondering if something's wrong. I could pick up some cucumber kimchee for supper.

"Breaker one-nine, one-nine! You copy?"

I start. Gary never calls when I'm off duty. "Roger dodger! What's up, Sarge?"

"We need someone to recon the core. I repeat. Recon the core."

My lips turn down. I've just finished eight hours of work! I like my job but eight consecutive hours of anything is enough for anybody.

"State your location, soldier!"

"Gary, I'm almost home." Hardly matters that I'm considering driving back to Bernie's. I still don't want to do extra work.

"Listen," Gary wheedles in a civilian's voice. "Laura couldn't finish her shift because she got sick. You don't need to pick up any carts. I just need a rough idea of how busy we'll be tomorrow."

"Laura? Who's Laura?"

"The new girl I hired. Laura Ng."

My small eyes pop wide. Stifle a guffaw.

"You'd know who she is if you came to more company barbecues!" Gary accuses.

"You're right," I agree. "I'll make more of an effort."

Gary, sensing an advantage, drops back into a military stance.

"I'll expect a report on your recon mission in O200 hours!"

I sigh. "Affirmative, Sergeant. Over."

"I'll give you time and a half. Over and out!" Gary sounds triumphant.

Laura Ng. Jesus god!

THE CITY CORE IS EMPTY OF PEOPLE. Abandoned, I can imagine a post-apocalyptic world of crumbling concrete, the struggle for clean water. Or maybe, when humans are gone, our myths will come alive, wander over the remnants of our uncivilization. Kappa, water dragons, yama-uba, oni. Selkie, golem, lorelei, xuan wu. The creatures we carry will be born from our demise and the world will dream a new existence.

My tailpipe rattles as I bump along stretches of back alleys. Not many of the abandoned at all. I keep a running tally while my eyes peer, flick from side to side. A man slightly bent over, pushing a half-filled cart. Maybe it's Jules? No. No German shepherd. I'd like to talk to that man and I owe him lunch. Well, with my job and his city-beautification project, it's not impossible to run into him again.

I meander through downtown. Smelly alleys, one-way avenues four lanes wide, I circle green spaces where people like to cram carts beneath spruce trees. Gary won't need to ask anyone to put in a double shift. Maybe I'll volunteer to do the core.

Whistling, I turn my milk van toward Bernie's market. Nobody makes better kimchee than Bernie. Mind you, maybe her father does the actual making.

Bernie's not behind the counter when I push through the heavy glass door. I glance down aisles but she isn't shelving stock or stickering pricetags. She must be eating her dinner in the room at the back.

I stick my head around the frame of the door.

"Bernie?"

A dark head, bent over a bowl of rice, looks up. My heart leaps. So like Bernie, but not at all. She must be at least four inches taller and thirty pounds heavier. Orange-gold rings adorn her thick fingers, curly strands of gray twist out of a sloppy bun. Slither'd be horrified.

"Who're you?" she demands.

Boy, Bernie and her sisters are a tough bunch. I straighten my shoulders as the woman runs her critical eye over my hair explosion, my dirty pajamas.

"Oh, you must be The One Who Eats Cucumbers," she answers herself and continues pushing rice into her mouth.

"I beg your pardon?!" I gasp. Has Bernie been talking about me? Laughing while she ate lunch with her sisters?

"Nothing personal, yeah? You're Bernie's favorite customer, don't worry."

"Humph. Where is she anyway?" No point in being polite, Bernie's sister wasn't the type.

"The kid's got a bad cold. Won't let anyone feed him rice porridge but her."

"Ohhhh." A twinge of an emotion. "Is Gabriel okay?"

222

"You kidding?!" the sister snorts. "Bernie's spoon-feeding him while he watches videos, the little brat. His grandfather's concocting mystery soup that takes six hours to stew." She serves herself some more rice from the cooker. "The store's actually closed, you know. I forgot to lock the door."

"Oh. Well, say hi to Bernie for me." I turn around to leave.

"I haven't cashed out yet." She waves with her thin, silver chopsticks. "You can still buy something if you want."

"Uh, thanks." Now I feel like I have to.

"There's fresh cucumber kimchee in the cooler. Our father made it yesterday." Bernie's sister surges to her feet, a few grains of rice sticking to her shirt. She thrusts out a big hand and I reach to shake. She squeezes down, hard, to test my strength and I clench with a cart collector's grip, a toothy grin spread over my face.

"Hm!" she nods, satisfied. "The name's Maple."

I nod back. Shuffle up and down aisles with a metal basket. I choose a small plastic container of spicy cucumbers. Grab a package of curry and some sesame osenbei. A jar of chili flakes. Would be rude to buy only one thing after Maple's offer, I snatch a bag of sweet bean buns as well.

"So," Maple says, handing me change. She's short ten cents but I don't tell her. "You be nice to my little sister or you'll have the Yoon sisters to answer to."

"What?!" I splutter.

Maple gives me a wink, carelessly dropping my groceries in a bag, not arranging the items heaviest to lightest.

"What are you talking about?"

Maple glares at me. Looks up and down my pajamas once more. "If you don't know, you're stupider than you look!" She crams the bag into my hands and scowls. Hurries me out the door and locks it.

"What?" I mumble, turning back. But Maple flips the sign from Open to Closed and switches off the light.

One Glorious Summer

W E GREW UP. We grew up on eggs and meshi, Spartan apples, and barley tea. I remained short, strong, while Slither stretched and curved into a shape called adulthood. She was gorgeous. I wasn't jealous. If strength wouldn't save her, maybe beauty would. PG and Mice grew taller than me by the time they were eleven, PG smoking cigarettes and drinking coffee by twelve. Mice stayed Mice-like despite her age. And what was cute at four was deemed extraordinarily odd for a prepubescent.

Slither moved out, finally free from doing time with our family, onto the big city. Where she could pursue her dreams of sustaining beauty for the sake of beauty. With Slither gone, the house was quieter, the rest of us able to gauge the buttons of our father's anger. We tiptoed past brief moments of peace. PG didn't have to protect herself with her childish mantras and Mice didn't have to be a dog. And I plucked fewer strands of hair, nourished by the knowledge that in one year, I would be free.

And that summer. What rains fell! Droplets as full as muscat grapes and just as sweet. The land flourished with greenage, never-before plants, prehistoric seeds that had lain dormant from another age. Bigwig scientists with nature shows flocked to the area, brought money into the economy. New motels were hastily constructed.

Dad's tambo flourished. He would stand out in the rains for hours, wet sliding down his face. He looked almost gentle, melting. The rice fields filled mud-thick, not parched gaping cracks of desperation soil. And he didn't need his nasal spray to help him breathe. All that summer he breathed with everyone else. The other farmers were confounded, potatoes drowning, rotting, wheat and barley turning to porridge before developing seeds. But Dad's slender nae grew bright, fresh green. Fledgling blades of tender rice, we replanted them all by hand, our bare feet in warm mud. The work was almost pleasant.

Janice would come by after dosing her chickens with antibiotics. Shake her head at "this unnatural sight," as she called it. Dad just laughing, "WA! HA! HA! HA! HA!"

Okasan making quick suppers of curry rice.

The weather was perfect. Raining every evening, Dad made drainage ditches so the water would flow, not rot stagnant. Nothing I had seen was as beautiful a sight, and I even phoned Slither to tell her that Dad's rice had finally grown.

"It's really happened. The rice is growing!" I was happy. I didn't know why.

"That's nice," Slither managed.

"*That's nice!* That's all you have to say? This is what we've been busting our butts for our whole childhood!"

"No!" Slither uttered forcefully.

I was stunned. Slither with authority? Slither the crybaby, the whiner?

"It's what Dad forced us to do. I never wanted to be a part of it. And I won't be a part of it now."

"Won't you come down for a look?" I asked, confused.

"No," Slither said softly. Like Okasan.

I SLEPT SHALLOW AND LIGHT. The evening rains, the heavy night air kept me from brittle prairie dreams. The air smelled like leaves. I rolled my butt out of bed, went into the kitchen. Damp. The dishes on the draining rack were still wet from the night before. I grabbed two pieces of soggy raisin bread and plunged my flat feet into stinky gumboots.

Green glow of tender rice. The blades lit up with a brightness that shone from a source within. The sun rising. I wasn't a morning person, but somehow the magic of the rice nudged me. Really, I thought, Slither was right. Why the hell should I care that Dad's rice finally came in?

Noticed.

A small footprint in the mud at my feet. Odd, not like any duck I'd seen before. The print was webbed, but not the wide-webbed indentation of an aquatic fowl, the shape was stretched longer, more foot-like. In size it was comparable to a five-year-old child's, only this print had four webbed toes instead of five regular ones. I peered closer, fascinated, then looked up, stunned.

Spread out before me, through the expanse of the green rice field, the moist mud tambo was literally covered by these small footprints. Like a gleeful creature had ran jubilantly over every inch of the amazing wetness, jumping, leaping, dancing, stepping exquisite toes, perfectly webbed.

"Dad!" I yelled, too excited for caution. "Dad, come see the tambo!"

He roared out of bed. From the second floor, the pounding of feet on thin floorboards, his furious energy. Enraged that some calamity had ruined the fruits of his pioneering labor.

"Come outside," I whispered. Cringing.

Dad burst from the house, no shoes. Stood time-bomb still. His rice undamaged, growing lush. He raised his hand and I leapt back, stammered to explain.

"D-dad. Look. In the mud."

He looked down at his feet, and his frightening eyes glowed with a strange light. He crouched down, grinned like a child, and I could almost imagine him before he had become the father I knew. Pressed one finger into the outlines. How handsome, I thought, he was handsome when he smiled.

"Kore wa kappa da yo!"

"Kappa?"

"Bakatare," he muttered affectionately. "Don't you remember anything I've told you?!" Shaking his head at all the lost information that children of immigrants could never take for granted.

"But how?" he murmured, "in this country, this climate? Where would it have come from? Emigrated like us?" Dad snorted in a self-deprecating way. He stood slowly and thoughtfully walked beside his lush field, the wonderful footprints in the mud.

I ran into the house. Up to Okasan's room where she slept, a small square of light on her curled-up form. Nudged her rounded shoulder with an impatient hand.

"Okasan," I hissed. "Okasan! Tell me about kappa."

She moaned softly, sighed. "Nanji?"

"I dunno, around 5:30. What's a kappa again? Is it some kind of duck?"

She clucked her tongue. "I'm sure we've told you stories."

"I don't remember," I muttered impatiently.

Okasan flung open the blankets and I almost fell back in shock. An act of welcome, with no strings attached. I was distrustful. Eyed my mother, the warmth of the bed, weighed the possible consequences of joining her for a moment.

"Come. Let me tell you about kappas," she smiled.

Curiosity stronger than self-preservation. I crept in beside her and held myself stiffly, cringing at the thought of contamination. Okasan cozied the blankets around my shoulders and clasped my feet between hers, an *ara!* of surprise at how cold they were.

And there, in the beam of dusty light, watching motes lift and bob with our breathing, Okasan retold tales I had forgotten. The sweet smell of Okasan's body, still soft with sleep. Her words rained softly onto my thirsty body. Kappa who drowned children and livestock, who caressed the buttocks of beautiful women. Evil kappa, heroic kappa, and always, their ties to water. Okasan told me kappa tales until Mice, and even PG, woke up asking for breakfast. PG crawling in between us and falling asleep again, her soft, even breath. Mice perched on the edge of the bed in case Dad should suddenly return. We listened to Okasan's kappa stories until she had told all that she remembered.

"But they're not *real*," I said, disappointed. "They're just mythical, like unicorns or something."

"Chotto chigauto omouyo," Okasan murmured, reaching her rough hand over PG's sleeping body to stroke the hair from my forehead. I flinched. Okasan lowered her hand and tucked the blankets around PG instead.

Come back, my heart said. No, said my face. I sneered. "How can it be different? I've never heard any scientific reference to them. How can kappa be real? Like a dish on its head with water in it? A turtle shell? Webbed hands and feet? And what about all of this anus-sucking? That's really unnatural, okay?"

"Not a dish *on* its head, but a head shaped like a dish," Okasan corrected.

"Dish on head, dish-shaped head, what's the difference? I know make-believe when I hear it!" I scoffed. "But it still doesn't explain what all of those footprints are doing in Dad's tambo."

Okasan sat up so suddenly that PG hissed awake and grabbed futilely for blankets.

"Kappano ashiatoga tamboni aruno?"

"It must be some kind of duck," I called to Okasan's back, her running outside in her nightie and bare feet.

THE RAINS FELL ALL SPRING and early summer. Every evening, showers spilled from the heavens so that the rice fields were perfect wet. And every morning, the incredible footprints of some unknown creature marked its existence. The kappa never manifested itself and I teased my mother with what I called her peasant beliefs. Dad and Okasan nodded their heads at each other, chummy and smiling. A sign of good fortune, they beamed in a way that made me hate them. How could Okasan smile at our enemy like that?

"But I thought they were troublemakers. Playing tricks, you said. And sometimes deadly! How can it be a sign of good luck?" I sat on the kitchen counter, kicking the cupboard doors until Okasan wearily asked me to stop. Dad was out in his field. Counting the footprints. Cataloging.

"Don't you think it's strange that a Japanese kappa would be here, in a place like this?" Okasan said softly, salting hakusai leaves to be pressed into otsukemono under the huge pickling rock.

"Yeah, assuming they exist, it'd be unusual to find one on this prairie continent, but what I don't get is why you'd think something that's trouble in Japan would be good here! There aren't any logical connections."

Okasan sighed and flapped her hand at me to get off my counter perch.

"There's not always an answer," Okasan muttered, stooping to lift the heavy rock.

THE RAINS FELL UNTIL THE SEEDS of rice started to form, then the rains stopped. The weather couldn't have been more perfect. The warm sun made the rice grow fat while all around us, other fields in devastation, stinking of rotten plants. The tambo was the only place of beauty. The strange footprints disappeared after the rains stopped falling, gone one morning. I couldn't help feeling a twinge of loss. But Okasan's and Dad's good-luck kappa must have left some green goodness behind, despite all my poo-poohing and cynical comments. We had an incredible crop, handpicked in the old-fashioned way, and each grain so sweet it flooded our mouths with juicy longing.

Dad's one and only ever rice crop. Something he wouldn't get over for the rest of his life. But we were thankful, that year, that summer, and at Christmas, I received a diving watch that could withstand water pressure up to fifty meters. Me inwardly snorting, when the hell had I ever gone diving? Where would I go that was fifty meters deep? Milk Chocolate River perhaps? The Old Man? But I was touched, all the same, and wore the gift constantly. Sending thanks to a questionable creature from a different clime. A creature much greener than Santa.

My world is shrinking.

Or perhaps I am simply growing. I had thought that this place I inhabit would house me forever, but the surface of my body aches for something which cannot be found here. How can it ache for what it has never known?

This living is a mysterious event.

Choices are fraught with risk and I am not so green-naive that I do not see. Life outside this wetly safe pool is a hostile place for the weak, the sensitive, the poor. But my eyes are over six hundred years old, time just a thin curtain between the same rooms called past and present. The coming close of a mortal's millennium. When the lonely turn to the cold space of the universe, to the hopeless sound of stars already collapsed, to the last song reaching mortal eyes as light. When humans weep without parting with tears.

There is a need, still, for creatures of fur, and for soil, plants, and above all, water.

M Y HEART IS FINE, really, and my pregnant life is the same as when I wasn't, only in a different way. Before I was expecting, I expected very little, and as a result, I got almost nothing. Now that I'm always expectant and nothing develops, I get even less.

No, that's a lie. Not everything is visible to the human eye, or the human heart. Our bodies are over seventy percent water. And the rest, memories. I don't understand how I recall a past I thought I never felt. Could the memories have lain hidden in the watery depths? And why does the long ago resurface now? The funny thing is, the longer I'm pregnant, the more my thoughts are pulled to my childhood. Long gone and unvisited for good reason. I thought I had earned the right to forget. But that doesn't save me from sudden memory cramps: Okasan's face being struck, never knowing when the blow would fall. Or on whom. No how or why, just reeling in the aftermath of delayed emotions. Just as well that I remember, now, to lock my door. Before Midori can thump down the stairs, I have time enough to grab a Kleenex and wipe away all signs of weakness.

"Thought you might have ODed on Nina Simone by now," she mumbles around the stinky Camel in the corner of her mouth. Knowing my tendency for overkill, my listening to the same tape over and over until it's smoothed into nothing.

She tosses me another homemade, this time Mercedes Sosa.

"Hey, girl. You're not returning our messages."

"Our?" I raise my eyebrows, Midori blushing. "You wouldn't be, so unseemingly, dare I say, suffering from *couple-ism?"*

Midori throws a slow-motion punch and I duck, jab with an uppercut. Midori, a girl after my own heart. I reel backward and slide down the wall. KO.

Midori slides down beside me. Smoke curling upward. Her panting breath, and, to my surprise, me not. Must be all the walking I've been doing.

"Moved in together. For better or for worse," she says without preamble.

Oh Midori.

"That's great!" I smile. Thump her on the shoulder. She goes to the sink and puts out her cigarette. Pads back, sitting beside me on the cool linoleum. The smoke still lingers.

"I'm really happy for you two. I never imagined you'd hit it off so well, I mean, who would have thought? I should have introduced you to each other years ago." My gap-toothed smile smiling.

Midori looks concerned.

"Genevieve thought I should come over and tell you. You weren't picking up the phone. She was getting worried. I was too."

"I'm fine. No, really, I'm FINE. In fact, I've never felt better in my life!"

"You look different. You okay?" Midori prods me in the stomach. "You been losing weight or something?"

"Maybe. I've been doing a lot of walking."

"Aren't you supposed to be gaining weight, being pregnant and all?" Midori glances at me, looks away.

"Never mind." My small eyes getting smaller with annoyance.

"Did you ever go to that ultrasound appointment?" Midori asks. "I'm, uh . . . sorry we . . . I never went with—"

"Don't go through any contortions on my account. I didn't bother going. There wasn't much point, was there?"

"Because you're not really pregnant?"

"Because it wouldn't goddamn show!" I shout.

Midori silent.

What is wrong with me? I stare at my hands, shocked to see they are squeezed into fists. Exhale and loosen my grip. "I'm sorry. That's why I haven't been keeping in touch. I've been sorting through my life. My baggage. It's been hard."

"How long?!" Midori demands. "When will you stop sorting through life and just bloody well act?!"

I reach, clasp Midori's neck, and pull her toward me. My ugly lips on her surprised mouth. Our eyes open.

I turn my back to her. Salt sting, hating the wobble in my chin.

"There! Are you satisfied? Now just leave me alone!"

Can't stand the ache in my chest, the hollow pit of nothing, hurting. I can't even stand up to walk dignified into my bedroom. Or offer a pot of ocha. I'm stone still and mentally hug myself beyond nothing while Midori sits beside me, juggling surprise, dismay, embarrassment, I don't know.

Razor-blade seconds tick longer than humanly bearable. Blood pounding hot in my face, my head. The room is hollow, tinny, and a bitter taste coats my tongue. Midori not even rubbing her hands over hands, her flurry of finger dandruff. How can we still be friends? What have I done? Can't I just leave well enough alone? I want to grab my head and tear out fistfuls of my hair. But I cannot move. I can barely breathe, my heart is so loud.

Midori moves her arm and I flinch.

"I didn't know you felt that way about me," Midori says gently. And she puts her arm around my shoulder, hand dangling instead of cupping, holding, like she would with a lover.

I almost shudder, with longing, loss, I don't know what, but I swallow. "Of course not," I manage. But I lean into the curve of her arm all the same. No pride left. And it doesn't matter. Midori grips tight with her hand, reaches with her other arm, circles me to the lean warmth of her body.

Hiccup, I think, what a time to hiccup, but the sound won't

stop. Wetness streaming from my eyes and I'm shaking so hard I can barely breathe.

"Shhhh," Midori murmurs into my ill-cut hair, holds me. "Shhh," she murmurs, not to shush me, but to let me know she is there.

Tears streaming, sliding down my flat face, between my lips. Onto my tongue.

It isn't until later that I realize they didn't taste of the sea, but were sweet as water, bubbling fresh from a mountain spring.

MIDORI HOLDS ME LONGER than I can remember anyone holding me. She holds me until my body stops shaking, tears dried on skin shiny with unused-to moisture. She holds me until my body slumps, exhausted. My tough, mouthy friend patiently leads me to my bathroom, warms a washcloth under the tap, wrings it, and wipes my face, my neck. Midori guides me to my bedroom, pulls open the blankets, and gently pushes me to my bed. Kneels, unbuttons, and removes pajamas wet with tears, sweat, the cool of cotton sheets against naked skin. "Lie back," pulls blankets snug around my curled-up body. Strokes my forehead with her eczema-rough fingertips, brief scent of Camel cigarettes. "Sleep now."

And I do.

I WALK THROUGH SUMMER into fall barely noticing the change. The brittle grass yellow crunch beneath my steps. Work slowing down, Gary only keeps the hard-core collectors on during the winter. The seasonals take the time off to finish their university degrees. Teenagers back in school, they have fewer opportunities to race down hot summer streets so fewer carts clutter the city center. I have three days off instead of two and spend the hours walking, walking. Not really acknowledging the passage of time. Until I get a call from Slither.

Why on earth would she phone *me*? I don't think we've ever talked on the telephone.

"I think there's something wrong," she murmurs, after asking if I'd called her beautician.

"Tell me something I don't know. I'm glad you figured it out." I nervously suck at a clump of hair.

"No, silly. I think there's something wrong at the house."

"No." My heart sinking. Not again. "What makes you think that?"

"Well, it was Thanksgiving and Okasan didn't call us home for dinner."

"Thanksgiving's over already?!" I look at my diving watch under a strange notion that I might find answers. "When was Thanksgiving?"

"Last week," Slither starts to whine.

Oh yeah. There'd been a sudden swell of shopping carts that weekend. "There's got to be something wrong. Okasan never misses a family dinner. A whole week's passed. Do you think there's trouble?" Slither whispers.

"Did you phone home?"

"No way," Slither's pitch starts to rise, but she catches herself. Actually catches herself and stops before the emotional ground beneath her feet crumbles into empty space. "I don't want to," she says soberly.

I'm amazed. She never had self-control before. What's going on? I mutter, "All right. I'll drop a line and see what's up," before I can stop myself.

I don't want to call, but if I don't, who will? And if nobody does, I won't be able to stand how I feel. An unhealthy dilemma all around.

I perk up with a thought. Maybe Janice will know what's happening, she seemed really chummy with Okasan.

"Yeah, I'll call. But you owe me. You never do anything for Okasan and I always end up taking care of the messes."

"Gee. . . ."

Fuck, I think. Did anyone else in the world still say *gee?!*

"I know what!" Slither chirps. "I'll come over and give you a makeover. I'll give you a proper haircut and then we can go shopping for some clothes."

"Never mind! Forget it. Don't worry about the family thing, I'll take care of it, you just have a nice weekend, hear?" And I hang up, heart pounding. A home makeover. Jesus god! I shudder and trot to the kitchen for another cucumber. English. The cravings are quieter, more infrequent. But I still like to eat cucumbers. I sit on my speckled vinyl chair, my toes bratwurst-bare and just as ugly. But my calves are nicely muscled, and hard as rock, pleasing, really. And I hum a little as I chew.

Get Janice's number from directory before I come down from my cucumber high.

The phone rings five times. I glance at my watch, fuck! 1:30 A.M., Janice, all country-time sleeping at 9:00 P.M. to get up predawn early for chicken feed. I consider hanging up, but then she'll be awake by now, might as well face the music. Besides, there's always the callback *69. She might even have call display. A voice answers on the seventh ring.

"Hello?"

Shock. Not because of the sound of the voice, but by how it inflects.

"Gerald?"

"Yes? May I help you?"

"Jesus, Gerald! It's me! What the hell are you doing there?"

"Oh, hullo. It's 1:32 A.M., you know, not that I was sleeping." He sounds like when he was a child, only older.

"Sorry. I'm calling for Janice. I need to ask her if everything seems all right with our Okasan."

"Well, it's a bit late."

"I know, I'm really sorry about the time, but this might be an emergency and I thought she wouldn't mind too much—"

"No," Gerald interrupts. "It's a bit late to phone for Janice and ask if your mom's all right! They left town over a month ago."

"What?!"

"Yeah, they up and left town. Janice phoned me in Vancouver and actually asked me to come look after her chickens. 'For a spell,' she said."

236

"Where'd they go? Okasan and Janice? Huh?"

Gerald laughs and the sound is so sweet I can barely stand it, makes me want to say silly things so I can hear his pleasure over and over again.

"Janice took the camper with them, on the crew cab, so they must be traveling. I got a call last week from someplace in Wyoming. I think they're making their way south."

"Like *Thelma and Louise?*"

Gerald laughs so hard he starts snorting, has to excuse himself to blow his nose. Can hear the murmur of voices.

"No, not like *Thelma and Louise!* Unless they get low on cash. Just kidding!" he adds after he hears my intake of breath. "Don't you know?"

"I don't know a goddamn thing!" I admit. It's true. I don't know anything at all.

"Your mom's a survivor of alien abductions."

Oh no. Not Gerald too!

"You believe that shit?" I scoff. "It's just hysterical manifesta—" I break off. Realizing. Who the hell am I to talk about hysterical anything? Sigh deep inside enough to cause the other to gently stir after a cucumber-inspired nap. "Okay. She's a survivor of alien abductions. Is she on the road so they can't find her anymore?"

"No, silly. Your mom is doing a support survey, an outreach program to see how many other recent immigrants from non-European backgrounds have been abducted. Janice says she's already got quite a following. People are asking her to do some talks."

"Wow." There is nothing else I can say.

Phone silence, intensely more uncomfortable than in-the-same-room silence.

"What—" we both say at the same time, like a really bad CBC late-night movie. "You first," I quickly interject.

"What have you been doing since you graduated from high school?"

Incredible, to be asked that, I'm stunned at the enormity, years and years of life, nothing I'm proud of, nothing I can hold up and say, here, look, I feel pretty good about this. And unconsciously, my hand slips, cups the unpregnant curve of my wide-waisted belly, as blocky as it was when I was a young and ugly child. A friendly nudge to my palm. I smile in a Mona Lisa way.

"Nothing much," I say.

Murmur again, a voice low, in the background. The pitch of intimacy. I blush at my lack of late-night, love-in sensitivity. Never being a recipient of it, I'm slow to pick up on cues.

"Jesus, Gerald! I keep on having to apologize. You have someone there with you and it's so late."

"Don't worry. I'm glad to catch up. I've thought about you, over the years. Janice said you always kept to yourself after I moved."

I gulp. Swallow something unpleasant from the past, not knowing that it had stayed in my mouth all this time. "Gerald. The horrible things I said to you. I am so very sorry, I have no excuse. You were so kind and I was—"

"We were children. And our lives were a mess. I forgave you a long time ago."

God, he's so sweet.

"Actually, the move was good for me. Going to my auntie's in Vancouver gave me options I never had in a small town. There were more people I could relate to. I made friends. Grew up. Had lovers. I'm happy, now, so don't worry."

"I'm glad," I whisper, a touch of envy. Wondering how much of a difference geography would have made in my own life, the lives of my family.

"Come down and see me," Gerald offers. "I'm staying here until the end of this month. If Janice's not back by then, I'm selling the chickens. I can't stay here forever."

"No. Yes. You can't stay forever," I repeat. Go see him! my heart says.

I don't know why, but I'm scared. "I'll try to get down there," I manage. "You know, work and stuff. I'd really like to see you, though."

"Sure," Gerald says gently. "You take care." And he hangs up.

I cup the receiver in my palm, warm. I don't want it to cool but I place it back in the cradle.

My bedroom is still dark when I wake up. I stroke my belly with my hand, the slight fullness a small comfort. Hard to guess the time and too lazy to bother looking at the clock radio, I lie a little longer savoring the moment between dreaming and wakefulness. The warm cave of blankets protects my peace.

My Okasan has become a person I never imagined. How is this possible? I shake my head to clear away troubling thoughts, but I've burst my comfortable bubble. I swing my legs to the floor. Run my fingers through my hair. Another workweek of hauling carts, another weekend of walking, walking. I'll visit no one and no one will visit me. I'm so used to being pregnant now I cannot imagine how I was before.

Brush my teeth, wash my face. The towels stink, I should do some laundry. I shrug into leisure pajamas made of gray sweatpants material and grab a short housecoat.

The sun is dimmer, falling into winter, and soon the weather will keep me confined to my burrow. Work will slow down, I'll go on part-time and who knows, I might look into a few evening classes. Audit a survey course on mythical folk creatures of Japan. I think this is the first winter I've ever had a plan. I'm not incapable of change. But get out of the basement, get out! Get out! Plenty of time to sleep when the cold brittle snap of winter convinces me indoors. I need to get my walking in before I have to resort to malls.

The air is brisk, sweet with decaying leaves. I breathe deeply. Exhale. My breath a small cloud although there's no frost on the ground. I stamp my feet and the keys in my pocket jangle. I ought to give the milk van a good fall cleaning, but my feet tap, directing me through the back yard and past my neglected vehicle. "Sorry," I mutter, and give the side of my van an affectionate pat. The last part of the P in *Palm* flakes off. "Oops," I giggle.

I've slept in, so there's not enough time for a decent jaunt in the countryside. My feet take me twenty-three blocks to downtown. A few people walk their dogs and the owners duck their head in greeting and I wave back. A dog might be nice, I muse, but not a needy one. Gracie, he's a fine canine.

I spot seven stray carts and mentally map their location. Type-A people zip by, bodies smothered in Lycra, Rollerblades spinning madly down the hill. My eyebrows rise. There's a river after all. Mulling over my current anxiety, Okasan's alien outreach, heading south with Janice. Really, I admonish. What can worrying about her help? But worry I do, all the same. Were the aliens who abducted her nice? Were they evil? Why didn't she tell us she was leaving? Why didn't she say good-bye? Why did she leave with Janice? I would have gone with her. . . . Eyes tired, they smart and I drag my arm over the weakness. I ought to tell Dr. Suleri about it the next time I have a physical. I might need glasses.

Wafts of oil-steam, noodles moist and fried quick with minced garlic and ginger. Pungent bamboo, black bean-sauced with beef and green onions. I raise my head. Chinatown.

My middle gurgles and there's a suggestion of a touch against my empty stomach. Good idea, I nod. I can mull over some decent food. I turn to the closest restaurant and deja vuuuuuuuu. It's the place where I met the Stranger. That green imp that skewed my life. The small hairs on my spine prickle prickle into my scalp, almost inducing a shudder of pee. What's in store for me now? There are always risks. If I turned away, how would my life path alter?

I step through.

The whole place has been renovated, a kind of retro motif, with pseudopillars and a chandelier, but the clatter-din of people remains the same, dim sum pushed on carts. The restaurant is brand-new clean, no sense of mystery, magic. Under New Management, the sign on the door says. I dart my small eyes in search of a seat, the place crowded with families, grandparents with grandchildren, squalling babies, bags of bought groceries.

Two heads held close in quiet talking. The familiar tilt, the perfectly cut hair slashing diagonally along an exquisite chin. The jut of a nose. Indignation burns hot and throbbing at the base of my throat.

"I'm joining a party," I wave to the hostess, and stomp my flat feet to where my sisters eat without me.

"We were waiting for you," Mice states without looking up and I'm too angry even to twitch at her strangeness.

"Don't give me that!"

Slither presses slender fingers over her lipsticked mouth. Looks guiltily at my face before scanning my gray sweats pajamas, my huge-headed hair, with critical eyes. Mice scoots over in the booth and I sit stiffly. Self-righteousness presses my backbone bible-straight and I only nod at the waiter when he brings me a place setting.

"Have some shrimp toast," Slither nudges some over with her chopsticks and I generously accept her offer. Nibble in an angry way.

"I gave a paper at the university. There's a multidisciplinary conference on Intelligence with a capital *I*." Mice chews around some sticky rice, pungent in a moist steamed leaf.

Hmmmph! Okay, so she has a good reason for being here, but that doesn't explain how she's so chummily eating dim sum with Slither! Slither the Superficial, Slither the Whiner. Slither the Incompetent. Why is Mice eating lunch with Slither when she could be eating lunch with me?

"Don't be maaaaad," Slither pours some tea into my cup. "It's just that no one knows where you live and I tried to phone you but you weren't in."

True. No family member knows my address, just my unlisted phone number. Because I don't want to deal with unwanted surprise visits from the people who are the most likely to hurt and disappoint me.

Yup. I'm quite the warm and cozy one.

"Yeah, yeah," I give in. Self-righteousness is a pretty thin companion and I'm too hungry to eat with the pinched mouth of bittered disappointment. "Pass the squid. What were you talking about all serious?" I chew around some legs.

Slither glances obviously at Mice and ducks into her bowl of tea.

"You." Mice not one to choose words out of nicety or tact. She stares into my eyes until I turn away. When I'm able to look back, she is already picking the shrimp from her toast, dipping her toast into her tea like it is English.

"Me? Me!? What's there to talk about!? What about Okasan! 'Heading south' with Janice. An alien abductee organizing support lectures for other immigrant survivors, for god's sake. My story is nothing compared to what she's up to."

"Okasan's quite fine," Mice beams and I impatiently snip the discarded shrimp from her plate. Cram them into my gap-toothed mouth.

"Quite fine?! You can't be serious! I just want to have a normal life! I just want to have a normal family! But I'm always tossed into this tornado, this Wizard of Oz meets Godzilla at the Little House on the Prairie! Jesus, god," I gulp, don't realize I'm so close to tears. All these years of sublimating my "weaker" emotions has truly and finally caught up with me, reducing me to maudlin melodrama. I don't even have a stinky cocker spaniel or a snooty long-haired cat, no, I have to be pregnant with some mysterious who-knows-what and I can't even pet it.

Mice and Slither look at each other, look back at me stuffing fried dumplings into my mouth to plug up the tears. I'm gorging and my stomach protests, it has shrunk with my new habits and exercise, has learned to enjoy food slowly. I set down my chopsticks and blow a sigh into my ugly bangs. Mice pats my hand with her sweat-sticky palm.

"PG phoned me."

"What!"

"She owns a houseboat," Mice nods. Like this is the sum total of what anyone would want to know. "Houseboats are better than mobile homes because most of this planet is water."

"Where is she? Is she all right?"

"She's on water," Mice says slowly, in case I need longer to process the information. Slither sees my impatience roll up my short neck toward my pumpkin face in a tide of red.

"PG's fine. She's doing some travel writing for a feminist magazine in the States." Slither wrinkles up her nose.

"Oh." I'd been all ready to worry about her forever, nurture in absence, but it sounds like she's okay. Really okay and not desperate, homeless, and obviously nowhere near wandering the dark alleys of this city like some forlorn ghost. I snort at my own projections. They're nothing but the reflections of my own sorry circumstances and I really need a kick in the butt.

I snort again. "Too bad, so sad," I chant.

Slither covers her mouth and giggles.

"What's so funny?" Mice utters. Picking grains of sticky rice off the table and eating them.

"Oh!" Slither says. A surprised exclamation. Did she spill something on her designer clothing?

"What?" I bark.

"I just realized. I wonder if Dad is okay?"

Oh.

"Who cares," Mice says coldly.

I'm shocked. Mice is strange, but never a mean bone in her body. Never capable of hurting another human being.

It isn't like *I* feel an overwhelming surge of affection whenever I think of our father, but, I don't know, an emotion I can't name stays small and silent in the depths of my heart. I can't cut off my feelings from him, my monster, my hero.

Let go, I think.

Slither leans across the table and softly touches my clenched fists.

"Don't worry. You don't have to do anything." She smiles. A steady strength in her eyes. I smile back, my famous gap-toothed grin, and she doesn't even glance critically at my teeth or suggest a good orthodontist.

Mice pulls her alarm clock out of her coat pocket.

"I've got to get back to the university. There are some panel discussions I want to attend."

How has Mice turned scholar when I only saw her as a dog? How has she taught herself discipline?

There's a shriek of childish laughter across the room and we turn our heads simultaneously.

A small, curly-haired child runs around tables, chased by an annoyed mother.

"Isn't he so cute!" Slither coos.

I slide low in my seat, my eyes beneath the level of the table. Why am I hiding?! I don't care. My ears burn hot and my palms are damp.

"Gabriel! We're leaving right now!" the mother shouts.

"There's lots of gum. I checked already," Mice states.

I shake my head. Stay slouched in my seat until Gabriel, Bernie, her father, and her tough sisters leave the restaurant.

Breathe a big sigh of relief. That was close. Close to what, I have no idea.

"Do you need a ride?" Slither stands up, jingling a Hello Kitty key chain. I shudder. Lunch might have been sister-cozy in a way I would have never imagined, but that still doesn't inspire me to be caught dead in an automatic Trans Am with CUTEGRL for a license plate.

"Uh, no. I have a few more things to do before I go home."

"Okay," Slither chirps, picking up the tab, Mice rolls the leftover sticky rice back into the leaf and deposits it in her pocket. With her alarm clock.

They wave out the door. I wave back, grinning. Notice a small rectangle of mauve on the table and pick it up. Slither has left her beautician's card again.

"Hmmmph!" Exasperated, annoyed, and also touched for her way of expressing concern, translated into, 'All you need is a decent haircut.'

I stand and all the tea I drank sloshes to my bladder, no way I'll make it back home in this condition. I navigate through crowded tables to the washroom in the back. Pause for a moment, head tilted to one side, before stepping through the door. It's empty and I laugh at my silliness. When I come out of the stall, I catch my reflection in the mirror. My pumpkin face is shining from eating good hot food. I lean over to wash my face, with one hand, Okasan always telling me how I wash up like a cat.

Water drip-slides over my closed eyes and I grope for the paper-towel dispenser with my hand. Someone pushes a rough square into my palm.

"Uh, thanks," I mutter. Drag the coarse paper over my face.

Open my eyes into the mirror, a reflection of pooled intensity mesmerizing from a mischievous, green face. Standing right behind me. Close enough to touch.

"Eeeeeep!" I spin around, crouching low into a karate-like stance for no reason other than watching too many kung-fu movies.

Nothing. No one. The room is empty.

I would have peed my pajama bottoms if I hadn't just gone to the can. I drag shaking hands down my face. Weary, I think. I'm just weary. I've got to get a grip on myself. I just need to rest. I turn slowly toward the door and eye-glance green off the sheen of glass.

"Fuck!" I resist the instinct to turn. Resist my desire to see the physical reality behind me and force myself to stare at what's reflected.

"Hello," the Stranger smirks.

"NOTHING WRONG with getting a haircut," eyes rounding at my scowled annoyance. I have much more pressing issues I want to talk about, like, say, the *pregnancy* for starters. But nooooooo. The Stranger wants to talk about hair.

"We don't come from a Samsonite culture."

I snort. "That's a suitcase company!"

"You're not listening. Listen. There's a barbershop around the corner, beside that gorgeous bakery. A haircut will feel good and you're wasting your great face with this odds-and-ends, deck-brush hair gone wild."

"Great face! Hmmmmph!" But I'm still pleased, although annoyed that I should feel this way.

"Okay! I'll go. But," I cup my middle, "what about my pregnancy?" A symbolic gesture, really, because the other is nestled in the warm curve of my left armpit. "Why am I pregnant? When will the child be finished?"

"You'll see," the Stranger blows a green-water–scented kiss toward the mirror and blinks dark, intense eyes. When I blink my own, the creature is gone.

"Fuck!" I eject, just as someone nudges the door open.

"Sorry," I mumble, blush-red up my short neck into my face.

ELEGANT HAIR
Design Emporium

The sign promise is totally compromised by the way the hairdresser looks, his balding crown, his messy sideburns, and the general hair-dust mess of the place.

"Yes," the sideburn-man nods, "you need a good haircut."

So do you, I think to myself, in a not unlike Slither-ish way, but I don't say it out loud.

"Well, whatever you think," I say gruffly. I close my eyes so I won't change my mind, just listen to the snik-snak of quick scissors, the itchy prickle of coarse hair on my nape, the tickling burr of the electric shaver. The cut takes all of five minutes.

"There. Much better," the barber beams with his voice and I cautiously open one eye.

Huh. I grin. Huh.

My pumpkin head. He's cut my hair short, shorter than it has ever been, and the weight is off my head, the bones in my face pronounced. My neck emerges from my shoulders, not graceful swan-like, never that, but a neck, definitely long enough to kiss. I shiver at the thought.

The barber shuffles over a hand mirror to show off the back of my head, something I can't ever remember looking at, always figuring that my eyes faced one way for a reason.

My cropped hair, buzzed along the curve of skull. A lovely, curved skull, I think. I look at my reflection again, the mirrored infinity all my selves there.

I grin even wider, my gap-toothed grin, and leave a five-dollar tip for an eight-dollar haircut.

I FIND OUT THAT SHORT HAIR needs upkeep to stay that way. Once it grows out, I try emulating what I thought the hairdresser did, but end up cutting depressions into some sections and leaving other clumps too long and it's impossible to do the back of my head. I go back to the elegant place and get a fine scolding.

I've learned to measure time in six-week intervals. The time it takes for another haircut.

"Your hair grows fast. Very healthy and strong!" the sideburn-man admires.

"Thanks." I'm gruff. "Just the usual."

I stroll around in Chinatown. Bits of hair bristle unpleasantly down my back, between my breasts, but I love the scenery. And the only place in the city where people cross the road regardless of traffic lights. I wander back and forth in front of cars with impunity. I haven't run into Bernie again and I'm not sure if I'm relieved or disappointed.

I love how light my head feels when I leave the barber's. I stroll a little jauntier, the wind sliding to caress my skull. Catch my reflection in plate-glass windows.

Now that I've changed my hair, should I change my wardrobe?

A chill wind whips between buildings and my pale blue cottons flutter, then press against my compact body.

Two girls and a boy slouch behind me, their images walking across the shop window. A girl whispers to her friends and they all look up, eye my haircut, then run their gaze down my clothes.

"Nice," one of them breathes, and they giggle. Not sarcasm. Not ridicule. The first girl who whispered blushes and I slow-smile. Her look of interest sends a rush of blood into the base of my throat.

The pajamas stay. Will always stay. A body might make some changes, but like some people are compelled to stay with basic black, I'm a basic pajama person.

I thought that with the Stranger's enigmatic, "You'll see," some mythic process was initiated. But my life continues as always, uneventful in my daily ruminations. Only now I have a better haircut. I guess that constitutes a change, minute in the scale of the universe, but even minutia affects the trajectory. Something someone said along the way has shaped my life.

People say "childhood" and "adulthood" with such absolute conviction. Like they are two entirely separate rooms of the four-room bungalow of life. I don't know. I don't know.

I'VE PUT OFF THE CLEANING of my milk truck for too long. Though the chill keeps the smell from getting too ripe, my forays haven't been as pleasant. I bundle myself into my rattiest pair of work jammies and throw on a tattered housecoat. Brrrr. Not the nicest weather to wash a van, I've no one to blame but myself.

"Hey," I say softly. But there is no answer. Shake my head. Shrug. Maybe the creature hibernates. Maybe on vacation. How long did I want to be pregnant anyway?

The cold weather keeps people from the car wash. Especially at dinnertime. I pull into a dock and bungee the van's back doors open. The hand-held wand sprays a jet of soapy water, peels off the caked remnants of vegetables, dissolves puddles of soured ice cream. When I wash the outside of my delivery truck, the last bits of the Palm sign fly off with the spray. I guess I can't pretend to be a milkperson anymore.

I wish the car wash had drying wands as well. I wipe the wet from the seats with paper towels, but run out of the two-ply sheets. My butt sticks in the most unpleasant way. At least the van is clean. Luckily, no matter how many washes my delivery truck gets, the perfume of sweet cream still lingers.

A dark green cast rises in the night sky and I shudder. Switch on the headlights. One by one, the mercury streetlamps shimmer into orange along the windy road that leads to my home. My stomach gurgles. Maybe I'll just order a pizza. I haven't been to Bernie's because I've been so busy. I don't crave the bittersweet fruit, I've become accustomed to eating them, that's all. Pizza and a salad. I can press the water out of the English cukes with salt and a heavy rock. Like Okasan. The keys jangle in my hand as I approach my underground home. In the growing night, a dog barks. Somewhere, a door slams shut. I stop.

A sound.

Coming from the inside of my basement suite.

I look around the door for signs of tampering, crowbar marks next to the deadbolt, a bullet-hole in the doorknob. Churned up mud and grass from large feet. Nothing. I could just turn around and get back in my van, drive to the cop station and ask for help. But what if the person inside is a friend? What if I've left my tape player on auto reverse and Nina Simone has been raging her fury all evening? I softly turn the doorknob. Still locked. But that doesn't mean someone isn't inside. Heart tripping, what should I do? Must not assume anything. Be ready, that's all. Eye the ground. Rocks. A Frisbee. An old hockey stick. I grip the handle, rise, and gently unlock the door. The click is over-loud and I wince, then shift the keys in my fist so that the points stick out between my knuckled fingers.

The sound is the muffled tones of the television. I never left it on, haven't watched TV for months. Who could it possibly be? Midori, broken up with Genevieve and come over for moral support? Not Slither. Maybe Mice?

I mince down the stairs, keys prepared in one hand, the hockey stick in the other. A muted blue light glows from the living room and I press my back against the wall, peer around the corner.

No one.

Stick my head in the kitchen but nothing. The cupboards are too small for anyone to hide in. I tiptoe to the washroom and fling back the shower curtain. Jump into my bedroom, flicking on the lights simultaneously.

"Ha!" I challenge.

Empty.

I kick open the closet door. No one hiding inside.

I exhale. Adrenaline-exhaust streams from my mouth.

"Jesus." Drop the hockey stick and loosen my deathhold on the keys. I shuffle back to the living room and slump onto the couch. I'm too old for this. And much too old for a poltergeist.

On the television, Melissa Gilbert, playing Laura Ingalls, runs across a stretch of prairie, whooping, leaping, jubilant. The music is sunny and playful. "Da da dada. Da da daaaaaa. Da da dada! Daaa da da—"

The hairs on my arms tingle, shiver, stand in a rush of goose-bumps.

The camera angle is wide and Melissa runs closer and closer. Until her face fills the screen. The music is gone. Only the sound of wind in the grass. And as I watch, her face hardens, the skin slowly browns, tightens, pressing against bones, her eyes glitter bright in her starving face, lips cracked with malnutrition. Her braids are messy, the hair dull and brittle. The child grins and her teeth are yellow and crooked.

"They changed the book, you know," she croaks.

I shake my head.

"They did! They got it all wrong." Laura Ingalls' lips are bitter. "Why do they do that? Oh, I know what they said. 'The book is for children! Children need happy stories!' Damn them all to hell!" Laura rubs her arm roughly over her eyes.

"Wha—"

"And I can't do anything about it!" Laura is fierce, heat exudes from her skin and I pull back from the intensity.

Laura stares at me and I'm afraid to blink.

"You can, though," she nods.

"You can."

The camera rolls back slowly, Laura receding to a far shot, even as her face begins to fill. Healthy, full, she transforms back into Melissa Gilbert as music swells in the background. My body starts shaking as the credits rise on the screen.

Return to
Little House on the Prairie

L ATE OCTOBER'S NOT THE BEST TIME for travel. Dark so quickly after work and I'm tired. The highway isn't icy, but brittle MSG snow blows fitfully against the windshield and my wipers flap, completely useless. I should have worn my two-ply flannels. My milk van's not warming up and I scrape ice build-up on the windshield from the inside. Hard to do while driving. I veer toward the direction I'm scraping and almost run over a cat.

The cats. Who is taking care of the cats?

Find myself blinking hard for no reason.

There's the smallest touch against my heart. Almost indiscernible. Have I imagined it? I smile. Sad. The movements grow fewer and the touch faint. Maybe the creature ages before being born.

I shake my head, surprised again at how light it feels.

MSG snow turns into eiderdown. Must have hit a warmer patch. The flakes stick heavily. Inch my way to the edge of seat, Portishead wailing on tape. Another homemade one, compliments of Midori, who'd been disgusted by my love songs from the seventies. I like Portishead, the singer a depressed woman after my own heart.

The oversaturated snow adheres to the glass, flakes so big they drift with slow-motion speed, downward spirals pulling my gaze from the highway. Portishead moans. Sudden shapes loom from the periphery. Dart past me. Anything can be anything. Cringing animals in the middle of the road. I steer around them only to discover they are shadows cast by my lights and the bounce of snow. I slow, slower, creeping in the vortex of total whiteness.

Stop.

Everything swirls around, cacophony of silence and motion, my head spins with vertigo.

I don't know where I am.

I unclench my hands from the steering wheel. Press thumbs into my palms to relieve the ache. Look back to see if anyone is coming from behind. Only darkness. My headlights slash a diagonal line and snow flows past in two beams. I can't hear the falling flakes, but they are loud all the same. Glare at my inadequate sneakers. The arrogance of drivers who never imagine they'll have to walk.

Press the light on my diving watch. The orange glow is a small comfort. 11:47 P.M. How long was I creeping, thirty kilometers per hour? I can't remember seeing a signpost. Who knows how far I came, blinking, bug-eyed? I could be in the middle of an open field for all I know. Just a few years ago, someone was caught in a snowstorm on a secondary road and left their car. Wandered and sank into the sleeping death of hypothermia. Not a demise that happened just to people in the olden days. It happens all the time. I switch off the engine so I don't use all the fuel and turn off the headlights. The hazards tick, tick, overloud. Is it my imagination or does the ticking seem slower? My fingers and toes are tingling and there's a hum in my ears. The snow enfolds.

Maybe I'm not meant to make this passage.

The CB!

I'm too far away for Gary to hear me, but maybe there's a trucker somewhere who can tell me if the storm is clearing up or settling in for the night. A late-night farmer longing for a friendly voice to break the quiet in a sleeping kitchen, waiting for the spin cycle to end so she can toss the daily load into the dryer, children long to bed and the dog scraping toenails in a dream chase.

"Breaker, breaker one-nine!"

Zap of static.

"Breaker one-nine, anyone copy?"

Crackle of phantom voices. I strain my ears but no connection. Like Major Tom, I'm stuck in my tin can. If I open the door, will I float in a peculiar way? Close eyes, rest forehead on the cold curve of steering wheel. Why bother? Why should I bother?

What do I want?

I open my eyes.

The night sky is purple turned to black and every star glitters, cool and distant. Dense. A thickness to the dark, almost as if I could peel back the skin of night. The sharp taste of stars biting my tongue. Heart thumping, I flick the headlights. I laugh.

There is no snow. Simply a storm of pathetic fallacy, one of my own creation, the pavement is dry and I am free to go. Anywhere I want.

I turn off my hazards and the engine starts with hardly a sputter.

Of course there are no lights on. The house's face is dark. For all I know, the place could be empty. Dad long gone, back to a warmer, moister climate so he won't have to blast medication up his nose. Maybe he slit his belly, all noble and tragic, his intestines spilling out, rank with food and rot, the cats, locked in with him, eating away his face. I shudder.

I fling myself out of the milk van before I can change my mind. I don't even know what I think I ought to do here. And now that I'm here, I'm at a loss I can't quite explain.

Back in front of the porch door. My hands are clenched inside the pockets of my quilted housecoat. The cold saps reason from my head, shorn and vulnerable to the elements. I should have worn a toque. I'm cold. I could turn around and drive home. There's nothing to keep me here, nobody saying I have to enter.

I'm still, hoping for some nudging clue from the creature inside. No. I back away, descend the three stairs but not to retreat to my van. Instead, I walk the perimeter around the house. There is a faint trail in the dry, yellow grass, probably from Mice's bicycle, and I smile. Tread thrice in one direction. Thrice back the other way.

Rattle of glass, squeaking slide of wood against wood. I tip back my head.

"Who's out there!" There is a quaver in his voice I don't recognize.

"It's me," I answer.

"Oh." Dad pulls his head back in from the window so that he is only visible from the middle of his nose, up. He must have sat on the bed. His head. There's something odd—

"You come to kill me, then?"

"What?!"

"Wa! Ha! Ha! Ha! Ha!" he laughs, like he used to. "Come inside."

I HOLD MY BREATH for a tide of stale air, tinted with rotten food and the after-aroma of goats that seems to plague the homes of men who live alone. But the house doesn't smell bad at all. It doesn't smell like Okasan's miso shiru and fried eggs, but this new smell isn't repulsive. My hackles lower. The laddered clotheshanger in the boot room is covered with Dad's laundry. A pile of dirty towels waiting to be washed next to the sink. The crutches are shoved in the back corner by the broken dryer, covered in a thin coating of dust. That's right. The golf cart wasn't out there. Maybe his leg is better now.

"Let me put on some hot water," Dad says, putters toward the sink. My eyebrows leap and I take a step back. His hair! His hair is completely white, every single strand, how could this be when just at Easter most of it was black?

"Uh, what happened to your hair?"

Dad raises his hand, gently touches. Like people do right after getting a new perm.

"Like Marie Antoinette! Turned white over night!"

"Really?"

"Huh!" he snorts. "You don't know everything," he mutters beneath his breath.

I sit at the table. I'm surprised how clean everything is. Would have thought the place would fall into disarray but Dad's even neater than I am. A cheap brochure on the tabletop, I pick it up and stare at the heading.

Hydroponics And You!
Farming For The Future

I flip open the leaf and skim down the contents. "Grow succulent cucumbers" leaps out from the page and my mouth waters.

"I thought you came to kill me," Dad continues, tapping tealeaves into the pot.

"Why would I do that?"

Dad turns his big, white head around and his black eyes glitter. "Your youngest sister did."

"No!" Little Mice? Who used to be a dog? Who's scared of the dark and of unaccountable noises? "Did she have a gun?"

Dad snorts, pours hot water over the tea, and the sweet-bitter smell fills the kitchen. "She had an ax! Lucky I still had the golf cart! She chased me all over the field, waving the ax. I was worried she'd trip and fall on it! That girl can run. I was driving full speed."

"Then what happened?"

Dad brings the tea to the table like Okasan used to do. He's even put some store-bought cookies into a little bowl. "She kept on chasing me. I was running out of batteries. I yelled out I'd buy her a new bicycle, the very best, then she stopped and went home."

"Jesus!"

"Jesus te yuwanaino."

I snort. "I wouldn't use an ax," I mutter.

"What?" Dad asks.

"I said I wouldn't use an ax!"

"Ohhhh?" He reaches for a cookie, changes his mind, slaps at his sweatpants pocket. Finds his nasal spray and inserts, blast, ahh-hhhh. Stares down at the plastic bottle in his hands. "What would you use, then?"

"I'd use my bare hands. I'd slap you stupid until you cried, then I'd start punching you, slowly, all over, then I'd finish you off with kicks until every bone of your body was shattered." I can't breathe. I grip the edge of table.

Dad looks up and stares into my eyes. "You are my child," he says slowly.

"I'm not like you," I manage. Shake my head in refusal.

Dad sighs, puts his nasal spray back in his pocket. He rubs his face wearily with both hands. "Maybe not," he agrees.

"Say you're sorry," I spit.

"Why?"

"You know why!" I shout. "You fucking know!"

Dad's face clenches. Red rises up his neck, bursts upward. "Don't," he says quietly. "Don't swear at me."

"Fuck you!" The blood burns hot in my eyes, I can barely see. A hot taste in my mouth. "You can't stop me anymore. So Fuck You!"

He bursts out of his chair with a roar. But I am quicker. My chair toppling, I throw myself on top of him and he crashes backward. His elbows try to break his fall, I dig one knee in his gut, press my forearm against his throat with everything I have.

"Say," I hiss, "you're sorry."

Dad gasps. Coughs. He slaps his hands against my head. I press down harder.

"Say it!"

Dad squeezes his lips shut. He won't. And I'm scared. I'll have to kill him. Blood roars in my ear, tinny sounds inside my head. There are spots in my eyes that explode into brightness.

What am I doing?

"I'm sorry," he croaks. Then barks a short laugh.

It's all wrong.

I yank back my arm and jump away from him. He sucks air, rasping, coughs and gasps again. Rolls to his side.

I stare at him. Panting. Suddenly cold, I wrap my arms around my middle.

Dad breathes hard, his shoulders rising up and down with the effort, then swallows hard. He pushes up, sits with legs sticking straight out, rubs his throat with one hand.

"You repay us," I say, weary. "All of us."

"How?"

I try to think of something. Something that will erase the past, right all wrongs, so we can be whole creatures again. Whole like we were, before ever being born onto this earth.

"I don't know," I mutter.

Dad picks up his chair and sits down at the table. Finds his spray for a nasal fix. "I did what I had to do," Dad states.

I shake my head. How can he believe that? "You're pathetic," I say sadly. And the words seem to crumple him in his chair.

My god. I was beating up an old man. My hands shake and I bite my lip. No, I won't start crying in front of him now. "What about what you did to Okasan. How can you think you're blameless?"

"Ha!" he barks. Crosses his arms and looks disbelievingly at the ceiling. "Don't worry about her! She can look after herself. Didn't you wonder why I was on crutches?"

"I thought you had a farming accident."

"Your mother!" His brows rise.

"No!" I lean forward. "How?"

Dad snorts, coughs, pulls a used hanky from his pocket and gives a blast. I wrinkle my nose and push my chair back. He wads the wet cloth and returns it to the same pocket.

"Your Okasan," Dad begins, recrossing his arms, "she's been sleepwalking ever since we moved here. She'd come walking home from who knows where. And she'd smell funny, too. Unnatural. Well, a few weeks before Easter, I woke up to terrible pain! I thought I was dreaming. Your mother was at the foot of my bed. She had a steak knife and she sliced through my tendon right above my heel!"

"Jesus god!"

"The knife must have been dirty. I got infected. Your mother didn't remember a thing."

I purse my lips to contain a sound. I don't realize what it is until the sound spills out as laughter.

Dad's eyes widen, incredulous that someone would laugh at him. I try to stop myself, but can't, I laugh until my eyes water.

"Hmmph." Dad uncrosses his arms, his lips turn down. "You said you didn't come to kill me." He rubs both hands over his face then stands. "I'm going back to bed."

His white hair is still a shock to me. He looks so old. He's over sixty, after all. And if Grendel was aged-frail by the time Beowulf caught him, would the hero have shown compassion?

Dad turns around and shuffles down the hallway, the slightest limp.

"You're grown up. You do what you want." He does not look back.

I want to have the last word. Tonight. I want the last word.

But there is nothing to say.

BLACK CAT AND ORANGE CAT waddle out from beneath my milk van. Dad must be overfeeding them, like people do who aren't used to caring for felines. I snort. Hop into my vehicle, the sun curving toward this face of the earth. There is a gray-green glow, a weight in the air that smells of snow.

What about Gerald? Is he still at Janice's? A tug somewhere, near my heart. Not the creature, but a tug all my own. When I think of Gerald, my heart squeezes painful in my chest.

I pull into their drive, heavy. How can I face him again when I was a monster myself?

But as I draw close to the house, I break a pool of silence, the stillness of people gone. I hop out of my van, anyway. Relieved and disappointed. Poke my head into the chicken barn, the ripe smell overlaid with dust. Gerald must have sold them all, I wonder if he had sense enough to haggle. The frozen grass crunches beneath my feet but the silence is uncanny. A nervous quality to the air without a wind, I wander to the house and peer into the living room window. The furniture all covered with white sheets. The lumps glow strangely in the darkness. I sigh. Breath clouds. The last stars of the night glitter. I can't imagine them as burning orbs, but then, their fires might already be out and I'm only looking at their past. Maybe that's why the stars look so cold. I'm only seeing their memories.

I have to peek into the kitchen before I leave. I rub a fist over the dusty window and press my nose against the glass. The room is cleaner than Janice ever had it. I rattle the door, just to be sure it is locked. Not only the knob, but a padlock's been added to deter teenagers looking for a place to party. I give the paneled wood a small kick. Notice. A fold of paper tucked into the frame of the blocky window. I tug and the piece pops out, falls to the ground. I crouch and unfold the message in the growing dawn.

Call me. 604-278-5144. Gerald

I'VE BEEN GIVEN ANOTHER CHANCE. I gulp. Shudder. Gasp. Can't contain the sound that spills out from between my clenched teeth and sink onto the cold ground, head tipped back, I wail for all that is gone. Everything I'm afraid to face. I bawl and the sound is glorious.

I CAN'T REMEMBER HOW I drove back to the city. Foolish. The sun feels hot through the glass windows and the scent of car soap mixes with the smell of milk. A blast of horn behind me. I jerk my head up and stare blearily at the lights. Turned green.

"Sorry," I mutter. Pinch my cheek, hard.

So very tired. My chin starts bobbing again. I shake my head. Don't be stupid. What if I hurt someone. Home, I think. Home is where the heart is. But if you don't know where your heart is, can you ever go home?

The basement's going to be so cold.

No. I have choices. I do.

I flick the signal lights, turn right, and drive across the bridge into Kensington. I've never been at her house before. Can barely remember her address, but my professional discipline kicks in and the location rolls into a mental image, aerial-view. I navigate the midmorning traffic and park right in front of the building in a spot marked Loading Only.

I stand in the foyer. Forehead pressed against a sheet of metal lined with names and black buttons. I press and a distant buzz bleats over the speaker.

"Hello!" She sounds so happy.

"It's me," I manage. "Can I come in?"

"Oh!" she gasps. The door clicks and I'm inside before I change my mind.

When I reach her apartment, the door is already opened. Her hair pulled up in a bun so she can put on makeup, she frowns with worry when she sees my face. I must be a mess.

She looks so much like Okasan my heart squeezes.

Slither grabs my arms and pulls me inside. Something floral fills the air. Potpourri? I think. Scented candles? Then Slither cradles me in her arms with such tenderness I shake my head in refusal. But my arms, they rise on their own and I'm clinging to her, to her quiet strength. My eyes are dry, grainy. And I sigh so long the air breaks into shudders.

"Shhhhhh," Slither breathes into my shorn hair. She runs her hand over my head, from the crown to my nape. Over and over, and the motion soothes. Until my breathing quiets and my arms dangle weakly at my sides.

"I'm really tired," I whisper.

Slither doesn't ask any questions. She gently puts her arm around my back, her other hand reaches in front of her body to hold my elbow. She leads me like an invalid to a brightly flowered bedroom. My sister pulls back the covers, takes off my housecoat, and tucks me in. She closes the door behind her and as I fall asleep, I can hear her talking to someone on the telephone.

There's a moistness to the room, warm and pungent. The walls, actually wet. How disgusting, I think, there must be a problem with plumbing or the heating system. Maybe Slither's boiling enormous pots of water. I rise to leave the room. The doorknob is slick and I pull my hand away in revulsion.

"Slither!" I call out. "Come here!"

A trickle of laughter outside. The sound fades and I can hear water dripping.

I drape the bottom of my pajama top over the disgusting doorknob and turn.

A light glares, burns into my retinas and bursts into tiny pieces.

The prairie is barren. Dust blows in fits, dies down to rise again. Rock juts from the ground in stark relief and the brightness is painful. I raise my arm to cover my eyes. No one lives here. How could they? As far as I dare to look, just the dryness of a dead prairie. No shrubs, no cacti, no clatter of insects. The wind howls and the hollow sound rings. I turn back to the door but someone, a child, stands in the way.

"Move!" I shout, the words snatched from my mouth. The wind leaves dust instead and I choke at the acrid taste.

The child wears a patched and sun-bleached pinafore dress. A large bonnet covers her face, her hands clasped behind her back. Her stillness is unsettling and I clamp my elbows to my ribs.

The child raises her head and I start.

She has no nose. Her face triangulates into an amphibian point, her skin a mottled green. Overlarge eyes bulge, all pupils. She unclasps her hands from behind her back and extends one, trembling, toward me. Her hand. Her green skin is like a mummy's, drained of all moisture. How can she be alive?

"Help," she rasps.

I step backward. What if she touched me? I would surely fall to dust.

"Please." She falters.

Drops her hand.

I close my eyes. Play my protection game. When I open them again, she'll be gone.

The child has fallen to the ground, curled in on herself, and the wind tugs the hem of her dress to expose the withered lengths of her legs. Her buttocks are fleshless, the bones of a residual tail jutting from the base of her spine.

"No." I step closer. She is dying.

I kneel in the hot dust and cradle the child to my chest, gently tug her skirt to cover her nakedness. Her eyes open and I start at their depths, the age and sadness of a thousand years.

"Thank-you," she whispers.

"What can I do?" I say fiercely. Because I know if she dies, something precious will be gone forever. "Tell me!"

The creature unfolds a long, scrawny arm and gestures to the expanse of dry death which surrounds us.

"Water."

I snap my head, look in every direction. How can I find water here? How many must die? So unfair. Why must we live to come to only this? And tears of frustration surge to my eyes, drip down my face.

The creature stretches her withered hand and brushes the track of wetness with a bony finger. Smiles.

"Don't cry," Slither whispers. "Everything's going to be all right. I promise." My head in her lap, she rocks back and forth. "You're going to be fine. You'll see."

I blink. The light in her spare bedroom has dimmed. The walls are dry. I drag the heel of one hand over my cheeks and stare up into my sister's gentle face. "I had the strangest dream."

"Was it sad?" Slither asks sadly.

"I'm not sure."

Slither starts stroking my hair.

"Do you like my new look?" I ask.

She frowns, pulls her head slightly back to get a better perspective. "Well," she pauses. "As a hair designer, I wouldn't have suggested this particular style. But it rather becomes you." She sounds surprised.

"Hmmm," I smile. "It's getting dark?"

"Around 6:00. You slept for a long time. I was worried."

"I went to see Dad."

"Ohhhhh," Slither sighs. And doesn't say anything else.

"Don't you want to know what happened?"

"Do I want to know?" Slither frowns.

"Probably not," I shake my head. Then laugh. Tell her about Mice and the ax.

"How horrible," she sighs, clasping her spider fingers together and bringing them to her lovely lips like an act of prayer.

"It actually gets worse. I kind of choked him until he said he was sorry."

"Oh," she says.

"Oh?! That's all?"

"When you first came in, I thought you might have killed him."

I shudder. How fine the line between fury and violence. I sit up and look down at my feet. "He's alive. He looks old, though. Smaller. His hair's turned completely white."

"Maybe it's because there's no one there for him to push against."

I'm amazed. Slither capable of insight. Did I think I had a monopoly?

"That doesn't mean he wasn't a hateful person. Aging doesn't negate the harm he did."

"I didn't suggest that," Slither says gently, me noticing that she has small lines of getting older in the folds of her eyes. We aren't kids now, for all that we, I, act otherwise. Far from it, in fact. I don't even know if there is anyone in Slither's life, someone she loves who loves her back. I've never cared to ask.

"If you don't let the hatred go, he continues to oppress your life, just like if you were still living in his house." Slither's fingertips brush my hand briefly.

"Where'd you hear that?" I scoff. "Therapy?"

"Counseling, actually, which is a little different."

"What about Okasan?! She let him beat us. And only leaves after we've moved away from home!"

"Is that what you really think?" Slither is stern. I'm taken aback.

"I don't know," I say, sullenly.

"Think about it," my sister demands.

"I don't know what to think!"

"You discredit her with your ignorance."

Her words sting. And I move slightly away.

Slither sighs. "Let Okasan have something for herself, now. I think she deserves it. We all do."

"Why can't she just call us!" I cry. "She doesn't have to come back. I just want to understand what she's doing."

Slither shrugs. "We don't need to understand. Can't you give her the space to act in her own self-interest? For once in her life she manages to imagine a better life for herself." Slither smiles. "We should be celebrating in her honor."

"PG too, I suppose."

"PG too."

"So you worked all this out in counseling?"

She discreetly takes a small, yellow, rectangular piece of paper from the pocket of her slacks. "It's made a big difference in my life."

I shake my head. Grin. And accept her offering.

"Do you want to stay overnight?"

I look around the guestroom. The walls are a creamy yellow and purple freesia, in a glass vase, grace the dresser. The floral bedspread is nothing I'd ever buy, but it is bright and cheerful. Her invitation is tempting.

"I'd love to," I really mean it, "but not today." I raise my eyebrows. "I'm going to go home and explore my ignorance."

"I didn't hurt your feelings, did I?" Slither asks anxiously. For a heartbeat, the face of her childhood fills my vision. Gone.

"No," I shake my head. "You've given me a lot to think about."

"Because I would never want to hurt you," Slither says.

"I know." I stand and Slither rises beside me. She walks me to the door and as I put on my shoes, she leans against the wall.

"Mice is coming into town next week."

"Really? Does she have another conference?" I ask.

"No, she's coming for a visit. Do you want to come over for dinner?"

"You know how to cook?" I tilt my head. I never imagined Slither cooking. But I guess that doesn't mean she hasn't been cooking all along.

"Yes!" she laughs. "Italian is my specialty."

"Has Mice ever come over before?" I ask.

"Yes."

"Why wasn't I invited?" I'm indignant.

"You never gave the impression that you wanted to see us," Slither defends. "But, then—I guess I shouldn't have assumed."

I flap my hand. "You're right. I wouldn't have come over. But I'd like to now."

Slither smiles. So beautiful. "I'll call with the details. By the way," my sister inclines her head so like Okasan my heart gives a little jump, "I would prefer that you called me Satomi. Slither was funny when we were children, but we're adults now."

"Yes," I say, thoughtful. "Yes, we are, aren't we." I glance at her face before looking down at my feet. "Are you happy, Satomi? Do you have someone in your life?" I gulp out before I change my mind.

Slith—Satomi's eyes widen. "Yes, I do. I have for a long time." She reaches to touch my shoulder and I don't flinch. "But I always wonder about you."

"Ohhh," I duck my head, "I've got some nice friends."

"From work?"

"No. Couple of girls I met by accident."

"What about love?" my sister asks.

"What about it?" I quip. "Why complicate a life that doesn't want or need complicating? I don't keep pets. My needs are simple. Love doesn't figure in my life, never did."

Sli—Satomi smiles soft-knowingly. Holds out my dirty house-coat and I shrug into the sleeves. "You'll see," she murmurs as I step out the door.

"Why does everyone keep saying that!" I call out, but she only flaps her slender hands to send me on my way.

I PREPARE MY GORGEOUS GREENS, cucumbers crisped in ice water, butterleaf lettuce, and baby spinach. Curls of radicchio and carrot shavings adorn the verdant bowl and I drizzle a miso sesame-seed dressing. My mouth eager for the freshness in the winter gloom of my kitchen. Another winter, and in January, my night classes start at the university. Another winter, but without the bitter Shakespearean edge that's plagued me in the past. Briefly wonder why, then shrug my shoulders. To enjoy a good salad, one must enjoy.

Huh, I laugh, snort at my own philosophical musings. If I'm not careful, I might become an optimist! Pour myself a glass of water and get chopsticks from the cupboard. A new tablecloth on the table. Not just new, my only tablecloth! Sli—Satomi must have inspired me. The light green cloth is actually trimmed with a row of yellow flowers and the colors of spring brighten my subterranean kitchen. I set my snack on the table carefully, so I won't spill oily dressing on the green cloth or my new book. Press play on my tape recorder, and the Portishead woman nasally sneers about being so tired of playing at love.

"Agh!" I flip my hands in the air. "You're tired! I'm tired! Everyone's tired!" I clatter through my stack of tapes and snatch another compilation. A sunny melody spills out, inanely optimistic and as perky as a cheerleader. I shake my head and smile. Who wouldn't like some afternoon delight? Especially in the seventies? I sit down and pick up my chopsticks, flip over my Ariyoshi novel.

Thud thud thud of a booted foot on my door. Heart-leap. Throat. Only one person would be irreverent enough to kick the door instead of knocking.

I consider my options. I can pretend I'm not home. I can let her in and see if we're still friends. I'll pretend I never kissed her. I can let her in and apologize about overstepping boundaries. Fuck! What if Genevieve's with her? Midori will have told her everything and I'll die of mortification. I can pretend I'm not home. I can—

Thud! Thud! "Open your goddamn door!"

Jesus! I trot up the stairs. Unlock and swing it open. Light reflects off banks of old snow, glares in my eyes. Midori is a lean shadow and I try inconspicuously to peer around her.

"I'm here too," Genevieve breathes and I sigh, despite myself.

"What do a couple of girls have to do to get invited in?"

"Oh," is all I manage, move to one side so she can thump down the stairs. Genevieve pauses. Glances in my eyes from beneath her bangs, then strokes her hand gently along my arm. I sigh again. Lock the doorknob slowly, and take my time with the deadbolt.

"You turning vegan on me?" Midori yells from the kitchen. Hear her crunching through a mouthful. "Hey, this is pretty good!" she garbles.

"Don't eat all the cucumbers!"

Midori sits in my seat, long legs stretched in front of her, waving the ohashi at my head.

"Wooweee! Nice do!"

"Get out! Shut up!" I burn in pleasure and sweet embarrassment.

"You look sexy," Genevieve breathes, leaning against the counter.

"I'm serious," Midori says. "You look very nice."

"Thanks," is all I can manage. I turn away, get two sets of chopsticks, put the kettle on the stove. We all eat together. Crunch of salad. The sweep of ohashi from bowl to mouths. We eat without talking, the kettle bubbling to a whine. Midori puts on some ocha. We sip. Zuru zuru of steaming tea sucked between lips.

Let go, I think. Is this what letting go means? "I've missed you guys." There is no going back. "How are you doing?"

Hear the crinkle of paper, wait for the bitter curl of Camel smoke, only what wafts over is the distinct pink scent of bubblegum.

"Trying to quit," Midori scowls, almost apologetically. And cracks a huge bubble. "We missed you too. What happened? You were a royal pain in the ass!"

Genevieve rests her hand on Midori's lean arm and I laugh with relief. We are still friends. And I need them. "Actually, I'm better. All things considered. Wait until I tell you what's happening with my mom!"

"What about your pregnancy?" Genevieve pushes her hair behind her ear. Her eyes concerned.

"You still pregnant?" Midori chews.

"Maybe, but it's okay."

"That's wonderful," Genevieve sighs. And enfolds me in the sweet circle of her breath. Genevieve rubs her palm lightly over the buzzed nape of my neck. Her touch is gentle and I lean over to kiss her on the cheek.

"Oh!" Genevieve gasps. Smiles. "You've never kissed me before."

A red heat rises up my face and I look away. "Sorry," I mutter.

"Silly prickly pear! I like it!"

Midori jumps up, slings her arm around my neck. "We've come here with an agenda."

"Political or personal?"

"Cosmic!" Midori laughs.

"What?"

"Come on!" Midori urges. Eyes bright. "Put on your housecoat. We've got a surprise for you!"

"Can we go for a ride in the van?" Genevieve smiles.

"Sure. Might take a while for it to warm up," I call as I shrug into my housecoat and boots, grab the keys off the nail in the wall.

"It's not cold," Midori says, "there's a chinook."

The west wind is as warm as breath and there are puddles everywhere. The engine starts without a hitch and before I can pop in a tape, Midori slides in another homemade. "Marisa Monté," she grins. "I think you'll like her."

"Thanks," I say, embarrassed. So many gifts in one day. "Anywhere in particular you folks wanted to cruise?"

"Let's leave the city limits." Midori slouches in her seat, extending her legs. I can almost hear the milk-rich walls of the van smoothing her coarse skin. Genevieve in the back. Maybe I can look into getting a seat installed. If I get a trailer, I won't miss the extra space for my carts.

The music spills over, sunny and warm. Sweet as honeydew melons.

"What's she singing?" I ask, my mouth beaming and I can't stop.

"I have no idea," Midori shrugs. "With a voice like that, she could be telling us to eat shit and die and we'd thank her for it!"

"Midori!" Genevieve scolds. "You're ruining it!"

I laugh. Marisa Monté's voice like candy.

I drive without thinking, my hands steering like creatures of habit. Down comfortable side streets, roads so familiar I don't notice. When I notice I'm not heading east, I'm already downtown. Bernie's shop and she's flipping the Open sign to Closed. I veer into the parking lot, Genevieve, tossed from one side to the other, laugh-screams behind me.

Bernie blinks in the headlights, frowning fiercely. Until I roll down my window and wave.

"Who's that?" Midori snickers, shuts up when Genevieve digs sneakered toes into her ribs.

"Bernie!" I call. Heart tripping. I hop from my van and trot to the door. Bernie unlocks the bolt and grabs both of my hands.

"Are you okay?"

Something hard bursts in my heart, a flow of sweet liquid fills my veins. I open my arms and she hugs me hard.

"I'm really fine," I smile. And I am.

Maybe the light from the van brings the color to her cheeks.

"Can you come out with us?" I ask. Hold nothing back. "I want you to meet my friends."

She looks surprised. Then grins. "Let me phone Gabriel and my father."

BY THE TIME WE DRIVE toward the prairie in the folds of a warm winter wind, the night is rich. The stars glitter. The orange glow of the city lights fade into the west and Marisa Monté sweetens the darkness. The creature inside me curls around my heart.

"Stop anywhere you see a big enough space," Midori says from the back. Having given up the front seat to welcome Bernie.

"Sure," I answer. Glance at Bernie and she glances back.

Genevieve leans over my shoulder in a cloud of sweet air.

"What's that?" she points.

A dirt track, and wonder of wonders, the barbed wire fence is down and the field is open. I drive into the spread of someone's pasture and park when I can no longer see the road.

"You still have your winter emergency kit?" Midori asks.

"Yeah, why?"

"Help me roll out the sleeping bag for us to sit on." She hops out of her side of the van and opens the back. I turn off the engine and the blast of warm western wind jerks the driver-side door from my hands. Midori has the back doors bungee-ed open so that the wind won't slam them shut. I grab the sleeping bag and Bernie helps me unroll.

Midori takes the sleeping bag from our hands, folds it in half, and covers the floor of the van right by the open doors. She sits, feet dangling outside, and thumps twice. "Come on up!"

I hop lightly and sit beside her, reach out my hand to pull Bernie up beside me. She makes a funny sound in her throat and I almost thump on her back, but realize she's croaking a laugh. My eyebrows rise and I smile in the darkness. Genevieve sits on the other side of Midori and our shoulders and thighs press heat into each other.

"Do you know what's happening tonight?" Genevieve smiles, pleased, tucking the swing of hair behind her small ear.

"Ummm, no, I don't think so."

"There's a conjunction," Midori says proudly.

"There won't be another one for a hundred years or so." Genevieve gestures to the heavens with a sweeping arm movement.

"What's a conjunction?" I ask.

Midori guffaws. Genevieve peals into a cackle.

"What's so funny?"

"You are! Here we thought we'd impress you with planetary alignment and you don't even know a thing about it!"

"Why would I know anything like that?"

"Because," Genevieve twines her hair around her forefinger. "you liked the eclipse so much. We heard about this on the news and thought we'd provide company."

"Oh, yeah. Huh!" I snort. "Look where the eclipse got me!"

"What happened during the eclipse?" Bernie asks.

"Everything impossible." I look up at the teeming stars with disgust and affection.

"But look at you now!" Midori crows. "A new haircut, a new attitude, a new girl—ugh!" Genevieve must have elbowed her.

"I've never seen a conjunction before," Bernie murmurs.

What's happened to Bernie? The showdown queen. The kicker of rude-customer butt?

"You're so quiet today," I whisper in her ear. "I've never seen you this way before."

"I'm feeling shy," Bernie whispers back. The heat of her breath tickling my ear, down my spine.

I blush with pleasure. A flutter in my ribcage. Was that my heart or my unexpected one? Now what should I do?

Her cool hand rises to cup the curve of my chin, my cheek. I am not frightened. I turn my lips and kiss the cup of her palm.

"Whispering is rude," Genevieve scolds, stern. Ruins the effect by laughing into her hands. I shake my head. My friends are silly and beautiful beyond belief. How have I been this lucky and not known?

"Where's the conjunction?" I ask.

Tipping her eyes to the curve of night, Bernie slips her arm around my waist and my silly heart tremors.

"I dunno," Midori shrugs. "We thought you would know!" and she starts laughing again.

"God!" I sigh. Smile.

The wind feels good, the stars glitter. And somewhere, planets align.

Then, a raindrop falls. Full and round, as big as a muscat grape. I look up but there's not a cloud. Where has it come from? A perfect orb drops on my lips, seeps to my tongue. Sweet. Then more droplets fall, plump, warm, soft as kisses, they rain down on us. We turn to each other, eyes wide with wonder.

We hold out palms to catch the wet in the cups of our hands, tip our heads, drink from the skies. We flip our boots off our feet, tug off socks, and with a whoop of joy, Midori rips off her shirt. We laugh, laugh, fling sodden winter clothing from our warm, wet bodies. We jump from the van and tear into the field. Moon to sea, sea to moon, earth to sky, earth to water. We leap, bound, in the sweetness, our laughter. Soaring, we leap skyward, leave perfect footprints in the rich mud. New green shoots of life twine at our feet, rising leafy in the warm night air. And in the collage of green, the movements of our bodies, I can see kappa rising from the soil. Like creatures waking from enforced hibernation, they stretch their long, green limbs with gleeful abandon. Skin moist, wet, slick and salamander-soft, kappa and humans dance together, our lives unfurling before us.

And the water breaks free with the rain.

I am a creature of the water.
I am a kappa child.

Come, embrace me.

Kappa   A water sprite (imp); a river monster; an excellent swimmer. –*Kenkyusha's New Japanese–English Dictionary.* Tokyo, Japan. 1997.

Description 1–1.5 m (approximation). Pale yellow to dark green. Aquatic, frog-like creature with webbed hands and feet, a small turtle-like shell, beaked mouth, and a bowl-shaped head. The water in the bowl is the source of its supernatural powers.

Breeding   Habits uncertain.

Habitat   Ponds, streams, rivers, lakes, base of waterfalls, laundry-washing areas of rivers, near outhouses, and rice paddies.

Range   Japan. Some sightings on mainland Asia. No other known sightings.

       This creature lives in the borders between natural and human environments. Most sightings have been made between dusk and dawn, only by the kappa's own volition. Primarily a trickster, all kappa should be approached warily as they are capable of drowning children and livestock. Noticeable traits include a fondness for cucumbers and initiating sumo-wrestling matches with humans. The kappa can be beaten only by spilling the water from its bowl-shaped head.

       –*The Aun Society Field Guide to Folk Creatures*

Acknowledgments

The path to this novel has been long and filled with adventure. I could not have traveled this path without the love and support of so many people. My thanks go first to Naoe Kiyokawa. You are my first hero. Tiger Goto, for showing me how never to give up, and Kyoko Goto, for teaching me through example the gracious arts of empathy, thank-you. I love you all very much.

Tamai Kobayashi, my gratitude for love and laughter shared, Mercedes Sosa and just being you. Snails are hermaphrodites.

My sisters, both born and met. Your love, friendship and support through the drama of life are gifts beyond measure. So thank-you, Ayumi Goto, Nozomi Goto, Naomi Goto, Susanda Yee, Rita Wong, Aruna Srivastava, Larissa Lai. And my life wouldn't be the same without my long-lost-separated-at-birth-twin-brother, Ashok Mathur.

Koji Tongu, Sae Goto and Tamotsu Tongu, for patience, love and impertinence I am eternally grateful. You bring joy to my life.

A special thank-you to Aritha van Herk, editor extraordinaire. Your keen eye and support is everything a writer ever dreams of.

My gratitude to Erin Mouré, Sonia Smee, Rosemary Nixon and my agent Anne McDermid.

I also would like to acknowledge Dr. Debra Putnam and Jesse Wayne Standing of the Calgary Airport Authority for their assistance in my background research. All errors of facts are my own.

Little House on the Prairie is an actual book. I would like to acknowledge Dr. Betsy Jameson for the enlightening panel discussion she gave at the University of Calgary on November 17, 1999. I could revisit the Little House books with new eyes. And thank-you to Red Deer Press, the Canada Council and The Alberta Foundation for the Arts. Your support is greatly appreciated.

Hiromi Goto's first novel, *Chorus of Mushrooms,* received the Commonwealth Writers' Prize for Best First Book in the Caribbean and Canadian Region and was co-winner of the Canada Japan Book Award. Her short stories and poetry have been widely published in literary journals. She is currently completing a collection of short stories, and her first novel for young adults, *The Water of Possibility,* has just been published.

CPSIA information can be obtained
at www.ICGtesting.com
Printed in the USA
LVHW090346150119
603912LV00001B/5/P